John Callander

**Two Ancient Scottish Poems**

The Gaberlunzie-Man and Christ's Kirk on the Green

John Callander

**Two Ancient Scottish Poems**
*The Gaberlunzie-Man and Christ's Kirk on the Green*

ISBN/EAN: 9783744711883

Printed in Europe, USA, Canada, Australia, Japan

Cover: Foto ©Andreas Hilbeck / pixelio.de

More available books at **www.hansebooks.com**

# TWO
# ANCIENT SCOTTISH POEMS;

## THE

## GABERLUNZIE-MAN,

### AND

## CHRIST's KIRK ON THE GREEN.

### WITH NOTES AND OBSERVATIONS.

### BY

## JOHN CALLANDER, ESQ. OF CRAIGFORTH.

By ftrange chanellis, fronteris, and forelandis,
Uncouth coiftis, and mony vilfum ftrandis,
Now goith our barge ———     G. Douglas.

## EDINBURGH:

PRINTED BY J. ROBERTSON.
SOLD BY J. BALFOUR, W. CREECH, AND C. ELLIOT,
EDINBURGH; DUNLOP AND WILSON, GLAS-
GOW; ANGUS AND SON, ABERDEEN;
W. ANDERSON, STIRLING; AND
A. DONALDSON, LONDON.

M,DCC,LXXXII.

# TO THE HONOURABLE

# SIR DAVID DALRYMPLE, BART

# LORD HAILES,

ONE OF THE SENATORS OF THE COLLEGE

OF JUSTICE.

MY LORD,

IN addreſſes of this ſort, it is almoſt equally difficult to avoid the ſervile tone of flattery, as to ſuppreſs the honeſt feelings of the heart, while we ſpeak to thoſe we love and eſteem. Happily for me, the public and private character of LORD HAILES will ever ſecure the author of the following obſervations from an imputation he diſdains, while he gladly embraces the opportunity of preſenting this little tract to the perſon who can beſt judge, whether an attempt to replace the Etymology of

A                                          our

our ancient language on a rational and ftable bafis, deferves any attention from the public.

Your Lordfhip has permitted me to look to you, as the patron and guide of my re-fearches; and it is a poor return to this con-defcenfion I now make, in fubfcribing myfelf,

MY LORD,

Your Lordfhip's much obliged,

And moft faithful humble fervant,

JO. CALLANDER.

CRAIG-FORTH, *April* 2. 1781.

# INTRODUCTION.

WE have publifhed thefe little poems, which tradition afcribes to James the Fifth of Scotland, with a few notes, as a fpecimen of the advantages which Etymology may derive from comparing thofe called *original*, and *fifter* languages, and their various dialects. The fcience of Etymology has, of late years, fallen into difrepute, rather, I believe, from the ignorance or negligence of fome of its profeffed admirers, than becaufe it is of little utility or importance to the Republic of Letters. But many attempts, and fometimes with fuccefs, have been made in this kind of inveftigation. The *Dutch* has been illuftrated by the *Frifian* and *Teutonic*; the *Englifh* by the *Anglo-Saxon*; and the *German* has been explained, with much labour and care, by Wachter, and others, from the ancient monuments of the Francs, Goths, and Alamahni. The learned Ihre, Profeffor at

Upfal,

Upfal, has illuftrated the ancient language and laws of Sweden, in his *Lexicon Swio-Gothicum*, a work that will ever be regarded as a noble treafury of Scandinavian antiquities. Men of learning need not be told how much Britain owes to the labours of Hickes, Junius, Spelman, and Lye. Thefe writers have followed, with indefatigable pains, the faint and almoft vanifhing traces of our ancient language; and have fucceeded, as far as it was poffible for men to fucceed, without the knowledge of thofe principles which alone form the bafis of true Etymology.

Not attending to this great truth, which we have recorded in the fcriptures, that the whole race of mankind formed at Babel one large family, which fpoke one tongue, they have confidered the different languages now in ufe all over our globe, as mere arbitrary founds,--- names impofed at random by the feveral tribes of mankind, as chance dictated, and bearing no other than a relation of convention to the object meant to be expreffed by a particular found. They were ignorant that the primæval language fpoken by Noah and his family, now fubfifts no where, and yet every where; that is to fay, that at the difperfion of the builders of Babel, each hord, or tribe, carried the radical words of the original language into the feveral diftricts

to

to which the providence of God conducted them; that these *radical* words are yet, in a great meafure, to be traced in all the different dialects now fpoken by men; and that thefe terms of primary formation are not mere arbitrary founds, but fixed and immutable, bearing the ftricteft analogy to the things they defcribe, and ufed, with very little material variation, by every nation whofe tongue we are acquainted with. The proofs of this great etymological truth rife to view, in proportion to the number of languages the refearches of the learned, and the diaries of the traveller, bring to our knowledge; and we hope, by the fmall collection we have been able to form, and which, at fome future period, we propofe to lay before the public, to fet the truth of our affertion beyond the reach of cavil. But this is not the place to enter further into the arguments by which we propofe to elucidate our hypothefis, and therefore we fhall prefent to the reader a word or two, felected from a vaft number of others which might be produced, as a fpecimen how far our principles are juft, and confonant to analogy.

Moon.----Goth. *mane.* Ulph. *mana,* A. S. *mona.* Ifl. *mana.* The primitive is the Oriental *mun,* enlighten, advertife. Hence Lat. *monere,* Engl. *monifh, admonifh.* Perf. *mah,* the moon. The

Turks

Turks write it *ma*. Gael. *mana*. Gr. μην, and Æol. μανα. Dan. *maane*. Alam. *mano*. In the ancient Arabic *manat*. Hebr. *meni*, in Ifa. 66. ii. and the Americans of Virginia fay *manith*, and in the Malabar dialect *mena*, a month. From *man* the Greeks formed μανια, madnefs, fuppofed to be occafioned by the influence of the moon. Hence our *maniac*, a madman; *Menuet, minuet*, facred dance, and of very high antiquity, reprefenting the movements of the fun and moon. The primitive *mun*, pronounced *man*, fignifies the *hand* and a *fign*. Hence *mon*, *men*, *man*, are applied to fun and moon, alfo to denote every thing relative to *figns*. Hence Lat. *manus*, and our *month*, &c.

Inftead of carrying on our refearches into the many other collateral meanings of this word, we fhall amufe our readers with another, fhewing that the fame principle of univerfality in language prevails in all.

MALADY:—Hebr, *malul*, evil, chagrin, grief; *moul*, patience. Perf. *mgll*, evil. Hebr. *mulidan*, to fuffer. Arab. *mel*, patience. Celt. *mal*, bad, corrupt. Hence Lat. *malum*; Fr. *mal*; *malade*; *maladerie*, an hofpital; the *malanders*, a difeafe to which horfes are fubject; *malice, malignity*.
                                                        Lat.

Lat. B. *male-aftrofus*, *ill-ftarred*, as Shakefpeare
has it, Othello, Act V.

Had the laborious Johnfon been better acquainted with the Oriental tongues, or had he
even underftood the firft rudiments of the
Northern languages from which the Englifh
and Scots derive their origin, his bulky volumes
had not prefented to us the melancholy truth,
That unwearied induftry, devoid of fettled
principles, avails only to add one error to another.

Junius, Skinner, and Lye, though far fu-
perior to Mr Johnfon in their knowledge of the
origin of our language, yet, in tracing its foun-
dation, feldom go farther back than the Celtic,
and Ulphila's Gothic verfion of part of the New
Teftament. Nay, the elegant and learned Ihre
tells us plainly, that it is unjuft to demand any
thing further. But ftill the queftion recurs to
an inquifitive reader, Whence were thefe Celtic
and Gothic terms formed? Every fmatterer
in Etymology knows that the Greek and Latin
are modern tongues, when compared to the
Oriental and Celtic dialects; and the blunder-
ing attempts of Euftathius, the author of the
Etymologicon Magnum, Varro, and Feftus,
prove, beyond a doubt, that thefe writers were
equally ignorant of the true meaning of their
mother

mother tongues, and of the originals from whence they were derived. Mifled by thofe blind guides, we find Voffius and Skinner very gravely afferting, that *Venus* is formed *a veni-endo,* quia omnibus venit ; *vulgus,* a volvendo ; *malus,* from the Greek μελας, black, and μαλακος ; *manus* from *munus* ; and *mons,* a mountain, *a movendo,* quia minimè movetur ; *mare,* quod amarum fit ; *mufcle* of the body, from *mus* ; and *mufquet,* from the Greek μοσχος, a calf.

It were eafy to fwell this catalogue, which any of our readers may augment at their plea-fure from *every* page of *every* Lexicographer, ancient and modern.

Of all the Nothern dialects none has been more neglected than the Scotch, though it tranfmits to us many works of genius both in poetry and profe ; and alfo fome gloffaries, which are not unufeful in pointing out the affinity of the ancient Scotch with its kindred dialects. Of thefe, the largeft is that annexed to Bifhop Douglas's verfion of the Æneid. But it wants many words which actually ex-ift in that tranflation, and a great many more are fo diftorted by falfe derivations, that they only ferve to multiply our doubts.

Our language, as it is at prefent fpoken by the common people in the Lowlands, and as it

appears

appears in the writings prior to the feventeenth century, furnifhes a great many obfervations, highly deferving the attention of thofe who wifh to be acquainted with the Scandinavian dialects in general, or the terms ufed by our anceftors in their jurifprudence and poetry, in particular. Many of thofe ferve materially to illuftrate the genius, the manners, and cuftoms of our forefathers. In Scotland, the Old Saxon dialect, which came over with *Octa* and *Nebriffa*, the founders of the Northumbrian kingdom, has maintained its ground much longer than in England, and in much greater purity. This muft be owing to the later cultivation of this part of the ifland, and its lefs frequent communication with ftrangers. In South Britain, the numerous fwarms of Normans and French, who followed William, and the Plantagenets, foon made their language that of the bar, and of the court. At the fame time, the long wars with France, and the extenfive poffeffions of the Englifh on that part of the continent, entirely changed not only the orthography, but alfo the pronunciation of the original Saxon; nor do we hefitate to fay, what we fhall foon endeavour to prove, that we, in Scotland, have preferved the original tongue, while it has been mangled, and almoft defaced, by our fouthern neighbours.

B                                    It

It is an undoubted fact, that the original language of this whole Island was the Celtic, now split into the several dialects of the *Gaelic*, *Welch*, and *Armoric*. In the present Scotch, we see indeed a few traces of this ancient tongue, which the inhabitants left behind them, when they fled for refuge to the mountains of Scotland and Wales ; but these are very easily distinguished from the now prevailing language of the country. In like manner we discover to this day, in the German, many marks of the same original, which were infused into it by the neighbouring Belgæ and Gauls, the posterity of the ancient Celts, by whom this Island was originally peopled. *Sufmilch* has proved this from the likeness of many German and Armoric words. Many more examples might be adduced from the Gaelic, in which the radical word is often preserved, though lost in all the dialects of the German language. Of this number is the word *fchleufe*, the root of which is only to be found in the Welch *Llaw*, the arm, or the hand. From this word was formed *Llawes*, which has been adopted into all the German dialects, in the same manner as *manica* from *manus*, or the Irish word *braccaile*, a bracelet, from *brac*, the arm, and *caile*, an ornament or covering. The word *treten*, has also greatly

puzzled

puzzled the German etymologifts, though it feems naturally derived from the Irifh *troed*, the foot, whence alfo comes our word *tread*.

The intimate connection of the Scots with the Teutonic, German, Iflandic, and other northern dialects, appears, firft, from the fimilarity of found, and enunciation. This is principally to be remarked in the found of the vowels, which retain the fame uniform tones in the broad Scotch, that they do in the languages above mentioned; whereas the fingular caprice of the Englifh pronunciation has varied and confounded them beyond the comprehenfion of rule. The German guttural pronunciation of *ch*, *g*, *gh*, is quite natural to a Scotchman, who forms the words *eight*, *light*, *fight*, *bought*, &c. exactly as his northern neighbours, and as the Germans do. How much the Englifh have deviated from this, we may fee from the few following examples.

| German. | Scots. | Englifh. |
|---|---|---|
| Beide, | Baith, | Both. |
| Eide, | Aith, | Oath. |
| Kifte, | Kift, | Cheft. |
| Meifte, | Maift, | Moft. |
| Brennen, | Bren, | Burn. |
| Gehe, | Gae, | Go, &c. |

We

We have to obferve, in the fecond place, that our language contains many words which were never admitted into the Englifh dialect. Thefe, a few excepted, which are derived from the Gaelic, are either pure German, or Scandinavian. We have annexed a few examples from our Scoto-Gothic gloffary as a fpecimen.

| Scots. | German, &c. | |
|---|---|---|
| Blate, | Bel. | Blode. |
| Dech, | | Deeg. |
| Barm, yeft, | B. | Barm. |
| Kail, | G. | Kohl. |
| Coft, | | Koeft. |
| Bikker, | G. | Becher. |
| Sicker, | | Sicher. |
| Kemp, | | Kampfen. |
| Haus, | G. | Hals. |
| Mutch, | G. | Mutz. |
| Skaith, | G. | Schade. |
| Slough, fkin, | B. | Shu. |
| Spill, | B. | Spillen. |
| Red, advife, | G. | Rathen. |
| Lift, fky, | G. | Luft. |
| Tig, touch gently, | B. | Ticken. |
| Forloffen, | G. | Weglaufen. |
| Bruick, | G. | Branchan. |
| Reek, | | Rauch. |
| Bouk, | G. | Baugh, the belly. |
| Fie, cattle, | G. | Vieh. |
| Kummer, | G. | Kummer, forrow. |
| Krummy, crooked, | G. | Krumm. |

Frend,

| Scots. | German, &c. |
| --- | --- |
| Fremd, | G. Fremd, ſtrange. |
| Low, flame, | G. Lohe, flame. |
| Leglen, | G. Leghel, a milking-pail. |
| Win, | G. Wohnen, to dwell. |
| Yammer, | G. Jammern, to complain. |
| Keek, | B. Kieken. |
| Girn, | Iſl. Girnd, deſire, anger. |
| Muil, | Iſl. Molld, pulvis. |
| Egg, | Iſl. Egg, aċies. |
| Awn, | Goth. Aigan, to poſſefs—*Aigin*, my own. |
| Elden, | Iſl. Eldur, fire. |
| Etter and ettercap, | Iſl. Eitur, poiſon, venom. |
| Dill, | Iſl. Dil, to conceal. |
| Ern, | Iſl. Ernur, large hawk. |

Theſe may ſuffice, though it were eaſy to add more examples.

The uſe of inveſtigating our Scottiſh dialeċt, will alſo appear from its retaining many radical words, which are either totally loſt in its ſiſter languages, or which are no longer enounced in the primitive ſounds. In this number is *gear*, or *gier*, which ſignifies dreſs, furniture, wealth. This word, like the Greek ἀιγίς, denoting originally *a goat-ſkin*, afterwards *a ſhield*, and laſtly the *ſacred ſhield* of Minerva, has greatly enlarged its primitive ſignification. From the original meaning of the Iſlandic *gera*, a ſheep-ſkin, this word came to ſignify covering, dreſs, ornament,

goods,

goods, riches ; cattle being all thefe to the
moft ancient nations.   Now this word is ufed
by our writers, in all thefe acceptations ; and,
though no longer found in the German, yet it
is the fruitful mother of many ancient and
modern words in that language.   From it are
evidently derived *haufegeraeth*, the Saxon *gerada*,
and the Swedifh *gerad* and *gerd*, tribute paid
both in goods and money ;  the etymon of
which neither Spegel nor Ihre underftood :--
(Vide Ihre, Lex. in *gerd, utgerd*).   The word
*graith*, in our language fignifying utenfils and
furniture of all kinds, is from the fame origin ;
as alfo the German *gier*, a mifer ; *gieren*, to defire anxioufly ; *geirig*, covetous ; *gern*, willing-
ly ; whence our *yearn*, with many others of
the fame family, the fignification being changed
from the *object* itfelf to the *defire* of poffeffing it,
and afterwards enlarged to exprefs any *defire* in
general, in the fame manner as in Englifh the
word *liquorifh*, from *liquor*, in its primary fenfe
firft denoted the defire of *drinking*, and afterwards any *luftful defire*.   Our word *gar*, make,
prepare, is another word not found at prefent
in the German language, in its original meaning.
But from it come the words *gar*, ready ; *garven*,
to prepare and curry leather ; with a great many
more in the old and pure German dialect; and

in

In the Alammanic *garuuin*, *garuuen*, whence *garue*, ready, prepared; the Iflandic *giorwer*; ready made; and in the ancient Runic Infcriptions, *gjarua*, *kiarua*, whence our *carve*, to cut up, *i. e.* prepare meat for eating. The Welfh fay *kervio*, and the Gaels *corrbham*. Cafaubon and Stephanus were certainly driven to the laft extremity, while they bring in this word from the Greek εγκυρα, or κυρα, a picture. But with thefe writers, the moft extravagant conjectures often fupply the want of folid principles.

To mention only one inftance more; our word *grean*, the muzzle or upper-lip of cattle, is the only root from whence the German *grynen*, to laugh, can be derived, the etymology of which has given rife to a variety of conjectures. Our *girn*, and the Englifh *grin*, are from the fame root.

Thefe few remarks may fuffice to fhew the great ufefulnefs and importance of inveftigating the terms and phrafes of our ancient language, fince thefe not only tend to elucidate the ancient manners and cuftoms of our remote anceftors, but alfo throw much light on its fifter-dialects of the North; by which we mean all thofe fpoken from the heads of the Rhine, and of the Danube, to the fartheft extremities of Scandinavia and Iceland.

It

It is high time that fomething of this kind were attempted to be done, before the prefent Englifh, which has now for many years been the written language of this country, fhall ba-nifh our Scottifh tongue entirely out of the world.

We cannot conclude thefe curfory remarks without congratulating our readers on the eftablifhment of a Society, which promifes to revive a tafte for the ftudy of national antiqui-ty. The worthy nobleman to whofe truly patriotic fpirit it owes its inftitution, and the gentlemen affociated for fo laudable a purpofe, it is hoped, will look with indulgence on this poor attempt to fecond their endeavours, in re-ftoring and explaining the ancient language of Scotland.

THE

# GABERLUNZIE-MAN.

## I.

THE pauky auld Carle came o'er the lee,
    Wi' mony gude eens and days to mee,
                     Saying,

*Gaberlunzie*] This word is compounded of *Gaber*, *Gab-ber*, a Wallet or Bag, and *Lunzie*, loin, *i. e.* the man who carries the wallet on his back, an itinerant mechanic, or tinker, who carries in his bag the implements of his trade, and ftrolls about the country mending pots and kettles. In fuch difguifes as this James V. (as is faid) ufed to go about the country, and to mingle, unknown, with the meaneft of his fubjects. Thefe frolickfome excurfions often gave birth to little amorous adventures, which our witty Monarch made the fubjects of his fong, as he was fecond to none of his age in the fciences of poetry and mufic.

The root of the word *gab* is the Celt. *cab*, fignifying to con-tain. Hence Scot. *gab*, the mouth, which contains our food; Englifh *gobbet*, a morfel; the French *gober*, to fwallow, and *gofier*, the throat. The large barks on Loch-Lomond for

C
                                       carrying

carrying wood, are called *gaberts*.    From *gab*, and *gab*, come English *gabble;* and *gabbing* is used by Douglas for idle talking, Prologue to I. Æn. p. 6. ˙v. 43. Rud. Edit.—and last line of leaf 3. Lond. Edit. 4to, 1553.

" Quhilk is nae gabbing southly, nor no lye."

In the same sense, Isl. *gabb;* Ludibrium, *gabba*, to deride; A. Sax. *gabban*, and many more words of the same import, *gaggle*, *gaffer*, and Old Fr. *gaber*, *gabbasser*, to mock; *gabatine*, mockery; Islandic *gamman*, drollery; Gal. *geubbeth*, falsehood; and *gaw*, *caw*, *gab*, cheating; Old Fr. *ganelon*, a traitor.    We have collected these words from various languages, as they not only explain the primitive idea of the word *gaber*, which none of our Etymologists have done, but prove what we shall every moment have occasion to shew, that the radical term once ascertained, throws light on all its derivatives, which are easily reducible to it, though scattered far distant from each other, among the various dialects used by different nations.    To this family belongs Lat. *capio*, whence our *capacity*, *capture;* the Scots *cap*, a drinking vessel; *cab*, a measure, mentioned in the Version of the Old Testament; and many more, all including the idea of *capacity*, or *content;* as *cabin*, Belg. *kaban;* Welsh, *cab*, *caban*, all signifying the same thing; Gr. καπαη; Lat. *cabana*, *cabbage*, from the form of its top, resembling a bason or large cup, which has much puzzled Junius; Lat. *cavus*, our *cave*, and the Fr. and Engl. *cabinet*.

*Lunzie*]    We have elsewhere observed, with Mr Ruddiman, that the Z, by the old Scots writers, is always used in the beginning of the syllable for the English Y.    The reason is, that the figure Z much resembles the Saxon G, which the English often change into Y, as *yard* from *geard; yea* from *gea;*

*year*

*year* from *gear*, &c. Thus *Yetland* is by us written *Zetland*, and *ye, year, young ; ze, zere, zyng ; ranzies, fenzies*, for *reins, feigns*, and the like.   This we remark once for all. In other fifter dialects Z has the force of S.   Thus Bel. *zour*, four ; *zuid*, fouth ; *zon*, fun ; Slav. *zakar*, fugar ; Ital. *zanni*, Gr. ϛαϰνοι, and in the Bar. Gr. ϳϛανοι, buffoons, whence our *zany*.

  *Lunzie*]   Lung, loin, lunzie'; *bene*, the thigh bone.   In Swed. *lend, land*, the loin.  In the Laws of Gothland, cap. 23. 4. *Synes lend oc lyndtr ;* fi appareant lumbi et pudenda. They alfo write it *Ljumske ;* Ihre, in voce. Ifl. *lend, boh, ledwi.* Ger. *lenden* and *lanken*, and hence our *flank*.  Welfh, *Llwyn;* and in Finland, *landet*, the loin.  Ital. *longia ;* Fr. *longe ;* Scot. *lend*.   Vide Not. S. Kirk. St.   From the ancient Goth. *Ljumske ;* the Lat. *lumbus ;*  Dan. *ljuske ;* whence our *lisk*.  The primitive is *Lat, Let*, broad, extended ; whence the Gr. πλατυ-, and the Latin *latus*.

  Thus the *Gaberlunzie-man* literally fignifies the man who bears a bag, or wallet, on his back or loins ; a pedlar ; Scot. a *pack-man*.

## STANZA I.

VER. 1. *Pauky*]   Sly, cunning, Bel. *Paiken*, to coax or wheedle.   Douglas, p. 238, v. 37.

  Prattis are repute policie, and perrellus *paukis*.

  *Auld*]   Old Ger. *alt*, as *eald*. Ifl. *aldradur*. Dan. *Eeld*. Scot. *eild*.  Cafaubon brings this from εωλος, vetus, and Lye from αλδεω, augeo ; as if our anceftors had no word to exprefs old age, till they got it from the Greeks.   But this is indeed an old wife's tale.  The primitive *E* denotes exiftence; every thing that lives.  Hence *Eve* is called emphatically, the mother of all living. Lat. *eft*. Fr. *etre*, being, *effentia*, whence our *effence*, what conftitutes the *being* of that thing.   Hence

Hebrew

Hebrew *hei*, life, and *God* emphatically; i. e. *He who lives.* *heie*, to live, life itself. Arab. *hei—hi*, to live, to be glad. In Zend, *gueie*, foul, life. · This word furnishes a remarkable example of the truth of our general principle, explained in the preface, and therefore we hope the reader will allow us to trace it a little further. The afpirate H, in the northern dialects, is changed into W, and Qu, and hence Swed. *weet*, *wight*, living animal; Engl. and Scot. *wight;* Goth, *qwick*, lively; *ewicka*, quicken, quick-filver, from its lively motion. In Sued. *qwick-filfwer*. The Latins ufed the V, and fo formed *vita, vivere, vivax, victus, victo, vis, vigor, vigeo*, and a thoufand more; as alfo the derivatives we have adopted from that language, *vivacity, violent, vivid*, &c. Voffius, able to get no further than the Greek, deduces *vita* from ϛιοτη : but ϛιος, life; ϛια, violence, ϛιακοπαι, ϛιοϖ, all come from one primitive, as alfo Gr. ις, the *vis* of the Latins, ισχυς, ισχυα, ισχυρος, only by fuppreffing the afpirate. In the more ancient dialects of Scandinavia, we find the fame word denoting the fame objects; Teuton. *vuith.* Ifl. *vætir.* a Sax. *vught, vight*, all fign. animals, living creatures; and the Alam. *quick, quickr.* Old German *queck.* Dan. *queg*, living, animal, every thing alive. Suab. *vich, viech*, animal. From the fame fource we formed *wife.* Bel. *wyf.* Swed. *wif.* Suab. *wib*, all fignifying *woman*, mother of a family.

Thus we have followed this word from the remoteft Eaft, to the fartheft extremities of the Weft and North. Such coincidences of found and meaning, demonftrate that language is no arbitrary thing, nor etymology that fallacious fcience it has been called, by thofe who find it more eafy to decide in hafte, than to examine at leifure.

*Carle*] The true fpelling is *karl* in all the Scythian dialects, in which it denotes a *man*, or *warrior*. The primitive is *car—kar*, ftrong. This root we have preferved in the Armenian,

menian, in which *car*, poffe, valere, et *carol*, potens. Not
attending to the univerfality of language, the learned Ihre
did not fee the juftnefs of this Etymology. From *kair, kar*,
the Mefogothic, *vair*, a man ; whence the Lat. *vir, vira*, a
woman, as from the Gothic *kas*, they formed *vas*, which
Voffius could make nothing of, though he has flung together
every paffage almoft, where this word occurs. From *karl* are
formed the Alamm. *karl;* Ger. *kerl;* A. S. *ceorl;* Ifl. *karl;* L. B.
*Carolus, karlus.* Vid. Cange Glofs. in V. From *kerl*, Sued.
*karlklader*, men's clothes ; *karlfmather*, and *karlfwag*, the high-
way ; and in the old Gothic laws *karlfbo*, man's habitation. The
word *karl* is oppofed to *gaffe*, a youth ; the former denoting a
man of ripe age. We find that of old, in the Gothic, as now
with us, *karl*, and *carl*, were ufed to fignify people of a low
rank, fuch as farmers, mechanics, &c. In the old laws, (ap.
Ihre glofs. Vol. I. P. 1033,) *karl oc konung*, plebs et princeps ; and in Gothr. Saga, cap. 86, *opter that I karls hufi er
ej er in congs ranni*, oft do we meet in a cottage, what we
feek in vain in the palaces of kings. In general, *karl* is ufed
to fignify a *husband ;* and in Sweden the country-women call
their hufbands *min-karl*. In the Swedifh tongue the gander
is called *gas-karl*. So in Engl. a *carle-cat*, is the male of
that fpecies. The Anglo-Saxons fay *ceorl*, for a hufband,
and *ceorlian*, to marry.

As this word was commonly ufed to fignify *ruftics*, the En-
lifh from it formed *churl, churlifh*. In the A. S. *ceorlborin*
is a man meanly born ; *ceorlife*, a ruftic ; *ceorlife blaf*, loaf
made of the fecond flour. In Dutch, *kaerle* a ruftic ; whence
the Italian phrafe, *a la carlona*, like a ruftic, ill-bred. The
Welch *carl* has the fame meaning. As *karl*, all over the
north, denotes an *elderly man*, from it we have formed *carling*,
an old woman of the loweft caft, a word which occurs in all
our poets.

The

Saying, Gudewife, for zour courtefie,
 Will zee ludge a filly poor man.

The

The Bar. Lat. *Carolus*, and our *Charles*, come from the fame origin, a name of high antiquity among the Germans, from whom we borrowed the name of the conftellation *Charles's wain*, in Gothic *Karlwagn*, and in Sax. *Carleas wagn;* Dan. *Karlvogn.* This proves the ignorance of thofe who will have this name given to thefe ftars in honour of Charles the Great, which was in general ufe many ages before Charlemain was born. The Welch alfo call this conftellation *Cart Wyn.*

VER. 1. *Lee,* or *lea*] An unplowed field, or a field formerly under corn, and afterwards laid down in grafs. Primitive *la,* and *le,* fignify broad, extended. A. S. *lea, leag, leah.* Old Ger. *la, lo, lohe.* Goth. *lee,* which Ihre explains, *locus tempeftatibus fubductus;* whence our *lown,* calm. In the northern parts of Germany, we have it in many names of places, as *Oldefloh, Kartla, Lohagen,* &c. vide Grupen Antiq. Van Den Bonnen. P. 556. Ifl. *logn,* and Goth. *lugn,* fign. *calm.* The Hebr. *lech,* denotes a meadow, green, verdure; and the Polifh *leka* is the fame, for all thefe are derived from the fame root, *la.* The Celtic and Gallic *las,* fign. grafs. 'Welch *Llys;* *bas,* Brett. *luzavan.* Hence *Lucern,* a fpecies of grafs growing abundantly in Switzerland. The Canton of *Lucern* has its name from this plant, not the plant from it, as the high antiquity of the word proves.

VER. 3. *Gudewife*] Properly the mother of a family; Goth. *wif,* a woman, a married woman. A. S. id. Ger. *weif.* This by fome has been derived from *wifwa,* to weave; by others from *wif,* or *hwif,* a woman's head-drefs,

in

in the fame way as the Swedes fay *gyrdel* and *linda*, the belt, and girdle for the *man* and the *woman*. They alfo ufe *hatt* and *hætta*, the hat and cap, in the fame fenfe. But the true primitive of this word is E, life, exiftence ; whence *Eve*, the general mother of mankind ; Arab. *heib*, the female fex, alfo modefty. This word *heib*, pronounced *hai*, gave birth to the ancient formulary of marriage among the Romans, *Ubi tu eras Caius* (fays the woman) *ego ero Caia*. None of their writers tell us any thing of the origin of thefe *verba concepta*. *Caia* was in reality a title of honour given to the Roman matrons, anfwering to that of *Thane*, ufed by the Etrufcans ; whence, it would feem, the Italian *Donna* came. So Pliny, l. 8. cap. 48. tells us that *Caia Kaikilia*, wife to the elder Tarquin, was called in the Hetrufcan, *Thana Quilis*. *He* and *hei*, the primitive, with the change of the H into G, the eafieft of all tranfpofitions, formed in Greek γαω, whence γεγαω, to generate, γενεσις, γενος, race, family ; γονευς, parent ; γυνη, a wife ; Lat. *genus, gigno, gens* ; Chin. *gin* ; Celt. *gen*, a man ; Greenl. *kora* ; Ifl. Teut. Dan. *kona*; Cuen. *quin*, woman ; and our *quean* and *queen* ; Gaelic, *quenaft*, to marry ; Slav. *fyena*, a woman ; and Fr. *guenon*, the female monkey.

From the fame root the *Earth*, the *nourifher* of men and animals, is, in every language, called by the fame appellation. Chinefe *chi* ; Gael. *gwe* ; Zend *gweth, enanm*; Pehlvi *gue, ka*, the world ; Gael. *gwaed*, riches, goods produced by the Earth ; Celtic, *gueth*, a poor man, one deftitute of thefe goods, compofed of *gue*, the Earth, and the negative termination *th* ; Ancient Gr. Αια, γαια, γεα, and γη, the Earth. Hence we can eafily trace the origin of the Latin *egeo* and *egenus*, which literally fignifies *to be without ground*, to be deftitute of the fruits of the Earth. *Inops*, from the negative

*in*

*in* and *ops*, the ancient appellative of our common mother, as in that verse of the old poet Accius, Ap. Prisc. Lib. 7.

" Quorum genitor fertur esse *ops* gentibus."

Plautus Ciftellar:

" Itaque me ops opulenta illius avia, imo mater quidem."

How little Voffius and Ifidorus knew the real origin of the Latin words, may be feen, apud Voff. Etym. in *Egens*. Nor has Feftus fucceeded a whit better, when he fays, *Egens*, *velut exgens*, cui ne gens quidem fit reliqua; and yet thefe writers are called *Etymologifts*. We leave them amidft thefe futile derivations, and proceed to obferve, that from this primitive *he*, life, nourifhment, are derived a number of Celtic words, all of the fame import; as *hei*, our *hay*, food of animals produced by the Earth; *heize*, barley; *hai*, trees, a foreft; *hei*, *wei*, pafturage, hunting; *he* and *kai*, habitation, literally the place *where we live*. And as thofe who abound in goods are, or fhould be *cheerful*, hence Gr. γαω, rejoice; Chinefe, *gao*, to laugh or be glad; Celt. *gae*, id. Latin, *gavifus*, *gaudere*; the French and our *gay*, and Scot. *gauf*.

We have extended our remarks on this word, as it ftrongly confirms our hypothefis relating to the univerfality of the primitive language, and the exiftence of its elementary parts, in every dialect fpoken by men, even at this day, from the remoteft parts of the Eaft, to the fartheft limits of the North and Weft. In all thefe languages, we have feen that this root, exceedingly fimple in itfelf, has proved the fruitful mother of many families in every quarter of the globe. Thefe may fhew, that the primæval language was not *eradicated* at Babel, but only *fplit* into a great variety of dialects, as the facred Hiftorian informs us; and that the feveral languages now in ufe, are fo far from being formed by the tribes who

speak

The night was cauld, the carle was wat,

And down azont the ingle he fat ;

My

speak them, that they are only branches of that primæval tree,
which flourished long before the deluge.

We might eafily accumulate more proofs of the truth of our
leading principle, were we to add the Hebr. *eia*, being ; Indian
*he* ; Perf. *aift* ; Gr. *ts* ; Lat. *eft* ; Bafq. *ifan* ; Celt. *es* ;
Teuton. *ifh*, *ys* ; Ital. *e* ; and Englifh *is* : But thefe we fhall
referve for our Gloffary, in compiling of which we have already made fome progrefs.

VER. 4. *Silly.*—Simple, without guile. In old Englifh *fely*,
*felie*. So Chaucer, Miller's Tale, and Reve's Tale, v. 992.
The *Sely Carpenter*, and elfewhere *felie-man*. This is quite
different from *Sely*, fign. *holy*, from Goth. *falig*, A. S. *fæl*.

VER. 5. *Cauld.*—In this word we have an inftance of
our following the original orthography. Ulphila writes *calds* ;
A. S. *ceald* ; Ifl. *caldur* and *kulde* ; Alam. *kalt* ; Dan. *kuld* ;
all fignifying *cold*.

*Wat.*—Engl. *wet* ; Prim. *u*, *au*, water ; Ulph. *wato* ;
Goth. *watn* ; Pol. *wat*, humid ; A. S. *water* ; Alam. *wuafzar* ;
Ger. *waffer* ; Pol. *wæda* ; Gr. *ὕδωρ*, which Plato (in
Cratylo) allows to be a barbarous word ; and he is in
the right, for the Greeks had it from the Celtic. Ifland.
*udr* is *water*. Hence Goth. *wattu-fiktig*, the dropfy,
literally the *water-ficknefs*. From the Ifl. *watfka*, the Eng-
lifh *wafh*. From the fame origin comes the Swedifh *O*, an
Ifland, becaufe furrounded with water ; *Aland*, *Æland*, an
Ifland in the Baltic ; *Ho-lland*, literally *a land of waters*.
There is a diftrict in Normandy called *Auge*, for the fame
reafon. *Eau* has the fame origin.

D

We

We fhall add fome other coincidences of language here, in fupport of our general principle, that the radical words of the firft tongue are to be found in dialects fpoken by nations, who never had any connection with each other fince the difperfion at Babel. Thefe are fo numerous, and deviate fo little both from the original found and fenfe, that it can never be fuppofed, without the groffeft abfurdity, to be the effect of chance. Thus the Chinefe *ho—hu*, fignifies *water* in general, a lake, and *hai*, the fea. The Tartar *Icho*, a river in Siberia; and in the fame language, *O-mo*, a lake, literally a *great water*, for *mo* is great. Greek ὕς, water; whence ὕω, to rain, ὕδωρ, ὕδρος, ὕδρια; yet Stephanús and Scapula tell us, that ὕδωρ and ὕω are radical words, not knowing that no radical word ever con-fifted of two fyllables. Indeed, we may venture to affert, that no example can be produced of a true radical word having more than one. The public has lately been told, in very pompous terms, that the Greek language is the work of philofophers, complete and perfect in itfelf. We can moft eafily fhew, that this wild affertion is fo far from being true, that no perfon, but one utterly devoid of all fkill in Etymology and the analogy of language, could have hazarded an hypothefis fo replete with abfurdity. So far is the Greek tongue from being the work of philofophers, that one of their beft philofophers, in one of his (beft) dialogues, ingenuoufly confeffes, that he is quite ig-norant of the origin of many of the moft common words in the language. Such is the word ὕδωρ mentioned above, and a vaft number of others, which he, with a true Attic fupercili-ous air, allows to have been borrowed from the Barbarians. True it is, thefe terms do derive their origin from the Scy-thians, Thracians, Phrygians, and Celts, whofe language ex-ifted many ages before Athens was even a poor village. The very meaneft of thefe people, whom he ftigmatifes with the name of Barbarians, could have informed him of the origin of

ὕδωρ,

ὑδωρ, as well as of many others of which he owns himself
equally ignorant. After Plato, it is almost needless to observe,
that those who were far inferior to this Athenian in the knowledge of language, were still more unfortunate in their explica-
tions. Let every page of Hesychius, Eustathius, Suidas, the
Etymologicon Magnum, Tzetzes, Harpocation, and the whole
herd of their commentators and lexicographers, bear witness
to their ignorance, and account for the disgrace into which the
useful study of Etymology has, by their means, fallen among
those who have rashly concluded, that because nothing good
was done by these Scioli in the profession, therefore nothing
better could be done. Let us leave this language of yesterday,
said to be formed by philosophers, to the admiration of those
profound philosophers, who have told us, that, in certain
Islands in the Eastern Ocean, the human race have tails, and
whose credulity can digest the account the natives of Attica
gave of themselves, pretending that they sprung, like mush-
rooms, from the very soil on which they dwelt. All these
pretenders to the highest antiquity, were outdone in Grecian
rhodomontade by the Arcadians, who asserted, that they inhabited their mountainous district long before the moon appeared in the heavens.

We hasten to return from a digression, which, we are
afraid, many of our learned readers will deem unnecessary;
though perhaps others may think, that the hints here thrown
out, concerning the Greek tongue, may help to loosen the
college-fetters of those, who, from their early youth, have been
accustomed to look upon nothing as genuine and valuable, unless found in some of the writers of classic authority; nor any
thing expressed with elegance and propriety, unless written
in Greek. The chronological blunders of those, who are perpetually deriving Scythian, Tartar, and Celtic words, from

a language which did not receive its prefent form, till many centuries after the others were fpoken and cultivated, deferve nothing but contempt.

We have faid that ὕδωρ comes from the primitive Celtic *A—U*, water, liquid. From the fame origin the Latins formed *udus, humidus, humeo, humor, hyems*, literally *the feafon of rains*, concerning which, fee the nothings of Voffius, in *Humor* and *Hyems*. From the fame caufe the 'Υαδες, *Hyades*, derived their name. The primitive *au* was fometimes pronounced *oua ;* whence Fr. *eau*, the Lat. *aqua*, and, with the termination *ter, ouater*, water.

VER. 6. *Azont.*—Beyond. A. S. *begeond, begeondan*. The primitive is *ga—ge*, to *go*, and *on*, forward, or beyond the place one ftood in. Ulphila, *ganga*, to go or walk ; whence our *gang, gae*, and *gete*, way, as in S. G. it is written *ga*. From *ga*, written *ba*, the Greeks formed βαω, βαινω, and all their derivatives. The Englifh *gad-about* is from the fame origin ; and Ihre explains the S. G. *gadda*, capita conferre, ut folent novas res molientes. The fame idea is found in the A. S. *gaderian, gadran ;* Bel. *gaderin ;* whence Engl. *gather ;* the Ger. *gatten* and *ehegatten*, married pair. Ulphila, Mark 3. V. *Ja fah gaiddja fitt mangeei*, the people were gathered together. Wherever in the Mæfo Gothic we find the prefix *ga*, it always denotes a *gathering*, or going together. So *gafinthja*, comitatur ; *garanznans*, vicini, from *razn*, a houfe ; *gadailans*, partaker, from *dail*, a part; *galhaiba*, contubernales, from *illaibs*, bread ; Alamm. *caleibo*, literally Eaters of the fame bread, whence Ihre deduces Fr. *compagnon*, companion. The Ifl. *kuon gaudur*, married, is from the fame origin, as Wachter rightly obferves, though Ihre does not approve of this derivation.

VER. 6. *Ingle.*—This word is commonly derived from *ignis*. In our language it denotes a fire on the hearth, or in

kilns

My dochter's fhouthers he 'gan to clap,
 And cadgily ranted and fang.

           O

kilns and ovens, and is ufed by Douglas in many places. It
is likewife preferved in Cumberland, as Ray informs us.

 VER. 7. *Clap.*—From the Ifl. and Goth. *klappa*, to clap
the hands. Dan. *klappe*. Belg. *klappen, cloppen*. This word
is plainly an *onomatapæa*, formed from the found made by clapping the hands. Hence too was formed the Greek κολαπτω,
*tundere.* Whence Junius idly derives our word *clap.* The
fpeaking by the fingers was an art well known to the ancient
Iflanders, who called it *clapruner*, or letters formed by the
motion of the hands, vide Worm. Litt. Run. p. 41. The
watchmen in Holland carry a wooden inftrument with two
leaves, which, by clapping together, produce a great noife;
whence thefe night-guardians are called *klappermen.* In the
ancient Alammanick, the tongue of a bell is called *clepel;*
whence our Scots word to *clep*, or talk idly, repeating the
fame thing over and over. The Dutch ufe the verb *klappen*,
in the fame fenfe. Goth. *klæk*, infamy, difhonour; *klæknamu*,
*klækord*, opprobrious language, nicknames. The ingenious
and learned profeffor Ihre takes *klæpa*, with great probability,
from the primitive *laf*, the hand; Suiogoth. *lofa, lofwa;*
Welch *llaw;* whence Scot. *lufe*, the palm of the hand; and
the Latin *vola;* Welch *lloffi, djloffi*, to ftroke with the hand.
Hefych.

 To ftricke, from the fame origin, as alfo *colaphus,* and
*alapa,* Bar. Lat. *eclaffa.* In a charter of the year 1285,
" Si mulier det ei unum *eclaffa*, non debet bannum." *Cunge
in voce.*

 VER. 8. *Cadgily.*—After the manner of the *cadgers,* or
thofe who carry about goods for fale in *cages*, by us called
             *creels*,

## II.

O Wow! quo' he, war I as free,
As firſt whan I ſaw this country,
How blythe and mirry wad I be!
    And I wad never think lang.

                        He

creels, on horſes backs, who uſe to ſing, in order to beguile
the tediouſneſs of the way.  Prim. ca, cad, cap, any thing
made for containing, as we have already obſerved.  Some
think it comes from the Gael. cadhla I.

VER. 8.  Ranted.—Made a noiſe.  Prim. Hebr. ran, to
cry.  Hence the Latin rana, a frog, and French grenouille,
its diminutive.  From hence Gr. γερανος, which Stephanus
in Βιθυνια explains πικρος βατραχος; alſo written γυρινος,
γερινος, as Euſtathius obſerves.

### STANZA II.

VER. 1.  Wow.—Interjection, from Ger. weh, alas; Iſl.
warla, with difficulty; Snorro, Tom. 2. P. 102. Swa warla
ſeck.  Brætit ut ægre dirui poſſit; written alſo valla, verkunna,
to have pity; and S. G. warkunna, id.  Douglas p. 158.
27.
    " Ut on the wandrand ſpreits wow thou cryis."
VER. 3.  Blyth.—Glad.  A. S. blythe; Belg. bly, id. Ulphila bleiths, pitiful.  Lucke 6. 36. Jah Atta iſwara bleiths
iſt, as your father is merciful.  In the A. S. it denotes meek,
placid, ſimple; Iſl. bluther, bludur, bland, affable.  Hence
the A. S. blithſan, bletſian, rejoice; whence our bleſs.  In
Douglas it is written blyith.

                        VER. 5.

He grew canty, and scho grew fain;
But little did her auld minny ken

What

---

VER. 5. *Canty.*—Cheerful. Belg. *hantig*, merry. *Een cantiger karl*, a gamesome fellow; and, as cheerfulness attends good health, the Chesshire-man says, *very cant*, God *yield you*, i. e. very strong and lusty. To *cant* too, is used for recovering or growing better; Yorkshire, A health to the goodwife *canting*, recovery after child-bearing. Douglas, *cant*, merry, cheerful; *cant*, the language of gypsies, vid. Spelm. in Egyptiani. Gaelic, *caint*, discourse; *canteach*, full of talk. From this Celtic origin comes Lat. *cano*, to sing; Fr. *chanson*, *chanter*, &c. Lat. *occento*, de qua voce vide Fest. It would have saved Vossius much labour, had he known the true Etymon.

VER. 5. *Fain.*—Full of wishes. Douglas writes it *fane*, glad; Ulphila *faginon*, id. Isl. *feigin*; A. S. *wægn*, *fægn*. Ulphila thus translates the Angel's salutation of Mary, Luke 1. xxviii. *Fagino anstaiaud ahasta*, "Rejoice, thou full of "grace;" corresponding exactly to the Gr. χαιρε; Isl. *fognudur*, joy.

VER. 6. *Minny*—mother. This word belongs to the Infantine Lexicon, being used by very young children to their mothers. The prim. is *min*, little, beautiful, pleasant. Hence Goth. *minna*, to love; Alamm. *minnon*; Fr. *mignon*, and *mignard*. From hence *mama*; Scot. *mamy*; Fr. *maman*; Goth. *mamma*; "vox" (says Ihre) "qua blandientes in- "fantes matrem compellant." Welch *mam*; Armor. *mam- maeth*, a nurse. Gr. Μαμμα. Aria. Helladius (apud Phot. in Bibl.) informs us, that in ancient Greece the mothers were called παππαι. Confer Cange in Gloss. Graec. who also observes that, in the middle Latinity, the *pap* was called *mamma*; and hence comes Fr. *mammelle*. Pelletier, in Lexi-

co

What thir flee twa togidder war fayen,

    Whan wooing they war fae thrang.

### III.

And O! quo' he, ann zee war as black,

As evir the crown o' your daddy's hat,

                          'Tis

co Brit. p. 570, juftly obferves, " *Ce mot eft peutetre* un des
" plus anciens du monde, car c'eft apres les cris, la premiere
" ouverture de la bouche du petit enfant, a qui la nature dicte,
" qu'il a befoin de nourriture, qu'il ne peut recevoir que de
" la *mammelle*, de celle qui lui a donne la vie." The Hebr.
*em* fignifies *mother*. From the Prim. *min*, little, is formed
the Lat. *minor*, (the *or* being the mark of comparifon), and
*minimus*. When we come to the Eighth Stanza of this Ballad,
we fhall explain the connection betwixt this and *winfome*.

    Ver. 2. *Wooing.*—A. S. *wogere*, lover, whence our *woo-er*. It has been thought, and with probability, that this word
was formed from the cooing of the dove, as Douglas fays, p.
404. 27.

      I mene our awin native bird, gentil Dow,

      Singand on hir kynde, *I come hidder to woo,*

      So prikking her grene curage for to crowde

      In amorus voce, and *wowar* foundis lowde.

    This is, at leaft, a better conjecture than that of Junius,
who deduces it from *woe*. The A. S. *wogan*, fign. to
marry.

### STANZA III.

    Ver. 2. *Daddy.*—Engl. *dad*, father. The prim. is *da,
di*, every thing elevated in dignity and power, and being

                            denote

formed by a ſtrong preſſure of the tongue againſt the teeth, it comes to be a part of the child's firſt language, addreſſing him whom he is taught to look up to with reverence. Hence this radical word has given riſe, in every language, to thoſe which denote *elevation*. Such is the Celtic *Di*, God, the Supreme Being; *dun*, a hill; *dome*, *dum*, *din*, a judge. Hence too the Gr. Δυναϛης, Δυναμις, power; and the Lat. *dominus*, *dominatio*; the Greek Δαμαω, to tame, *i. e.* bring into ſubjeƈtion; our *dame*, miſtreſs.

In many dialeƈts the *d* is changed into *t*, and moſt often, in thoſe ſpoken in the North, though we alſo find it in the Weſt, as in the Lat. *totus*, totality; Fr. *taſſer*, *entaſſer*, to heap up. *Ta*, *tata*, father. From the idea of fatherly protection, were formed *di*, *ti*, prince or proteƈtor; and the Lat. *tego*, *teƈtum*, whence the Engl. *proteƈt*, pro-tec-tion; and many more.

We ſhall here colleƈt a few more infantine words, plainly derived from the ſtruƈture of the vocal organs, and the moſt eaſy movements of their ſeveral parts. Such are, *pappa, mamma, dad, atta*; Fr. *bon*; *bobo, bibbi, puppet*; Fr. *poupee*; *buſs*. Thus Cato, de Lib. Educand. talking of this part of language, "cum " cibum et potum, *buas* et *papas*, vocent; matremq; *maman*, " patrem, *papam*." We may add to theſe, *pap, baba*, and even the ancient ſtory of the word *bek*, pronounced by two children educated by Pſammytichus king of Egypt, remote from all commerce with mankind, as Herodotus informs us. Confer. Preſident de Broſſe's Mechaniſm du Language, tom. 1. p. 231. ſeqq. To evince the univerſality of this truth, we might cite the Hebr. *phe*, and Chald. *phum*, mouth. Whence the *fari* of the Latins; the Hebr. *phar*, or *par*, ornament. Whence Latin *paro*, and Fr. *parer*, *parure*; Hebr. *pulful*, herbage. Whence the Lat. *puls*; the Gr. Βοω, and Βοσκω, to feed; Βορα, meat; Lat. *voro, devoro*, and our *devour*;

E  Βαιος,

'Tis I wad lay thee be me bak,
    And awa wi' thee I'd gang.

                                And

*Caios*, little; and the Ital. *bambino*; the Hebr. *bag*, nourish-
ment, from the Prim. *bek*; from which is derived the Teuton.
and Ger. *becken*, a baker; Babble, Ger. *babbelen*.

But how happen all thefe coincidencies? To this vain queftion we will only anfwer, in the words of the learned Prefi-
dent laft quoted, " L' homme parle, parceque Dieu l'a
" creé *etre parlant*." The vocal organs are conftructed a-
like in every tribe of mankind, and all children pronounce
thofe founds firft, which are moft eafily formed by the mo-
tions of thefe wonderful inftruments. The founds they vary,
and multiply, in proportion as practice makes them better acquainted with the organic powers, and more ready in the application of them. For the fame reafon, too, we find all the
radical words in every tongue we are acquainted with, to be
*monofyllables*, thefe being the firft effays of man in ufing the
vocal organs.

To the lift of languages, in which *dad, tat*, fignifies *father*, let us add the Gael. *daid*; Welch *dad*; Cornifh *tad*;
and Armorick *tat*.

Verfe 4. *Awa*] Engl. *away*; A. S. *an wæge*, from
*wæg*, a way. Douglafs, p. 124. l. 4.

" And the felf hour mycht haif tane us *awa*."

*Gang*] From *gae*, to *go*. This is an inftance where
our fouthern neighbours have vitiated the true old pronounciation. The primitive letter G, being a guttural, is therefore
painted in all the ancient alphabets like the neck of a camel, or
with a remarkable *bending* in its figure, as in the Gr. Γ; the
                                Hebr.

Hebr. ɔ. Hence it neceffarily denotes every thing in the form
of *canal* or *throat*, and every thing that runs or paffes fwiftly.
We hope to produce many examples of this in our Scoto-
Gothic Gloffary. Mean while, we only obferve the likenefs
in the following inftances. Ulphila fays *gaggan*, to go; and
*gagg*, a ftreet or road. Though this word occurs very often in
the Codex Argenteus; yet Junius has omitted it in his learned gloffary on Ulphila's verfion of the Gofpels. Ger. *gechen*;
Belg. *gaen*; Dan. *gaa*. From hence comes the Lat. *eo*,
without the *G*; and the Gr. κ-ιειν. Plato (in Cratylo, P.
281, *Fic.*) owns that κ-ιεν is a barbaric term. The other
correfponding word ἐω, is undoubtedly Celtic; and here Voffius (in *eo*) ftops, being quite ignorant of the primitive word,
and that no true radical term has ever more than one fyllable.
Ihre's deep refearches into ancient languages enabled him to
difcover this truth; " Lingua" (fays he, Glofs. Vol. I. Col.
646.) " quo antiquior, eo monofyllabicarum vocum ditior
" eft." Pity this very ingenious Etymologift had not carried
this obfervation more into practice. The Armor. for *ga*, fay
*kea, ker*. The Goths call rogation days, *gandagar*; literally,
*walking days*, from the proceffions that then were ufually made
round the corn-fields, during the darknefs of popery. Ihre
juftly terms thefe *ambarvalia chriftiana*. Rolf, the firft who
led the Scandinavians into Normandy, being a man of great
ftature, could find no horfe ftrong enough to carry him. Being therefore always obliged to march on foot, from that cir-
cumftance he was furnamed *Ganga Hrolf*, by the Iflandic hiftorians. *Gangare*, in the old Gothic laws, is " equus tolu-
" tarius qui tolutim incedit." In one of the refcripts of King
Magnus, *anno*. 1345, the bridegroom fends to his future
fpoufe, *en gangare fadul, betzil, armakapo, och hata*, a horfe,
faddle, bridle, cloak, and head-drefs. Money of allowed
currency is called *gangfe*; and *gangjarn*, hinges; and hence

the

And O! quo' fho, ann I war as whyte
As er the fnaw lay on the dyke,

I'd

the Fr. *gond*. Perhaps our old word *ganze*, in Douglafs, a *dart*, or *arrow*, comes from the Prim. *ga*, p. 461. 48.

" So thyk the *ganzies* and the flanys flew."

And p. 343. 46.

" Als fwift as *ganze* or fedderit arrow fleis."·

VER. 6. *Snaw*] Snow; another inftance of the Englifh perverfion of our ancient language. Ulph. *fnaiws*; A. S. *fnaw*; Allam. *fne*; Ifl. *fnior*; Swed. *fnio*; Prim. *aw*; water, ever foft and flowing gently. Hence Gr. ναυειν; Hefich. ναυει, 'ρεει, ϲρυϲει, fluit, manat; A. S. *fniwan*, to fnow. How ridiculous are Junius, and the other lexico-graphers, who deduce our word from the Greek? Surely our anceftors had feen fnow long before they faw Greece. The ancient Goths were fond of prefixing *f* to many of their words; and hence the Prim. *aw*, water, became with them *fnaw*; Sclavon. *fneg*; Pol. *fnieg*. When the *f* is taken away, it became *niv* with the Latins, and *neve* with the Italians; fo the Gr. νιπας, denotes a thick falling fnow.

*Dyke*] This has been prepofteroufly derived from τειχος, a wall. The true primitive is the Celtic *digh*, folid, ftrong, powerful; applied particularly to every rampart, whether to keep off enemies, beafts, or inundations. Hence the τειχος of the Greeks; Ger. *teich*; Belg. *dyke*; French *digue*; the Ger. *dick*, folid; whence our word *thick*. The other German word *dight*, fign. folid, connected; A. S. *dic*, rampart; *dician*, *gedician*, to build a rampart. Hence our

*ditch*;

I'd cleid me braw and lady like,

　　And awa wi' thee Ild gang.

IV.

*ditch;* A. S. *diker,* a ditcher; the Gr. *Σικελλα,* a fpade; *Σικελλιτης,* a digger, one who ufes the fpade.

Ver. 7. *Cleid*] Engl. *clothe.* Our *claith* is the true pronounciation, not the Englifh *cloath,* our word being immediately formed from the Goth. *klaede,* clothing, and *klaeda,* to *clothe.* Prim. *kla—kle,* covering; A. S. *clath.* Obferve, that the ancient Scandinavians faid, *Eff par klæder,* a pair of garments, for a complete fuit of clothes; the one formed the breeches, and the *troja,* or veft, the other. The old Teutonic Verfion of the Gofpels (app. Ihre, vol. 1. col. 1076.) Luke xv. ver. 22. " Hemtin mik fram thet bafta *par klæder* jak " hafwer;" Bring forth a pair of the beft garments I have. Chron. Ryth. p. 121. " Eff hofweligt ors, ok *klæder* ett " par;" An excellent horfe, and a pair of garments. The Iflanders pronounce it *klæde;* the Germans *kleide,* arm; *arm klade,* a fcarf worn on the arm; *jaga klader,* a monk's gown.

*Braw*] Handfomely, elegantly. Prim. Celt. *bra,* ftrength, might, elegance; every thing having thefe qualities. Goth. *braf;* honeft; Scot. *bravery,* fumptuous apparel. In the Bas—Bret. *braw,* arm, id. Hence the Fr. and our *brave;* Ital. *bravo.* Hence too the Goth. *brage,* a hero, and *Brage,* the name of one of the companions of Odid, of whom *Edda, Agietus ad Spæki,* &c. He was very elegant, and wife, and a great poet; fo that from him all perfons, both men and women, who excelled in thefe arts, were called *Bragmadur.* From the fame fource the *bragebækare,* or large cup, drunk off by the new King, juft before he a-

fcended

## IV.

Between the twa was made a plot,
They raife a wee befor the cock,

And

fcended the throne, while he folemnly vowed to atchieve fome
great deed in arms, of which many inftances occur in Snorro,
and the other hiftorians of the North. This ceremony gave
rife to the ufage, according to which the knights, in ancient
times, made vows of the fame kind at their folemn banquets.
The learned and accurate Annalift, to whom Scotland owes
the elucidation of many hiftorical difficulties, obferves (ad an.
1306) that Edward made a vow after this form, by which
he bound himfelf to punifh Robert Bruce.—See alfo St Palaye
Mem. De l'ancienne cheval. tom. 1. p. 184, and 244.

### STANZA IV.

VER. I. *Twa*] Ger. *twee*; A. S. *twa*; Welch *dau*,
*dwy*; Armor. *du*; Cimber. *tu*; Sued. *twa*; Celt. id.
Whence Gr. *δυε*, and Lat. *duo*. Hence our *twin*; Dan.
*twilninger*; Alam. *zuinlinge*; A. S. *getwinn*. Douglas
calls fheep of two years old *twinleris*, p. 130, v. 34.

" Fyfe twinleris Britnyt he, as was the gyis."

Confer page 202, ver. 16. as being two *winters*, i. e. two years
old ; Ulphila *twai*, two. Hence to *twinne*, ufed both in
Scotland

And wylily they fhot the lock,
    And faft to the bent ar they gane.

                              Up-

Scotland aud England to fignify, to feparate, divide into two
parts. Chaucer, l. 518.

    " The life out of her body for to twyne."

Pard. Prol. 167 :

           ——" He muft ytwin
    " Out of that place."——

VER. 2. *Wee*] Little. This is an infantine word, denoting every thing *little*. Ger. *wenig*. Hence our *wean*,
i. e. *wee-ane*, a little child. Of the fame family, as I conjecture, is the word *weaena*, which the learned Lord Hailes
fhewed me in an Englifh book, where it denoted a *fimpleton*,
or unlearned man; little of underftanding, as the Dutch ftill
fay, *Klein van verftanda*.

VER. 3. *Wylily*] Cunningly. A. S. *wile*, whence our
*guile*, the *W* being often changed for *G*. Belg. *gylen*, and in
the Lower Germany they fay *begigeln*, to *beguile*. Dan. *ad-*
*willa*, to deceive. Ifl. *viel*, deception; hence *Willurunnur*,
Runæ deceptrices. Sax. Chron. ad an. 1128, *Thurh his*
*micele wiles*, " Through his many *wiles*, or tricks." In a
church-yard in Scotland are the following lines on the tomb-
ftoue of a Magiftrate :

    " He was baith wyss and *wyly*,
    " For which the town made him a bailey."

                             Under-

Upon the morn the auld wyf raife,

And at her leifure pat on her claife,

Syne to the fervants bed fcho gaes,

     To fpeir for the filly poor man.

                            V.

Under-waiftcoat is by Douglas called the *wylie-coat*, p. 201, v. 40.

  " In doubill garment cled, and *wyle-cot*."

As this inner-veft (fays Ruddiman) cunningly, or hiddenly, keeps us warm.

    VER. 4. , *Bent*] Properly a marfhy place, producing the coarfe grafs called *bent*, from its fmall limber ftalk eafily *bent*, fays Minfhew ; but may it not be rather derived from *ben*, a hill, as this coarfe grafs is common on the fides of hills, and on the rifing ground on the fea-fhore, or fandy hillocks, in Scotland ? In Gaelic *ban* fignifies wild or wafte ground, on which this fpecies of grafs is generally found.

    VER. 6. *Claife*] Vide Note to Stanza III. Ver. 7.

    VER. 7. *Syne*] Afterwards, then. Douglas writes *fen*, p. 100, v. 1.

  " *Sen* the deceis of my forry hufband."

*Senfyne*, fince that time, id. p. 44, v. 26.

       ——" *Senfyne* has ever mair

  " Backwart of grekis the hope went."

Teuton. G. *fyn* and *findes*, whence our *fince*. Alam. *ejnzen*; and *Otfrid*, Lib. 3. cap. 26. *findes*.

    Joh tharbetin thes *findes*,
    Their heiminges.

                        " And

" And were deprived of their country *from that time.*" Ulphila, Luke 17. v. 4. *Sintham.* Ubi confer Jun. Suio-Goth.
*naganſinn,* and more ſhortly *nanſin* ; *nanſtin,* ſometimes ;
*hwatſin,* how often ; *ſinnam oh ſinnɔm,* by degrees, gradually. Whence the Lat. *ſenſim,* underſtood by none of their
Lexicographers.

As particles in general form a difficult part of language, a
philoſophical enquiry into the origin of theſe might highly
deſerve the attention of the critic. It is thought that many
of them, being *monoſyllables,* will be found to be *radical
words.* Such are, Engl. *if* ; Scot. *giff* ; A. S. *giſ, gyf* ; Gr.
*ει,* enlarged by compaſition to ειπεϛ, and ειτϵ ; and many
others might be named. To derive *if* from *giff,* as ſome have
done, is ridiculous, and ſhews that ſome writers will rather
adopt the moſt futile conjeɛtures, than ingeniouſly confeſs their
ignorance. The limits we have preſcrib'd ourſelves in theſe
notes, do not permit us to enlarge on this at preſent.

Ver. 8. *Speir*] Prim. is *pa—ſa,* the mouth. Hence
*ſpeech* ; Germ. *ſpuren,* to enquire. The learned and ingenious
Mr Gebelin, to whom we confeſs ourſelves indebted for the
only rational principles of Etymology we have ſeen, in his
*Monde Primitive,* tom. 5. p. 790, has ſhewn, that the P,
in all the ancient alphabets, figures *the mouth opened,* viewed
in profile ; and, by neceſſary conſequence, all the aɛtions of
that organ, as *ſpeaking, eating, drinking,* &c. And this poſi
tion he has evinced to demonſtration, by innumerable examples. We confine ourſelves here to what regards the word
*ſpeir.* We have already obſerved, that the general meaning
relates to *ſpeech* ; Lat. *ſari* ; Fr. *pa-rler, ſa-ribole,* vain and
idle talking. Afterwards it was uſed in the North for *wiſdom, prudence.* Hence Iſl. *ſpakr,* a wiſe man ; in Goth.
*ſpak,* the ſame ; *ſpakum bonda,* a prudent man ; Iſl. *ſpakmæle,*
the ſayings of the wiſe ; Alam. *ſpaker,* and *ſpeke,* wiſdom.

F                                          Tatian,

## V.

She gaed to the bed whar the beggar lay,
The ftrae was cauld, he was away ;

She

'Tatian, cap. 12. *Fol fpahidu*, full of wifdom.  Ifl. *fpeja*, to fpeculate, or confider.   In reftricting the general meaning, it came to fignify only, to *divine*, *prophecy*.   Ifl. *fpa*, to prophecy ; whence our *fpae*, to foretell future events.   From this the Latins have formed *fpecio*, *aufpex*, *arufpex*, and the like.   Douglas, p. 101. 50 :

   " O welaway, of *fpaimen* and divines
   " The blind myndis."——

And p. 80. 26 :

      —— " The harpie Celeno
   " *Spais* unto us an fereful takin of wo."

The *Volufpa*, containing the theology of the Scandinavians, has its name from thence, and literally fignifies a poem artfully contrived, *or with much wifdom*, compounded of *wola*, *wool*, art, and *fpa*, poem or fpeech.  Hence Ifl. *wolundr*, artificer ; and *wolundarhus*, a labyrinth.

### STANZA V.

VER. 2. *Strae*] Engl. *ftraw* ; A. S. *ftreow*, *ftrew* ; Al. *kiftreiew*, to ftraw ; Mæfo-Goth. *ftrawan* ; A. S. *ftreawian*. The chamber *furnifhed* in Mark xiv. 15. is called in Gr. εϛρωμενοι, and by Ulphila *gaftrawith*.  The ancients not
only

Scho clapt her hands, cry'd, dulefu-day!
　　For fome o' our gier will be gane.

　　　　　　　　　　　　Sume

only filled their beds with ftraw, but on folemn days the
floors were covered with it; and we remember to have read,
that Queen Elizabeth's ftate-rooms were ftrawed with green
grafs or hay. It was alfo a part of the holding of feveral
manors, both in England and Scotland, to furnifh ftraw for
the Royal apartments, when the King made a progrefs. In
the Scandinavian writings, the ftraw ufed at the feftival of
*Yule*, was called *Iulhalm*, vide Ihre in V. So in Olaf's
*Trygwas*. Saga, p. 1. p. 204. it is faid of Thorleif, *Seeft han
nither utarliga utarfiga i halmin*, He fat down on the
furtheft part of the ftraw. Snorro tells us, tom. 1. p. 403.
that when Olaf, fon of Harald, came to fee his mother,
*Tweir karlar, baro halmin i golfid*, Two fervants brought ftraw
into the apartments; and, in the Hiftory of Alf, p. 41. one of
the Princes in the Court of King Hior, *Their voru i halmi-
num nidur a golfinu*, They fat on the ground on 'the ftraw.
It would appear, that this was commonly done in winter;
for the fame reafon we ufe carpets to keep the feet warm:
For it is remarked of Olaf Kyrra, that he had his apartments
covered with ftraw, winter and fummer; *han let giora ftragolff
um vetur, fem um fumur*. The fame mode was obferved in
France. In a charter of the year 1271 (ap. Cange in *Jonchare*)
" Item debet et tenetur dictus Raulinus pro prædictis, Jon-
" chare domum D. Epifcopi quando neceffe eft." Vide id. in
*Junkus*. Confer Spelm. in *Straftura*.

　　Ver. 4. *Gier*, or *gear*] Clothes, furniture, riches. To
what has been faid in the preface of this word, and in the
notes to Stan. 4. ver. 5. we have little to add. The prim. is

Sume ran to coffers, and fume to kifts,

But nought was ftown that cou'd be mift ;

                               She

*Ge* ; Gr. γη, the *earth* ; fource of all our riches. Hence ufed by the Scots indifcriminately, to fignify every thing we value, goods, tools, apparel, armour. So Douglaſs fays, *graithed in his gear,* armed at all points. *Gear,* in fome of our old poets, is ufed for the *membra viri genitalia.* A. S. *gyrian,* to clothe. Cædmon, 23. 7. *gyred wædum,* put on his weeds or garments.

Ver. 5. *Kifts*] Engl. chefts. The primitive of this is found in the form of the letter *c,* (for which the northern dialects generally ufe the *k*) fignifying every hollow, like the hollow of the hand ; as *cavus, cavea* ; Gr. κοιλος ; *cavity, cave, &c.* This obtains in every language, as we ſhall prove at fome length in our Scoto-Gothic Gloffary. With refpect to this word, we formed it from Goth. *kifta,* a cheft ; whence *kiftafæ,* precious goods which are kept in kifts ; Iſl. *kiftu* ; Welch *cift, cyft* ; Ger. *kaften* ; Fr. *caiffe* ; Gr. κιϛτη ; Lat. *cifta,* the origin of which fimple word is not to be found in the many Greek and Latin Dictionaries we have. Hence too *cifterna,* our ciftern. The etymon of this word by Feftus is too curious to be omitted ; *cifterna dicta eft, quod cis ineft infra terram.* Such are the reveries produced by ignorance of firft principles. We add further, that the Perfians call a *cheft,* or *kift, caftr.* In the north it fignifies a prifon where thieves are confined ; *teif kifta.* The Latins ufed a fimilar phrafe, *In arcam conjici,* vid. Cic. pro Milone, cap. 22. The Iflanders call a coffin *leikiftu,* as we alfo do, and the Anglo-Saxons. Luke 7. 14. *Iha cyfte æthran,* He touched the coffin.

                                        Ver

She dancid her lane, cry'd, Praife be bleft !
I have ludg'd a leil poor man.

### VI.

VER. 6. *Stown*] Engl. *ftolen* ; Prim. *ftill*, tacitly, hiddenly ; Goth. *ftilan* ; A. S. *ftelan* ; Swed. *ftiala*, to fteal ; Tueton. *ftille*, quiet, fecret. Hence our Scots *ftowth*, ftealing, which we find applied to amorous pleafures, as being fecret, by Douglafs, p. 402. 52.

" Hys mery *ftowth*, and paftyme lait ziftrene."

So the Latins, *Veneris furta*. *Stiala* is ufed by the Northerns in the fame fenfe as we fay, to *fteal away ; fo ftiala fig bort* ; and *komma ftialandes uppa en*, to come privately upon one. They alfo ufe it to denote *hiding*, concealing, the meaning of the primitive. Hift. Alex. M. Apud Ihre, v. 2. 267.

*Jordan kan eij gullit fwa ftiala.*
The earth cannot fo hide the gold.

Ulphila's *hliftus* fignifies a *thief*, from *hliftan*, to hide. Hence our Scots *to lift*, to fteal. From the primitive *ftill* is the Gr. ςειλαςϑαι, to hide ; and the Lat. *celo*, the *ft* being often added in the Scythian words ; as *ftrafwa*, for *rofwa*, *fpoliare ; ftræcha*, for *ræcka*, *tendere*, &c. The Iflandic *ftiarlare* is a *thief*, a *ftealer;* and hence the Latin *ftellio, ftellionatus, ftellatura*, occult fraud, as the ingenious Ihre has juftly obferved, and thereby unfolded the true etymon, about which all the Latin Lexicographers were puzzled.

VER. 7. *Praife be bleft*] God be praifed. This is a common form ftill in Scotland with fuch as, from reverence, decline to ufe the facred name.

VER.

## VI.

Since nathing's awa, as we can learn,
The kirn's to kirn, and milk to earn,

Gae

VER. 8. *Leil*] Loyal, honeſt, truly. Dougl. p. 86. 46.

" The *ceremonies leil,* i. e. holy ceremonies."

And p. 43. 20.

" ——by the faith unfylit, and the *lele* lawte."

### STANZA VI.

VER. 1. *Awa*] Engl. *away.* Angl. Sax. *an wæge,*
from *wæg,* a way. Dougl. p. 124. 4.

" And the ſelf hour mycht haif tane us *awa.*"

VER. 2. *Kirn*] Churn. This is the ſame with the
Ger. and Scot. *quern,* a hand-mill for grinding corn, butter
being produced by the continued action of turning round. In
the A. S. *quearn,* or *cwyrn;* Dan. *handquern,* hand-mill. The
prim. is *gur, kyr,* any thing circular; Arab. *kur,* a round tower; *ma-kur,* a turban; Hebr. *gur,* to aſſemble; and *ha-gur,*
a belt; Iſland. *gyrta;* whence our *girth,* and the verb to
*gird.* Hence too Gr. γυρ-ος; Lat. *gyrus,* and *girare.* The
Fr. *ceinture,* and our *girdle* are from the ſame root, and the
Gaelic *cor,* whence *cord;* Ger. *gurt,* a belt; and *gurten,* to
gird about; Welch *gwyr,* bent; Bas. Bret. *gouriſa,* to be-
gird; Baſq. *gur,* around; *girata,* to roll about; *gurcilla,*
chariot wheel; *guiroa,* the ſeaſons, *i. e.* the revolutions of the
heavens. The Gr. κυρ]ος, *vaulted,* and κιρκος, *round,* have
the ſame origin; alſo ἀγορα, a place of public aſſembly where

the

Gae butt the houfe, lafs, and waken my bairn,
And bid her come quickly ben.

The

the people ftood round the orators. In Varro we find the ancient Latin *guro,* to make round ; and the common, words,
*circus, circulus, circum, circuitus,* and many more, all deduced from the fame root. The *gier-falcon* has its name from
the circular flight he makes ; and the Ger. *kurbis,* a gourd ;
and the Lat. *cu-cur-bita,* cucumber ; Gr. ſopuγος, a quiver.
It were eafy to add ten times this number of words, all taking
their origin from *gyr ;* but we only further mention *gir,*
the Scots name for the *hoop* the boys drive before them with
a rod along the ftreets.

Our pronounciation of this word *kirn,* is more correct than
that of the Englifh ; for the Gothic verb is *kernais,* to *churn ;*
Fenn. *kirnun ;* and the churn itfelf is called in Eflhonia *kir-
nu,* and in Iceland *kernuafk.* The round Tower of Stock-
holm is called *Keerna* by the ancient writers, as the learned
Ihre informs us (Gloff. vol. 2. p. 1057.) to which we only
add, that the Gr. κιρναω *mifceo,* has the fame origin, though
it has not been obferved by Junius, or any other.

VER. 2. *Earn*] To thicken or curdle milk. Ger. *gerin-
nan,* to coagulate. The root is only found in the Armorick,
in which language *go* fign. fermentation ; *goi,* to ferment.
Hence the Goth. *gora,* effervefcere ; *drinkat gores,* the ale
ferments, or works ; Ger. *gœrung,* effervefcence ; and the
Swed. *gorning,* whence our *earning,* rennet.

VER. 3. *Butt*] From Belg. *buyten,* without; oppofed to
*binnen,* within. Thus Douglas ufes it, p. 123. 40.

" In furious flambe kendlit, and birnand fchire,
" Spredant fra thak to thak, baith *butt* and ben."

The

The primitive is found in the Goth. *bur-ho*, habitation; Ancient Goth. *bua-bu*, to inhabit; whence *bur*, and Iſl. *byr* and *bycht*, habitation. A. S. *bur*, a chamber; and Ray ſays, that in the North of England it is ſtill pronounced *boor*, and *bor*. Swed. *burtont*, floor of the houſe; *iung ſrubur*, apartment where the daughters of the family ſleep; βυρσον, οικημα, habitation. From the Goth. *byr*, we form *byre*, a cow-houſe. This primitive is alſo found in the Hebr. *beth*, and Perſ. *bat*, a houſe; Teuton. *bod*, whence the Engl. *abode*; Gael. *bwth*, *bottega*, a ſhop; Fr. *boutigue*. That part of Edinburgh where the merchants have their ſhops, is called *Lucken-booths*, rather *Lockenbooths*, from the booths, or ſhops, being locked up at night.

VER. 3. *Waken*] To a-wake. Prim. *wak*, *watch*. Hence Ulph. *vakan*, to awaken; *vaknandans*, vigilantes. All the Nothern dialects uſe this word. Goth. and Iſl. *waka*; Ger. *watchten*; Alam. *uuachan*. The Goths ſay alſo *wakna*, to watch; Iſl. *wekia*, *watch*, and Goth. *waht*, id. Ulphila ſays, *wahtus*; Alam. *uuaht*; B. Lat. *wacta*, cap. 3. an. 813. c. 34. "Si quis wactam aut wardam demiſerit." Vide Cange in *Wacta*. Hence in our old Scots Laws, to *watch and ward*, duty of citizens to defend their town, and for which they often obtained ſingular privileges from the Crown. *Wactar*, a watchman: It ſignifies alſo to *beware*; *Wacta ſig for en*, to be upon one's guard. From this, too, come the Lat. *vigilo*, *vigilium*; the Fr. *guetter*, and *garder*, our *guard*. The waiting a dead body before interment, is called in Sued. *wahſtuga*. Hence our phraſe *to wake a corpſe*, and *leikwake*, compounded of the two words Goth. *leik*, a dead body, and *wakna*, to watch.

*Bairn*] Child. Prim. Gael. *bar*; A. S. *bearn*; Alam. *barn*. Hence comes Gaelic *beirn*, and Goth. *baera*, both ſignifying *to bear*. We find our primitive in the Hebr. *Bar*,

Creator,

The fervant gaed quhar the dochter lay,
The fheits war cauld, fcho was away,

And

Creator, and *Bara*, creare. In the fragment of Sanchonia-
thon, *Beruth*, or *Berut*, is called the fpoufe of *El-ion*, or the
Moft High, becaufe God alone creates; and hence allegori-
cally *Creation* is called the *fpoufe of God*. In the Syriac, *bar*
fignifies a fon. We fay *bairn-team*, brood of children, from
the Saxon *team*, progeny; hence a *teeming-woman*. In our
old poets, *bairn* is often ufed to fignify a full-grown man.
So Douglas, p. 244. 33.

" Cùm furth quhat e'er thou be, *berne bald.*"

And elfewhere:

————" And that awfull *berne*,
" Berying fchaftis fedderit with plumes of the erne."

The fame author ufes *barnage* for an army, or troop of war-
riors; but Mr Ruddiman was far miftaken in deriving it from
the Lat. *baro*. We find the ancient Englifh poets ufed *child*
in the fame fenfe. See the ballad of the *Child of Elle*, in
Percy's Collection, vol. 1. page 107.

" And yonder lives the *childe* of Elle,
" A young and comely knight."

Vide ibid. p. 44. where two knights are called *children*.

VER. 4. *Ben*] The oppofite of *butt*, in the former verfe,
fignifying the inner-part of the houfe. From the Dutch
*binnen*, within, oppofed to *buyten*, without; A. S. *buta* and
*binnen*, butt and ben.

VER. 5. *Gaed*] Vide Note to Stanza I. Ver. 6.

G                                      *Dochter*]

And faſt to her gudewife 'gan ſay,
  Scho's aff wi' the Gaberlunzie-man.

### VII.

O fy gar ride, and fy gar rin,
And haſte ye find theſe traiters agen :

For

*Dochter*] Engl. *daughter ;* Ulph. *dauhtar.* We here obſerve how cloſely our ſpelling agrees with the Anglo-Saxon, in which it is wrote *dohter, dohtor,* and *dohtur ;* Alam. *dohtor, dohter,* and *thohter ;* Belg. *dochter.* The Gr. Θυγατηρ has a manifeſt affinity to all theſe.

VER. 6. *Cauld*] Another inſtance of our care in following the original orthography. Ulphila writes, *calds ;* A. S. *ceald ;* Iſl. *kaldur* and *kulde ;* Alam. *kalt ;* Dan. *kuld ;* all ſignifying *cold.*

VER. 7. *Faſt*] Quick or ſwift. Prim. Welch *fleſt,* agile, haſty. This is a quite different word from the Engliſh *faſt,* fixed or ſtable, which comes from the Mæſo-Gothic *faſtun,* to keep or hold faſt.

'Gan] For *gan, began ;* and thus Douglas elſewhere uſes it, as well as our more ancient poets.

VER. 8. *Aff*] Off; but all the other Northern dialects write this word with an *a.* Ulph. *af ;* Dan. *aff ;* Belg. *af.* The Lat. *ab,* and the Gr. *απ,* are quite ſimilar, eſpecially when we obſerve that the Greek word, before another beginning with an aſpirate, is written *αç.*

### STANZA VII.

VER. 1. *Fy*] Fy upon. Prim. Welch *fy,* and *hei,* whence *hiadd,* abominable ; Iſl. *ſue,* rottenneſs ; Belg. *ſcey ;*

hence

hence the Lat. *vah*, Ital. *vah*, Fr. *fi*.   The Gr. φευ is by the
Grammarians called φωνη χιτλ.αϛιχη, Vox ejus qui fe in-
digna pati conqueritur.   In old Englifh this · particle always
denotes *averfion*.   Chaucer, La. Prol. v. 80.

" Of fuch curfed ftories I fay *fie*."

And N. P. T. v. 73.

" *Fie* ftinking fwine! *fie* foul mote the befall."

'From hence the Scots formed *Fyle*, to foul; and the Engl.
*Defile*.   We alfo fay *Fych*, on feeling a bad fmell, or feeing
any dirty object, from the Celt. *cach*, *kakoa*, and *caffo*,
ftinking.   Hence our *kakie*, ventrem exonerare.   From
this origin, too, comes the old French appellation *cagots*,
*cacous*, *cakets*, given to lepers, who being confidered as a-
bominable, were fhut out from all fociety in the middle ages.
Thefe miferable wretches were found in great numbers about
the 12th and 14th centuries, fpread over Gafcony, Bearn,
and the two Navarres, on both fides the Pyrenean mountains.
Thefe were not allowed to traffick with their fellow citizens;
had a feparate door to enter into the churches, and a holy
water-font, which they only ufed; were forbid the ufe of
arms; nay, fuch was the univerfal horror of mankind againft
them, that the States of Berne, anno 1460, applied for an
order to prohibit their walking the ftreets bare-footed, left
others might catch the infection, and to oblige them to
wear on their garments the figure of a goofe's foot,
which, it would appear, they had neglected to do for
many years paft.   In the ancient *For. de Navarre*, compiled
about the year 1074, we fee them called *Gaffos* and
*Cakets* at Bourdeaux.   We find, among the Laws of the
Dukes of Brittany, anno 1474 and 1475, orders given, that

G 2                                          none

none of the *Cacofi-caquets*, or *Cacos*, fhould appear without
a bit of red cloth fewed on the outer-garment. They were
forbid even to cultivate any land but their gardens, and were
confined to the fingle trade of carpenters. Bullet (*Diction.
Celt.*) gives the following account of the rife of the public
hatred againft thefe poor people : " Cacous (fays he)
Nom que les Bas Brettons donnent par injure aux Cordiers et
aux Tonneliers, contre lefquelles le menu peuple eft fi prevenu,
qu'ils ont befoign de l'autorité du Parlement de Bretagne
pour avoir le fepulture, et la liberté de faire les fonctions du
Chriftianifme avec les autres, parce qu'ils font crus fans
raifon, defcendre des Juifs difperfés apres la ruine de Jerufa-
lem, et qu'ils paffent pour lepreux de race.—Les *Cacous* font
nommés *cacqueux* dans un arret du Parlement du Bretagne."
Here we have a people, living in the moft deplorable ftate of
flavery, from age to age, like the Gibeonites fubjected to the
Jews, and treated in the fame manner as the Gauls were, after
being conquered by the ancient *Franks* of Germany ; the
very name they went by, implying the moft rooted averfion,
though nobody ever gave any account of the reafon of this
appellation ; for the frivolous differtations of *Marca* and
*Venuti* leave us quite in the dark as to this, as well as to
the caufes of this extraordinary hatred againft a devoted race
from age to age. We therefore adopt the account of it given
by the learned and moft ingenious *Gebelin*, (Monde Primitif,
tom 5. p. 247) that they were the fcattered remains of the
original inhabitants of Gafcony and Lower Brittany, who, being conquered by thofe now called *Bretons*, and the Cantabri,
who invaded Brittany and Berne, were reduced to this miferable ftate by their Lords, in order to leave them no means of
revolt, and to render them ufeful as flaves. Du Cange informs us, that the celebrated Hevin firft obtained, from the
Parliament of Rennes, a repeal of thofe cruel and ridiculous
conftitutions

conftitutions againft the *Cacous.* But the word *Cagot* ftill remains a term of reproach, and now fignifies a *hypocrite.* Had
we leifure, it would be amufing to compare the miferable ftate
of the poor *Cagots,* with that infamy which is entailed, in
Hindoftan, on the caft or tribe of the *Sooders.* But we have
already made this note too long ; and all the apology we can
offer is, that we flatter ourfelves the reader will be glad to find
here an account of a fet of men, whofe very name is little, if
at all, known in this Ifland, and againft whom far more in-
tolerable feverities were exercifed, than by our anceftors againft
the lepers, who abounded both in England and Scotland
during the middle ages.

*Gar*] Force one to act, to conftrain. Prim. Celtic *gor,
gar,* force, ftrength, elevation, abundance ; vide Dict. Celt.
de Bullet in *Gorchaled,* and *Gor.* Hence Breton. *gor,* tu-
mour, elevation ; Gaelic *gorm,* nobleman, grandee. In the
language of Stiria and Carniola, mountain ; *gora,* in Sclavon.
id. Polon. *gora-hegy,* a cape or promontory ; Lapland, and
Finland, *kor-kin,* high ; Hebr. *gor,* to heap up ; Arab.
*ghurur,* pride, ambition ; whence Gr. γαυϝος, proud, elated ;
Old French *gaur,* id. Celt. *gorain,* to cry out with vehemence,
which greatly illuftrates the primitive fignification of our *gar ;*
Welfh, *gorchfygiad,* to force or conftrain ; Suio-Goth. *gora,*
antiq. *gara,* faccre ; vide Ihre in *gora,* where this elegant e-
tymologift has obferved the agreement betwixt this word and
our *gar.* Adde Lye addit. Etymol. Junü ; but none of thefe
writers have gone back to the Primitive Celtic ; Aremor.
*gra,* facere. From this root, too, comes the Latin *gero,* applied fometimes to war, *gerere bellum ;* vide Livy, l. 39. c.
54. Ifl. *giora,* to act ; Alam. *garen, garuuen.* The reader
may turn to our Introduction, where he will find fome other
obfervations on this word, to which we only add, that *carve*
comes from this root.

VER.

For ſcho's be burnt, and hee's be ſlean,
   The weirifou' Gaberlunzie-man.
Some rade upo' horſe, ſome ran a-fit,
The wife was wude, and out o' her wit;

                       Scho

---

VER. 3. *Scho's—Hee's*] She ſhall—He ſhall; a contraction frequently in the mouths of our country people.

VER. 4. *Weirifou*] *Fou* for *full*, it being cuſtomary in Scots to change the *l* into *w*, as *roll*, *row*; *ſcroll*, *ſcrow*; *tolbooth*, *toubooth*; *pol*, *pow*, &c. Ruddiman. From *fou*, we form *fouth*, plenty, abundance. So Douglaſs, p. 4. v. 6.

    " That of thy copious fouth or plentitude."

Thus from *deep*, *depth*; *rew*, *reuth*, &c. This is alſo remarked by Mr Ruddiman, Gloſſ.

VER. 6. *Wude*] Mad. Ger. *wuth*, rage; A. S. *wod*, mad; Teut. *ueueuten*, to be mad; A. S. *wedan*, id. Whence perhaps the Scandinavians called their Mars *Woden*. Doug. p. 16. 29.

    " The ſtorm up bullerit ſand, as it war *wod*."

And p. 423, 16.

    " Wod wroith he worthis for diſdene."

Dutch *woed*, fury; Ulphila, Mark v. 18. *wods*, poſſeſſed with a Devil; A. S. *wod*, mad; Iſl. *æde*, furor; Alam. *unatage*, furious. From this root the Gr. ϕυταν, vulnerare, pugnare; and ὑδαιveιr, to ſwell with anger.

                          VER.

Scho cou'd na gang, nor yet cou'd ſcho ſit,
   But ay ſcho curs't and ſcho bann'd.

## VIII.

Mein tym far hind out o'wr the lee,
Fu' ſnug in a glen whar nane cou'd ſee,

                 Thir

VER. 7. *Gang*] Mæſo Goth. *gagga*, pronounced *ganga*; as in the Greek when two *gammas* follow each other. Vide ad Stan. I. v. 6.

VER. 8. *Ban*] To curſe. Goth. *banna*, ſign. ſimply to forbid; *forbanna*, Divis devovere. The primitive Celt. *ban*, a *tie*; whence our *bond* and *band*. ▮Hence marriage *banns*. The Iſl. *forbanna*, ſign. to excommunicate or put out of ſociety. Hence our *ban-iſh*, and the Ital. *bandito*, our *banditti*; *a-ban-don*, to give up our claim to any thing, to looſen our tie to it. The bond by which the king's vaſſals are obliged to follow their ſovereign to the field, is, in France, called the *ban*, and *arriere ban*. Thus to *bann* one, literally ſign. to put him *under the bond of a curſe*. Hence Gael. *bana*, tied; Fr. *bande, bander*, our *band* or *company*, perſons linked together by one common tie, or bond; *bandage*, to bend; Fr. *ruban*, whence *ribbon*, literally, a fillet of a red colour. Hence, too, in the French, the barbarous *droit d'aubaine*, by which the lord of the ſoil inherited all that a ſtranger died poſſeſſed of in his territory. We find, in the Bar. Lat. *albani*, and *aubani*, a ſtranger; concerning which word many idle conjectures have been publiſhed, as derived from *advena*, and *Albanus*, a Scotſman. But it is compoſed of *al*, another, and *ban*, juriſdiction, literally a perſon living under *other laws*.

*laws.* The Iſl. *bann,* to curſe, is ſtill uſed in the north of England.

## STANZA VIII.

Ver 1. *Hind* ] This is the primitive of *behind, hindermoſt* ; Scot. *hindmoſt* ; and is found in all the ancient dialects of the north ; Ulphila, *hindar, hindana,* back, after ; *hindumiſts,* hindermoſt ; A. S. *hindan,* behind. Hence comes the verb to *hinder,* to impede ; Dan. *hindre, forhindra* ; Belg. *hinderen, verhinderen.* From this root comes the A. S. *hinderling,* properly one who comes far behind his anceſtors, *familiæ ſuæ opprobrium.* In Ll. Edw. Confeſſ. c. 35. Occidentales Saxonici habent in proverbio ſummi deſpectus, *hinderling* ; i. e. omni honeſtate dejecta et recedens imago ; the ſcandal of his family.

Ver. 2. *Snug* ] The primitive of ſeveral northern words, all ſignifying *hiding, concealment* ; Dan. *ſniger,* ſubterfugio ; *ſnican,* to crawl about hiddenly ; whence Engl. *ſneak,* a ſneaking fellow. Lye was miſtaken in deriving it from Iſl. *ſnoggur,* celer. The Gael. *ſnaighim,* is the ſame with the Saxon *ſnican* ; Dan. *ſnige ſig aff veyen,* to ſneak away. The Scots *ſnod,* neat, trim, may come alſo from this ſource, as it is evidently the ſame with the Gothic, *ſnug,* ſhort and neat ; *en ſnug piga,* a neat girl ; Iſl. *ſnylld,* elegance. Ray ſays, that in the north of England, they pronounce it *ſuog ; ſnogly geard,* handſomely dreſſed.

*Glen* ] Old Engliſh *glin,* or *glyn* ; Gael. *gleann.* It denotes a large, level tract of ground, bounded on each ſide by ridges of ſloping mountains. Hence we have in Scotland *Strathmore, Strathſpey, Strathern.* There is this difference between the Saxon *Dale,* and the Gaelic *Strath.* The former denotes a narrow valley, bounded on each ſide by a
ridge

Thir twa, wi' kindly ſport and glee,
    Cut frae a new cheeſe a whang.

                                    The

ridge of ſteep mountains, commonly with a river running
through the middle ; the latter anſwers the above deſcription,
which needs not to be repeated.

VER. 3. *Twa*] Ulphila *twai* ; A. S. *twa* ; Welſh *dau*,
*dwy* ; Gael. *do* ; Swed. *twa* ; Iſl. *tueir*. Hence the Gr. δνω,
and *twain* ; our Scot. *twin*, literally ſign. to ſplit into two
parts, to ſeparate. It is alſo uſed by Chaucer in this ſenſe, R.
R. 5077.

"Trowe nat that I woll hem twinne."

And Troil, 4. 1197.

"There ſhall no deth me fro' my ladie twinne."

From this root, too, is formed *twine*, thread, *i. e.* to double
it ; A. S. *twinen* ; vide Exod. c. 39. 29. Sued. *twynna* ;
Dan. *tuinder*, to ſpin ; *tuinde trade*, twined thread ; Belg.
*tweyn draed*. In Teutoniſta, *twern yarn*, *duinum tuinum* ;
A. S. *twinne*, to twine.

*Glee*] Mirth, gladneſs ; Iſl. *gled*, *gladde*, I have made
glad ; *mig gladur*, it is a pleaſure to me ; Sax. *glad*,
and our *glad*. With Chaucer *glee* denotes a concert of vocal
and inſtrumental muſic. Sir Top. R. v. 126.

"His merie men commanded he
"To maken him both game and glee."

Fa. Lib. 3. 161.

"There ſaw I ſitt in other ſees,
"Playing on other ſundric glees."

                    H                        The

The A. S. Verſion of Paſtor. 26. 2. *David deſeng his hearkan, and geſtilde his wodthraga mid tham gligge.* David took his harp, and ſtilled his madneſs with muſic. *Gligman,* mimus, ſcurra; *Gligmon,* id. Junius rightly conjectures, that *glig* was firſt uſed to denote inſtruments inflated by the breath, though afterwards indiſcriminately applied to every muſical ſound. This is confirmed by the Iſlandic *gliggur,* flatus, breath. A certain ſpecies of *catch* is ſtill called a *glee.* A. S. *gle,* joy, and without the *g* the Goth. *lek,* to laugh; we ſay *gaaff,* to laugh loudly, and with the open mouth. From the idea of joy, *gle* and *gla* came to ſignify every thing bright, ſplendid. Hence a multitude of words, Iſl. *glaumur,* joy; whence our old Scots *glamur,* often employed to ſignify *incantations,* becauſe, by ſuch arts, the mind was thought to be greatly moved, and to look on things indifferent as of great conſequence. Goth. *glans,* and Alam. *klanz,* ſplendour; whence our *glance,* from *gla,* light; *gloa,* to ſhine. From this laſt the Eng. *glow, glow-worm*; A. S. *glowan,* to glow; Swed. *glod*; Gael. *glo*; A. S. *gled*; Ger. *glut*; all ſignifying a *live coal.* Iſl. *glia*; Friſl. *glian,* to ſhine; Sax. *gleij,* ſplendidus; and hence the Gr. αιγλη, ſplendour; which none of our Lexicographers have been able to explain. Hence, too, Engl. *glitter,* by Ulphila written *glitmunjan*; Iſl. *glitta*; Ger. *gleiſſen*; Swed. *gliſtra, gniſta*; Sax. *glinſtern,* and the Gr. αγλαιζεϑαι; Iſl. *gliſt,* and *glaſt,* nitidus. So Snorro, v. 1. *Glaſt med gulli, och ſilfri,* ſhining with gold and ſilver. Gr. γελειν, ſplendere; and Heſychius explains. γελας, αυγην ηλιυ, a ſun-beam; αγλαος, ſplendidus; γλαυςςω, ſplendeo; γλαυκος, γλαυρος, ſplendidus; Goth. *glaſſa,* and our *glaze*; Iſl. *glas,* our *glaſs.* We call the ſlipperymucus, growing on ſtones in the river, *glitt*; and *glatt* in Gothic is nitidus, lævis. Hence Engl. *gloſs*; Goth. *gles,* Succinum. Vide Tacit. Mor. Ger. cap. 45. Plin. H. N. lib. 26. c. 3.

From

From the fame root are derived Goth. *glimra, glindra*, to fhine, whence our *glimmer* and *glimpfe ;* Engl. *gleam*, a ray of light ; Ifl. *glimbr*, fplendour. Taking away the *g*, we have the Gr. λαπτω, to fhine ; Ifl. *liome*, light ; Ulphila, *lauhmon*, lightning. And with the *g*, Swed. *glo*, to fee ; Gr. γλαυσσω; Sax. *gloren*, fplendere ; hence Scot. *glowr*, to look intently at any object. So in the old Ballad :

> " I canna get leave
> " To luke to my luve,
> " My minny's aye *glowring* owr me."

Ifl. *gloggr*, and Goth *glau*, fharp-fighted ; Gr. γληνι, pupil of the eye; Fr. *glaire*, the clear or white of the egg; Ifl. *glæ*, the fhining of the ocean in a calm. Hence Gr. γαληνη, ferenitas ; γαλνοα, fereno ; γλνϊα, res nitidæ, prætiofæ ; γλνρος, a ftar; Swed. *gran*, fhining; whence the *Apollo Gryneus*, literally the *Splendid Sun*. We are much deceived if the many coincidences we have here thrown together, (and to which more might eafily be added) do not prove very ftrongly, a primitive and univerfal language. We have not room to alledge the many examples the Eaftern dialects furnifh to us ;—thefe we referve for a larger work. Mean while, the reader may look at Ihre, Lex. voce *Gloa* and *Glo*.

VER. 4. *Frae*] Engl. *from*. But we have kept the true orthography. Swed. *fram*, prorfum, adverbium motus de loco pofteriori in anteriorem. The *pro* of the Latins is from this root, and has the fame meaning in *prorfum, procedere, prodire, profferre ;* and the Swedes fay ga *fram*, gifwa *fram* ; Ulphila, *iddja fram*, proceffit ; Luke xix. 28. *framis leitl*, a little further. So, too, in the compounds, *fram-wigis*, femper ; and Luke i. 18. *fram-aldrozi*, ftricken in years ; Alam. *frampringan*, producere. Tatian, cap. 73.

v. 1. *franor*, further. We find in Wilking. Saga, p. 3.
*Hugprydiac fpæki, oc framwifi*, a genius wife and prudent ;
from *fram* and *wis*, wifdom ; and hence *framvis*, a diviner,
conjurer ; Ifl. *framygdur*, a wife man ; Goth. *framfus*, a
petulant fellow, ever putting himfelf forward ; whence Engl.
*frumpifh*. To return to the Scots word *frae*, as correfponding
to the Goth. *fram*, from.   Chron. Ryth. p. 444.

> " Huar monde *fram* androm fly."
> Qui ab altero feceffit, aufugit.

*Framgangu*, going from, departure ; Swed. *fran*.   From
*fram* the ingenious and learned Ihre derives *framea*, a dart
ufed by the ancient Germans, mentioned by Tacitus, M. G.
cap. 6. Haftas, vel ipforum vocabulo, *frameas* gerunt ; from
*fram* and *frumen*, mittere, jaculari.   Hence, in Ulphila, we
find, Joh. x. 5. *Framthjana ni lajsjand*, a ftranger will they
not follow.   Alam. *framider* ; Ger. *fremd*, a ftranger ; and
Scot. *fremdman*, one come from far.

Douglas writes this word fometimes *fra* and *fray*.

*Whang*] Prim. *tan*, a binding or cord.   Hence every
thing of a long narrow fhape.   *Whang*, a flice of cheefe, cut
in a long narrow form.   Ulphila, *twang* ; Ifl. *tange, vinculum* ; Swed. *tang*, a ftrap hanging at the handle of a knife.
They alfo call an ifthmus *tang*, and we fay a *tongue of land*.
Ifl. *thuing*, a band ; A. S. *twang*, whence our *whang*.

The primitive *tan* is found in all the Scythian dialects, and
thofe derived from them.   Swed. *tan*, nerve.   Leg, Goth. cap.
22. *Thau en fundr er than hels edanacca* ; Si abfciffus fuerit
nervus colli.   Welch *tant*, chorda ; Ger. id. Alam. *than*, a
leather ftrap ; A. S. *tan*, vimen, virgultum ; and hence *tan-
blyta*, fortilegus.   Swed. *tanor*, filaments in flefh.   The Gr.
τενω, is formed from *tan*, fign. a nerve.—Odyff. 3.

" — πελεκυς

The prieving was good, it pleas'd them baith,
To lo'e her for ay, he gae her his aith,

Quo'

" —— πηλαχυς δ'ιεκοψε τενοντας,
" Αυχενος.——

Securis abfcidit nervos cervicis. The Iflanders call the
nets for catching birds *thaner*; and hence Latin *tenus*, *teno-*
*ris*, in Nonius; and Plaut. Bacchid. v. v. 6.

" Pendebit hodie pulcre; ita intendi *tenus*."

It is needlefs to obferve that our *tendon* is derived from
the fame fource. The Goths call the fwaddling bands of children *tanom*; Chron. Rythm. p. 561. *Barn then fom an i ta-*
*nom lag*, Children that lay yet in their fwaddling bands. The
Greeks called them τενια, τενιδια. Vide Jun. Glofs. Ulph.
p. 330.

VER. 5. *Prieving*] The proof, the firft tafte of any thing.
Primitive is *por*, *pro*; Celt. *por*, what is *before*; as *por* fignifies alfo *face*. Hence *porro*, *probo*, *probation*; Fr. *preuve*,
*eprouver*, the *prow* of a fhip; Gr. τρωϊος; Lat. *primus*,
*prior*, *princeps*, and a vaft number of other words. At prefent we confine ourfelves to the northern dialects, where we
find, in the Celtic, *prid*; whence our *price*, or value of any
thing; Ger. *preis*; Lat. *pretium*; Italian *apprezzare*; Goth.
*pris*, id. and metaphorically, glory, honour, high efteem;
whence Engl. *praife*. The truly learned and elegant Ihre obferves, that, in the old Swio-Gothic, they ufed *prifhet* in the
fame fenfe. In Chron. Ryth. p. 442.

" *Och innan ftrid ftor prifhet was*."
In war he was greatly prized.

With

Quo' she, to leave thee I will be laith,
    My winsom Gaberlunzie-man.

IX.

With them *prisa*, sign. *to prize, apprize*; and these words
clearly indicate their northern origin. Hence, too, Fr. *priser,*
*mepriser*; *winna priset*, to win the prize. In our dialect
*prif, prieve*, is proof, or trial, as here; and in Douglass, p.
309. 49.

   " Thus rude examplis may we gif,
   " Thocht God be his awin Creauture to *prieve.*"

We also use the verb, to *prie*, to taste.

   VER. 5. *Baith*] Engl, both, by a faulty pronunciation;
for the primitive is found in Ulphila's, *ba, bai*, i. e. *baith*,
not *both*. So Luke 5. v. 7. *Ba tho skipa gafullidedun*, they
filled both the ships; and Luke 6. v. 39. *Bai in dalga dri-
usand*, both will fall into the ditch. A. S. *ba, butu*; Alam.
*bedu, beidu*; Isl. *bathur*. It is diverting to see Junius gravely
supposing that our word comes from Gr. αμφω, as if our an-
cestors could not reckon *two*, till the Greeks taught them.
The savages of Kamschatka do more than this; for they follow the number of their fingers and toes up to twenty, and
having got thus far, they stop, and cry, Where shall I find
more ? See the account of this country, published at Peters-
burg, and translated by Grieve, p. 178. We just add, that
the same observation may be applied to the words, *aith, oath,*
*laith, loth*, which occur in the verses immediately following,
and which have been equally vitiated by our southern neighbours, as this word *baith*.

   VER. 7. *Laith*] Loth. But ours is the true pronunciation, as derived from Al. *leid, luad*; Alam. *lath*; Belg.

*leyd,*

*leyd,* odious, ugly, troublefome ; Old Danifh, *tha the lœwas and lœdedon iuch,* who hate and perfecute you. The primitive of all thefe is found in the Celt. *lad, loc,* to cut, pain, or wound ; Bafg. *laceria,* misfortune. We cannot deny our-felves the pleafure of following this original through fome of its many defcendants ; hence come Gr. λησειν ; Fr. *lacerer* ; Lat. *lacerare,* our *lacerate* ; Fr. *loqueté,* cut out in flices ; whence our *lock* of hair, or wool ; Celt. *laza,* to kill ; and hence *lay,* a poem on any tragical fubject ; fo Dougl. 321. v. 5.

" The dowy tones, and layes lamentabil."

Ital. *lai,* and our *lament,* the true Scots appellation of E-legiac fongs ; A. S. *ley,* id. which neither Menage, nor even Skinner underftood ; Ger. *lied,* a fong, but properly a me-lancholy ditty ; as the B. L. *leudus* alfo fignifies ; Fortunat. Epift. ad Gregor. Turon. ad Lib. 1. Poemat. Sola fœpe bom-bicans barbaros *leudos* harpa relidebat. Id. Lib. 7. Poem 8.

" Nos tibi verficulos, dent barbara carmina *leudos.*"

Hence, too, Lat. *leffus,* and the Baf. Bret. *lais,* a melan-choly found or cry ; *e-legia, e-legy, lefion* ; and the Fr. *leze majeftee,* high treafon. We could eafily bring many more proofs of the truth of our account of the term *elegy,* as that paffage of Proclus, in Chreft. ap. Phot. Bibl. Το γαρ θρηνος, ελεγιαν ελεγων οι παλαιοι, veteres luctum vocarunt ελεγον. Ovid gives us the fame idea, Ded. de Lib. 3. Eleg. 1.

" Flebilis indignos elegia folve capillos,
" Heu nimis ex vero nunc tibi nomen ineft."

Voffius (in Elegia) has quoted thefe paffages, but gives no Etymology, as indeed the root is loft both in the Greek and Roman languages. But we muft ftop, after obferving that the

Fr.

## IX.

O kend my minny I war wi' you,
Ill-fardly wad fhe crook her mou',

Sic

Fr. words *læid*, (which of old fignified, offence, injury, and now *uglinefs*,) *laideur, laidron*, and the Gr. λοιδορεω, to de- fame, are all of this family.

VER. 8. *Winfom*] We have have already fhewn the mean- ing and origin of this word, in the note on Stanza II. ver. 6. In the old ballads we find it often ufed; fo in the old fong of Gilderoy, (Percy, vol. I. p. 324, 325.) My *winfom* Gilderoy; Ger. *minnefam*, from *minne*, love, which we have already ex- plained; Alam. *wino*, a friend; A. S. *vine*, beloved.

## S T A N Z A  IX.

VER. 1. *Kend*] The primitive *kan-enen*, fignifies art, knowledge, dexterity. Hebr. *gwanen*, an inchanter, and the verb *gwenen*, to divine; Gr. κοινειν; Gaelic *kann*, I know; *kunna, kenning*, knowledge; *kennimen*, knowing, learned men, priefts; Ulphila, *kunnan*, Mark 4. v. 11. *Ifwis attiban ift, kunnan runa thiud angardjos Goths,*—To you it is given to know the myftery of the Kingdom of God. Ifl. *kunna*; Alam. *kennen, chennen*; from *kunna*, the Englifh *cunning*; in fea-phrafe, to *cunn a fhip*, is to direct her courfe; in Fr. *maitre gonin*, a fharper. See the poor efforts of Menage to explain this word. Hefych. κοιννειν, ςυνιεναι, επισαϑαι, to underftand. We fay here *kenfpeckled*, eafy to be known by particular marks. The Goths ufe a fimilar phrafe, *Kenefpak, qui alios facile agnofcit*; Ihre in *kenn*.

VER. 2. *Ill-fardly*] Ill-favouredly, in an ugly manner. In Engl. well-favoured, handfome, well-looking; and thus

our

our tranflators of the Bible ufe it, Gen. xli. v. 3. 4. Primitive is *fa*, to eat, to feed on good things, as defcended from the family of *fa*, denoting every action belonging to the mouth, as eating, fpeaking, &c. So the Latin *fari*, whence Fr. *faribole*, idle tale, and the like. From *fa* comes Latin *favus*, honey-comb; *favere alicui*, to favour one; our *favourite*, *favour*; Fr. *favorifer*, *fauteur*, and the Latin *fautor*. The common word *infant*, Latin *infans*, comes not from *in* and *fari*, one who cannot fpeak, as our herd of Lexicographers fay, but from *fa*, to nourifh, to feed, whence *fari* itfelf is derived, which being a diffyllable, can never be a primitive, thofe (as we have elfewhere obferved) being all *monofyllables*, in every language. From this root, too, we have *fawn*, a young deer. N. B. The animals do not fpeak, therefore it is impoffible that *fawn* can come from Latin *fari*: but we muft ftop here, left we offend thofe who hold, that the *Ourang-outans*, a fpecies of the monkey, belong to the human race; and that, though they have paffed above fix thoufand years without framing a language, it is ftill *very rationally expected*, that they will yet form one, (vide Origin and Prog. of Lang. vol. I. p. 189. 272). Whenever we are happy enough to poffefs a Dictionary, collected by fome learned Ouran-outang, and a Grammar of this new fpeech, we nothing doubt, but we fhall difcover many primitives of language yet unknown. But this by the bye.

We find *favour*, in the Welch, *fleafor*, *flawr*, and in the Greek, φαω, φημι; and in what Feftus writes, *faventia*, bonam ominationem fignificat; *favere*, enim, eft *bona fari*. Hence the folemn form, *Favete linguis*. Voffius has faid much, to no purpofe, about this, in *Favere*; but he had no principles. We fee new proofs of the truth of our Etymology in the *hinnuleus* of the Latins, and the Gr. ιννος, fig. παιδος, a boy or *young one*. Vide Salmaf. Plin. Exercit. p. 106. and

I

Spelman; in *Feñatio* and *Foinefium*. Lye mentions *fauntekin*
as an old Englifh word, fignifying an infant or little boy, which
he rightly derives from the Iflandic *fante*, a young man ;
whence the Italian *fante*, a page or fervant, and the French
*fantaffin*, a foldier who ferves on foot, and of thofe whom we
call *in-fantry*.

Ver. 2. *Crook*] Prim. Celt. *Crok*, fignifies every thing that
takes hold ; and as nothing can take hold but what deviates
from the ftreight line, this word has formed a very numerous
family : Goth. *krok*; the Gael. *krock*, *kruick*, an earthen
pot or vafe ; Goth. *kruka*, id. We in Scotland call the iron
on which the kettle hangs a *crook*. Shepherd's *crook*, from
its bent form ; and, for the fame reafon, *crotchet* in mufic fignifies a note, with a tail turned up. Hence, too, come the
French *crotcheteur efcroi*, a thief who feizes every thing he
can lay hands on ; *croffe*, the fheep-hook, with which bifhops
are invefted; *acrocher*, to feize or lay hold of. Gebelin obferves, with his ufual acutenefs, that the French peafants
who revolted in 1598, were called *Les Croquans*, becaufe they
plundered and carried off every thing wherever they came.

*Mou'*] Mouth. Prim. *muth*, *mun* ; whence Ulphila
has *munths*, the mouth ; Celt. *mu*, id. alfo the lips.
Hence Fr. *mot*, what is fpoken with the lips ; *motet*, Bafq.
*motafa*, found of the voice ; Gr. μυδος, and *mythology* ;
*murmur*, i. e. mu-mu, fmall found made by the mouth.
Our old word *mump* comes from the fame origin ; alfo *mant*,
to ftammer   From the ancient Celtic and Welch *mant*, fignifying the jaw-bone, comes the Latin *mandibula*, and the
ancient *munio*, *munito*, to eat ; Feft. *munitio*, *mortificatio*,
ciborum ; alfo *mando*, *manduco* ; the Fr. *manger* ; Ital. *man-
giere* ; Gr. μαδιζειν, loqui. Ihre informs us, that the
mouths of rivers are called *Mynne-a-mynne*, and Ifl. *munne*,
from *mun*, the mouth. They fay alfo, the *mouth* and *lips* of

a

Sic a pure man fhe'd nevir trow,
  After the Gaberlunzie-man.

My

2 wound, as we do: Ll. Scaniæ, p. 22. *Far man far gonum lar, allar lag, allar arm, fwá at that havir twa munna*, If any man's thigh, leg, or arm, be fo wounded as that the fore fhall have two mouths. In the fame fenfe the French ufe *balafre*, a great wound, which Dutchat rightly derives from the old French *balevre*, bilabrum: Ce qu'on appelle *balafre*, eft proprement une grande playe, qui fait une efpece de *bouche*, et par confequent *deux levres*. The Gothic *munhufteis*, a fet form of words, and ufed in their ancient Jurifprudence. Vide Ihre, Lex. in voce, vol. II. p. 207.

We have in this word a clear example of the method the firft men took to exprefs oppofite ideas, without multiplying the primitive words. *Muth* firft denoted the mouth and fpeech. They formed the negative by ufing the fame word in the oppofite fignification, and thus *muth* came to fignify a *dumb perfon*; Gr. μυδος; Lat. *mutus*, whence our *mute*; The Hebrew *muth*, a dead man, one who fpeaks not. In another work we have collected many examples of this kind, which we have no room for here. Such is the word *alt*, high; whence the Lat. *altus*, fignifying *high*, and alfo *deep*.

VER. 3. *Trow*] The verb, *to believe*; Belg. *truen*, id. Douglas ufes *trueles*, for faithlefs. Prim. Goth. *troft*, truft, fidelity. Hence, metaphorically, a *bold man*, on whom we may well rely. So Chron. Ryth. p. 311.

  " *Thet var en godn troft man.*"
  He was a good and trufty man.

Ifl. *trauftor*, Alam. *gidroft*, Engl. *trufty*. Otfrid, L 5. cap. 23.

I 2                " Zi

My dear, quod he, zere zet o'wr zoúng,
An' hae na learn'd the beggar's tongue,

To

" Zi themo thronoste,
" Sie sint al *gidroste*."

In their service all were faithful. Germ. *triest*, and Swed. *dristig*; vide Ihre in *Dristig*. From this root, too, the Greeks formed Θαρσος and Θαρρειν, *to dare*, or more properly, *to be confident*, by a literary metathesis of the same kind as that used by the Goths, while they say *toras*, to dare; *jators*, I dare, and then *trost*, our *trust*. So the ancient Greeks said indifferently, Θασος, Θρασυς, Θαρσυνα, and Θρασυνω, audacem reddo. Ulph. *thrasslian*, to confide or trust, and *dauran*, dare; Mark xii. 34. *gawdarsta*, audebat, which the Allemans pronounced *gidorsta*. In one of the Church Hymns, n. 127, *The lofwade Gud med gladje och trost*, They praised God with gladness and confidence. We observe, by the way, that our Scots phrase of *loving* God, used for *praising* him, frequent in Robert Bruce's Life, and other ancient poems, is formed from the Goth. *lofware*, to praise. In the Barb. Latin Laws, we find often the phrases, *Trustis regius, Esse in truste regia, Trustinus;* and the like; all denoting loyalty. Vid. Cange in *Trustis*. Marculf. For. l. 1. 18. These men were also called *Antrustiones*. Vid. L. Sal. Tit. 32. cap. 20. edit. Heroldi. Marculf. Lib. 1. n. 47. ibi Lindenbrog. Gloss. The *Antrustiones* were of dignity in the King's Court, as we gather from the article of the Gaelic Law last cited. We have the verb *traist*, to trust, frequent in Douglas. So p. 52. v. 25.

———" And there traist coistis nyce."

And p. 213. 37.

" His traisty faith."———

VER.

To fallow me frae toun to toun,
    And carry the Gaberlunzie on.

## X.

Wi' kauk and keel I'll win zour bread,
And fpinnels and quhorles for them wha need,
                                    Whilk

VER. 7. *Frae toun to toun*] By *toun* here is not folely
meant *city*, in which fenfe we now ufe it; but the Scots apply this word to every little village, and even to a farm-houfe,
where there is an inclofed yard, after the manner of their
anceftors, from the prim. *dun*, A. S. *tun*, Alam. *zun*, all
fignifying an inclofure. Hence the Belgic *tuyn*, a garden,
literally an inclofure; Gael. *dun-dunam*, to inclofe; A. S.
*tynan*, *betynan*, id. The firft cities of our Celtic and Saxon
anceftors were only farm-houfes, or a few ftraggling hutts,
inclofed with rails. Tacitus de M. G. cap. 16. Nullis
Germanorum populis urbes habitari notum eft, nec pati quidem
inter fe junctas fedes, (forte ædes) vicos locant, non in noftrum
morem connexis et coherentibus ædificiis. Thefe *vici* were
feparate houfes, like our farmers *fleddings*, which we ftill
call *towns*. In fome diftricts they are called *mains*, from
*manfio*, the B. Latin *manfus*, a *manfe*, now reftricted to
our parfonage houfes.

## STANZA X.

VER. 1. *Kauk*] From the primitive *cal*, *cel*, every thing
hard and proper to inclofe with. Hence Latin *celare*,
                                    *cellarium*,

*cellarium,* our *cellar;* French *celer,* our *con-ceal;* the Celtic *cal,* a hut or ſtable. Hence *kal* came to denote the materials for incloſing, *viz.* ſtones, and eſpecially that ſoft kind of ſtone, eaſily divided into ſmall pieces, which the Engliſh call *chalk,* and we, more properly, pronounce *kauk.* Iſl. *kalk;* Gael. *calch;* Alam. *calc;* A. S. *ceale, ceale, ſtan.* From this root, too, comes the Greek χαλιξ, explained by Suidas, μικρον λιθιδιον, a little ſtone, and more clearly by Heſych. χαλικες, οἱ εις τας οικοδομας μικροι λιθοι; of the ſame kind was the χαλιξ, mentioned by Thucidides, in his Account of the Walls of the Pyreus, built by the Athenians, in lib. 1. We are indebted to the induſtry of Junius for this remark; yet he does not even attempt an etymology of the word χαλιξ, which has baffled all the lexicographers.

*Keel*] A red calcarious ſtone, uſed by carpenters for marking their lines on wood. The promiſe here made by the feigned Gaberlunzie-man, to get a livelihood for his ſweet-heart by *kauk* and *keel,* alludes to the practice of fortune-tellers in Scotland, who uſually pretend to be dumb, to gain credit with the vulgar, and therefore have recourſe to ſigns made with kauk and keel, to explain their meaning. The primitive is plainly the ſame with that of *kauk; col, cel,* a ſmall ſtone, (of a red colour).

*Win*] In the more modern acceptation, ſimply ſignifies to gain. So the Goths uſe *vinna* of one who *wins* at play, or in making bargains, or by gaining his cauſe in a court of juſtice; *winna et kæromal,* in cauſa ſuperiorem eſſe; vide Ihre, vol. II. col. 2020. But of old it ſignified to *gain our bread by hard labour,* and induſtry. This is ſtill its common meaning in the Iſlandic. So Exod. 15. *Winna alladina winna,* Thou ſhalt work all thy work. Hence *winnubiu,* a labouring man. Numbers, cap. 30. A. S. *vinnan.* So the Dutch ſay *land winnen,* to plough the ground. *Winnende leeden,* membra genitalia;

Iſl.

Id. *vinna*, labour; in the A. S. *vinfull*, induſtrious; *win-lagga*, ſign. to give one's ſelf a great deal of trouble.   Hence it is uſed to denote ſuffering.   So Ulphila, Mark viii. 31. *Skal ſunus mans ſilu vinnam*, The ſon of man muſt ſuffer many things: And Luke ii. 48. *Sa atta theins, ja ik vin-nandona ſokidedum thuk*, Thy father and I have ſought thee ſorrowing.   Hence it is transferred to child-bearing : Swed. *Hon har wunnet en ſon*, She has born a ſon; and Belg. *Kinderin gewinnen*, to bring forth children.

As the ancients knew of no other honourable gains, be-ſides the ſpoils acquired in war, hence *winna* came to denote conqueſt, victory in war; and hence our phraſe *to win the battle*, to win the field.   In Matth. xxiv. 7. Verſ. Ulph. *Theod vinth ongean theode*, Nation ſhall fight againſt nation.   *Gevinn*, war ; *gevinne*, battle.   Tatian, cap. 195. 4.   *Mine ambathti wunnin*, My ſervants would fight.   In an old Runic inſcription, quoted by Ihre (in *Winna*), *Vant Selalant ala*, He con-quered all Seland.   The moſt modern ſignification is that in which it is applied to *gain* in general.   From *winna*, applied to war, comes the Latin *vincere*.   Strange ! that Voſſius did not ſee the true etymon, though he has mentioned the Goth. *winnen*, in *Vinco*.   But he ſeldom or never looks further than the Greek or Latin.   Still more abſurd is Varro's etymon, lib. 4. de L. L. *Victoria*, ab eo quod ſuperati vincuntur.   Yet this Varro pretended to give us the origin of language ; and he is generally called *Romanorum Doctiſſimus* ; and ſo, per-haps, he was.

Ver. 2. *Spinnels*]  Goth. *ſpindel*, Machina tornatorum, in gyrum verſatilis, ſays the learned Profeſſor of Upſal. *Slenda*, fuſus, *ſpincok*, fuſus, colus; and hence our *rok*, a diſtaff.   A. S. *ſpinel*; and from ſpindle the Greek ςπονδυλος, as the ſpindle is of a long ſlender form ; the Goth. *ſpinkog*, ſig. *ſlender* ; and, by a ſimilar figure, we ſay *ſpindle-ſhanks*,

of

of a man underlimbed. The prim. is *span*, to ~~extend~~, or draw out to length,. as the thread is extended from the ~~mass~~ on the diftaff. Hence our *span*, of the hand *extended*. Vid. Bullet, Dict. Celt. in *Span*. We have much to fay concerning this primitive, which we referve for our Scoto-Gothic Gloffary. Suffice it to obferve here, that the word *span*, to extend, and hence to meafure, is found in all the dialects of the North. A. S. *span*, *spon*, *sponne*; Alam. *spana*; Ifl. *span*, *spon*; Ital. *spanna*; Fr. *espan*, *empan*. Vide Hicks, Gram. Franc. p. 98. The Swed. verb *spanna*, to meafure. Hence they call grain in general *spannemal*, as being fold by meafure. Of a young flender girl they fay, *Hon at fa fmal, ati man kan spanna om benne*, She is fo fmall, that with two fpans you may encircle her; *spanna konut*, mulieres contrectare. We are not fure whether we are to connect with this the Goth. *spann*, a bracelet; Ger. *spange*, B. Lat. *spanga*, de qua Cange. From this word comes Swed. *spanna*, to bind. Feftus has *spinter*, armillæ genus. *Spannabalt* was the ancient defperate mode of duelling, when the combatants, bound within the narrow circle of one belt, which furrounded both,. attacked each other with fhort daggers. From *spin*, *span*, a number of words have their origin, all denoting what is long, flender, and fharp. Such are Goth. *spik*, whence our *spike* and *hand-spike*, the wooden leavers by which feamen heave at the capftan. The Lat. *spica*, *spiculum*; Gael. *speice*; *spoke* of a wheel; Ital. *spighe*, della rota; Ger. *speiche*. In the Armor. *spec* and *anspec*, fign. a fmall leaver. The Gothic *spik*, a fpear; whence the *spiculum* of the Latins. Confer Cange, in *Specillum*, a probe.

*Quhorles*] A perforated piece of circular ftone, fixed on the fpindle to give it weight in turning round; literally, *whirlers*, to encreafe the motion in *whirling* round. Scyth. *whirra*, *horra*, *wherta*, turbare, tumultuari, furfum et deorfum ferri.

Goth.

Whilk is a gentle trade indeed,
  To carry the Gaberlunzie on.
I'll bow my leg and crook my knee,
An' draw a black clout owr my eye,

         A

Goth. *huirfwel,* our *whirlwind,* from *hwerfwa,* Ifl. *huerfa,*
in gyrum agere. From the Goth. *horra,* the Englifh *hurry.*
Prim. *girwhir,* circle. A. S. *ymbbærtan,* to be turned round.
Belg. *werwen, wieren.* Hence the fea-phrafe, *to wear fhip,*
to bring her round. Fr. *virer* and *verve,* by which they
denote the *furor poeticus,* which ftrongly agitates the mind ;
and this affection the Iflanders, among whom of old it was
very ftrong and frequent, call *fcaldwingl.* From this primitive the Greek γυρϟιʹ, and the Latin *gyrare.* It is remarkable that the old Latins faid *vervare,* for *circumagere ;* and
*urvare,* to draw the circular line with the plough, to mark
the boundaries of the future city. The word is pure Gothic ;
but neither Feftus, nor any of his commentators, underftood
it. Confer Acta Sueciæ Litterar. vol. IV. p. 386. Junius
has given us no etymon of *whirl.* Vid. in voce.

 VER. 6. *Clout*] Goth. *klut,* panni fruftum, a rag. The
prim. is *clo-clu,* covered, fhut up. Hence Lat. *claudo, cludo,*
*in-cludo,* and our *clofe, inclofe, difclofe.* Douglas ufed *cloys*
for *cloifter,* place where monks and nuns are fhut up. In
the Gael. *cl f,* in A. S. *cleof,* fignify joining of a rent.
A. S. *geclutad hraegl,* a clouted garment. " Ex his con-
jicere licet (fays Ihre) *klut,* prima et antiquiffima fignifi-
fione denotaffe panni frufta ad farciendas veftes immiffa." In
Englifh, a *clouterly fellow,* a mean man, a fellow in rags.
Belg. *kloete,* a fool ; Swed. *klutare,* a botcher of old clothes.

      K      VER.

A cripple or blind they will ca' me,

    While we will be merry and ſing.

VER. 7. *Cripple*] Lame man. A word found in all the Celtic dialects. Welſh *crupl*; A. S. *crypl*; Belg. *krepel, kreupel*; Swed. *krympling*, paralytic, membris captus ; whence our *cramp*, binding of the ſinews. The primitive is *craſ, criſ, craw*, to bind. Hence Gaelic *crampa*, French *crampon, cramponer*. The ſhell-fiſh *crab*, from its claws, and the French *crapaud*, are of the ſame origin. Hence, too, Greek γρυπαινειν, in-curvari, γρυπαλιον, a man bent down or crippled with age. Gloſſ. Philoxeni κραιπαλοντες, vacillantes. Junius odly deduces *cripple*, a κραιπαλη, crapula :—But we are weary of his blunders ; and ſo, perhaps, is the reader of ours.

    ——*Jam ſatis eſt, manum de tabula.*

A D D E N D A.

# ADDENDA.

FOR the following elucidations of the general principles laid down in the Preface, and exemplified in the Notes on the foregoing Ballad, the Public and I are indebted to a learned and worthy friend of the Author*, whose extensive erudition is only equalled by the modesty and candour conspicuous in his whole deportment. I am sure our learned readers will regret with me, that he has not pushed his researches further than he has done. But, from the little he has here given us, the general principle of Etymology I have endeavoured to establish will derive new force, and our readers new entertainment.

## TO THE READER.

IN the following strictures, I have, in a manner, confined myself to the Oriental languages. My knowledge of the Northern tongues is too much bounded to qualify me for pursuing the coincidences of words through their various dialects. I shall, perhaps, be blamed for terminating the origin of too great a number of words in the Hebrew. This, however, I did, from a conviction that their radical syllables and significations appeared most obvious in that language. In a few instances I have taken the liberty to differ from the

learned

* *Mr David Doig,* Rector of the Academy in Stirling.

learned and laborious Author of the Notes. I have not, however, the remoteſt intention to detract from his well-known abilities and merit. I imagined it might neither be diſpleaſing to himſelf, nor his readers,-to ſee, upon ſome occaſions, the ſame individual term placed in various points of light. If the unlearned philologer ſhall acquire one new idea by the peruſal of them, I ſhall think myſelf abundantly rewarded for the pains I have taken in throwing them together.

Before I proceed to the additional notes, I ſhall take the liberty to preſent to the reader one ſingle word, which, in my opinion, furniſhes a very ſtriking evidence of the truth of the Author's leading principle, with relation to the exiſtence of an original univerſal language.

*Ur, aur, our*] Theſe words ſignify *fire, light, heat,* and ſeveral other things nearly connected with theſe ideas. They occur frequently in the Hebrew, and its ſiſter-dialects. In the Chald. we have *Ur,* the name of a city, where, it is thought, the Sun was worſhipped by a perpetual *fire.* Alſo *Or-choe,* the ſeat of the Chaldean aſtronomers called *Or-cheni,* Strabo, l. 16. p, 739. We find *oreitæ,* or *oritæ,* in different parts of the Eaſt, the Chald. *Atun B-ura,* the furnace of *fire,* occurs, Dan. chap. 3. ver. 6. &c. In the Gentoo language *war,* which is only a ſmall variation, imports *day, light, ſee*—Halhed's Pref. to his Tranſlation of the Gentoo Laws. In the ſame tongue, the moſt ancient Dynaſty of the Gentoo Princes were called *Surage,* from *Sur,* a name or epithet of the *Sun*—See Halhed's Pref. and Col. Dow's Introd. to the Hiſt. of Hindoſtan.

In the old Perſian, or Pehlvi, the word *hyr* ſignifies *fire,* the ſame with *ur,* only with the aſpirate prefixed.

*Hyr-bad,* a fire, temple; *Az-ur,* Mars, i. e. the *fiery* planet, compounded of *Az,* or *Aſt,* fire, and *Ur,* heat or light. *Hur,* or *Chur,* is a common name of the Sun in that
language.

language. *Kur, Raſch, Horéſh,* Κυρος, Gr. which laſt,
Plut. Vit. Artax. ſignifies the Sun. From the ſame word we
have the firſt ſyllable of *Or-mazd,* the God of Light, the
chief Divinity of the Perſians. Here, too, we find *Purim,*
ſignifying *lots,* denominated from the ceremonies of *fire* employed upon theſe occaſions—Eſth. chap. iii. ver. 7. &c.

The Arabian *Uro-talt,* Heſod. l. 3. cap. 8. is compounded of *ur,* light, and *jalath,* high. In Egypt we find *Orus,*
or *Horus,* Apollo, the Sun, Herod, l. 2. Diod. Sic. l. 1.
Plut. Iſis and Oſiris, Horapollo, Paſſ. In the ſame language
we have *Athur,* the name of a month, partly anſwering to
our October, on the 17th day of which Oſiris was put into
the coffin, a word compounded of *ait,* or *at,* or *ath,* heat,
and *ur,* or *or*—See Plut. ubi ſupra. The particle *pi* was
common in the Egyptian tongue, ſee Kirch. Prolegom. Copt.
page 180, 297. Jameſon's Spicileg. cap. 9. parag. 4. Hence
*pur,* fire, and ſometimes the Sun. Of this word, and the
Hebrew *chamud,* or *omud,* columna, is compounded the
term πυραμις, pyramid, edifices, erected in honour of the
Sun.

The πυρ of the Greeks, according to Plato (Cratyl. p.
410. Serr.) was borrowed from the Phrygians. Theſe laſt
had received it from the Perſians by the Armenians, who
ſpoke nearly the ſame language. The word πυρ produced a
numerous family, all deſcendants of the oriental term *Ur.*

*Or*] Another modification of the ſame word, produced
ὡρα, tempeſtas, a ſeaſon, with a numerous train of connections.
Alſo ὡρα, beauty ; αορ, a ſword, from its glittering, by
the ſame analogy that the Scandinavians call it *brandt :* Alſo
ὁραω, video, and many others.

From *aur* we have the Eolic αυρα, αυρου, afterwards adopted by the Latins. From *our* we have ουρος, ventus ſecundus,
with all its compounds and derivatives; alſo κυνοςερα, the
North Pole-Star, which the Greeks have corrupted in a
ſhameful

shameful manner. It is really compofed of the Hebrew or Phœnician *kanes*, congregavit, and *ur*, light, i. e. **an** *Affem-blage of Light*. From the fame root we have ουρανος, cœlum. The laft part is probably the oriental *en*, fignifying an *eye*, a fountain, the Sun being the eye of Heaven, or fountain of light.

In the Latin tongue we have a numerous tribe of words defcended from *ur; or; aur;* fuch are *uro, buro, burrum,* ap. Feftum pro *rufum, purus, purgo.* From the fame root we have *furo,* to rage like fire ; *furia,* a fury. Perhaps this laft word may be a native of Egypt, from whence the Greeks derived their ideas of the infernal regions. See Diod. Sic. l. 1. juxta finem. The Latian Jupiter was called Jupiter *Puer.* I fufpect this epithet is diftorted from *pi-ur.* In ancient times, it is probable, this Deity was no other than the *Sun.* See Macrob. Saturn. cap. 17. His Minifters were called *Pueri ;* and becaufe they were generally handfome young men, felected for that office, in procefs of time, I fancy, the word *puer* came to fignify a young man in general. At Prenefte, *Jupiter Puer* was in high veneration ; he prefided over the celebrated Sortes Preneftini, defcribed by Cicero, de Divinat. l. 2. From *or* we have *orior, ordior,* and perhaps *oro ;* from *aur* we have *aura, Aurora, aurum,* &c.

The words *fire, air,* &c. plainly defcended of the fame ftock, under various forms, and with new modifications, pervade all the German and Scandinavian dialects ; an affertion which the Author of the Notes would certainly have demonftrated, had that term occurred in the text of the Ballad.

In the French we have *jour,* with all its compounds, from the very fame root. In the Celtic, *ere,* or *aur,* fignifies *gold,* concerning which, Voffius (Etym. V. *Aurum)* has told a heap of abfurdites. The name *ore* is given it in allufion to its fhining quality, a word which we have adopted,

                                     **and**

and applied to fignify any metal before it is purified
and refined. *Aur* alfo in Celtic fignifies *yellow.* Vid,
Bullet in *Aur.* Thofe who are well acquainted with
the remains of the ancient Celtic, can, no doubt, produce
many other cognates of the fame original term. If the above
detail fhould be thought tedious, the beft apology I can make
is, that I am confident I have, for the fake of brevity, omitted at leaft one third of what I could eafily have produced :
At the fame time, all thefe analogies might have been confirmed and elucidated by a variety of quotations from ancient
and modern authors, had the bounds I have prefcribed to myfelf admitted fuch enlargements.

## T I T L E.

*Gaber*] In fome places of Scotland, this word, among the
vulgar, denotes an idea very different from that affigned by
the Author of the Notes. When a thing is dafhed to pieces,
they fay it is driven to *gaberts,* or *gabers.* According to
this acceptation, the *Gaberlunzie-man* will imply a fellow
whofe clothes about his loins are all rags and tatters, all
worn out, *&c.*

The character exhibited throughout the Ballad, feems
rather to be that of a common *beggar* than of a *tinker,* though
indeed both profeffions were often united in the fame perfon.

*Gab* feems originally to denote the roof of the mouth or
palate. In fome of the Eaftern languages it fignifies an *eminence,* a *protuberance, gibbous,* &c. Hence Arab. *gebal,* a
hill ; alfo the Lat. *gibbus,* hump-backed. According to this
idea, it was appropriated to fignify the *roof of the mouth,*
which, indeed, rifes in a *gibbous* form or arch over the tongue
and lower part of the mouth. From the notion of a rifing
protuberance, it was probably transferred to fignify *cabbage,*
and whatever elfe imports *eminence, elevation,* or *gibbofity.*

Hence

Hence *gabah*, *fcyphus*, a kind of cup, fo called from its *gibbous protuberant* belly, perhaps the origin of the Scotch word *cap*, and of all its German and Scandinavian *cognates*.

*Caph*, Hebr. the *hollow of the hand*, or any other *cavity* fitted for containing. By changing the *ph* but a very little, we have *cav*, *gau*, *cow*, and *gow*, fyllables which occur in a number of compounds, both in the Eaft and Weft. Plut. in Alex. tells us that *gau-gamela* fignifies the houfe of the camel. It were eafy to trace this word through many different languages. It is the origin of the English word *cave*, Scotch *cove*, and Welch *cowe* ; Lat. *cavus*, *a-um*, hollow. Here, I believe, we may difcover a compofition of the word *cœlum* very different from that ufually affigned. *Co* is a houfe, and *El*, or *Il*, a Phnœician name of the Deity. Hence we have Ennius's *Allifonans Cœil*, Annal. L. 1. and alfo the following verfes :

" *Cœilum* profpexit ftellis fulgentibus aptum.
" Olim de *Cœilo* laivum dedit inclytus fignum,
" Saturnus quem *Cœilus* genuvit.
" Unus erat quem tu tollas in coirila *Cœili*
" Templa."

Hence it is probable that *Co-il* originally fignified the Houfe of *Il*, or *El*, which is perfectly conformable to the notion of Heaven commonly exhibited in Scripture. The idea annexed to this word carries us back to a very uncultivated ftate of Society. The fame word being applied both to fignify a *cave* and a *houfe*, intimates that the original men often dwelt in *caves*. Vid. the Poems of Offian, paffim.

" Domus antra fuerunt,
" Et denfi frutices, vinetæ cortice virgæ."
*Ovid. Metam.*

As

As *gow*, *gaw*, *caw*, *cow*, originally fignified a *houfe*, in procefs of time it came to import a collection of *houfes*, a *village*, a *city*. This was the cafe both in the German and Celtic tongues. Thus we have *Cra-cow*, *Tor-gaw*, *Wormes-gaw*, *Nord-gaw*, *Rhin-gaw*: See Cluv. Germ. Antiq. l. 1. cap. 13. p. 91. Confer Bullet in *Gouri*, and *Gowrin*. In Scotland we have *Glaf-cow*, or *Glaf-gow*, *Linlith-gow*, &c. In the old Britifh dialect, *gowe*, or rather *cowe*, fignified likewife *low*, *hollow*; Scotch *howe*. From *gow*, or *cow*, and *ri*, a *river*, we have *Gowrie*, a low fer-tile tract of ground, lying on the north bank of the river Tay. In ancient times, this diftrict lay between the rivers Tay and Erne.

*Lunzie*] We call a bulky parcel, which one carries on his *haunch*, under his coat, a *lunchick*; perhaps the fame with the Englifh *luncheon*, both derived from the word *lunzie*.

## STANZA I.

VER. 1. *The*] This particle has a moft extenfive range both in the Eaftern and Weftern parts of the Globe. Hebr. *zah*, or *zahah*; Chald. *da*, *di*, *dik*, *din*. Arab. Syr. much the fame. Perf. *di*. From the Chald. *da*, the Greeks formed their το, the article of the neuter gender. It is the fame with the Latin *de*, though of a different fignification. The fame article runs through all the Gothic dialects, with very little variation.

*Over*] This prepofition, however meanly it figures in our dialects, is, notwithftanding, one of the terms which made a part of the original language of mankind. In Hebrew we have *chabar*, or, as fome pronounce it, *obar*, tranfivit, tranfgreffus eft; *heber*, tranfitus; Chald. *cheber*, *chiber*, from which word, fome think the pofterity of Abraham were called

L *Hebrews*,

*Hebrews, transfluviani,* men from beyond the river. Syriaa *chabara,* or *abara,* whence *Beth-abara, the house of the paſſage, the ferry-house,* John, chap. i. 25. Hence alſo *chebar,* in Ezek. From *Chabar,* trans, *over,* were denominated the *Chabareni,* a people beyond the mountains of Armenia, Steph. Byzan. in Voc.

From the Chald *Chiber,* we have all the *Iberi* in the Eaſt. In Spain we have *Celt-iberi,* i. e. the Celtæ beyond the mountains; the river *Iber,* now *Ebro,* denominated, I ſuppoſe, by the Gauls who ſettled in that country.

The word *aber,* ſignifying the *mouth of a river,* pervades all the Celtic dialeĉts, and differs almoſt nothing from the *Chabar* of the Eaſt.

From the ſame word we have the Greek υπερ, and γεουρα, a *bridge.* Alſo the Lat. *ſuper, ſupra,* with all their connecĉtions. Upon the whole, hardly any particle has pervaded a greater number of dialeĉts, both in Europe and Aſia.

*Lee*] Over all the North of Scotland they pronounce this word *ley,* which comes very near the Greek λειος, λευιων, λειε, &c.

Ver. 3. *Gudewiſe*] Good, Scots *gude,* runs through all the Northern dialeĉts. Its primitive is found in the old Perſian language, where it is *gath,* good. It is the root of the Greek αγαθος, good.

*Wiſe*] Of all the etymologies of this word, none ſeem to me more plauſible than that which refers it to the very word *chevah.* It is only changing the letter *heth* into *w,* and throwing away the *he* at the end; but the profound etymologiſts will rejeĉt this derivation, were it for no other reaſon but becauſe it is obvious.

*Kaiu, Kaio*] Theſe words are originally Perſian. *Kai,* or *Hei,* was a title given to a dynaſty of their Kings. Hence the

the Princes of that family were called *Kaianides*, which fignifies the *splendid*, or *illuftrious*. The word *hai*, *hei*, fignifies
*fulgur*, a flafh of lightning. Hebr. *kai*, or *kei*, uftio,
aduftio; Gr. καιω, aro. From the fame root the Latin
prænomen *Caius*, borrowed, I fuppofe; from the Etrufcans,
a colony of Lydians, which laft had it from their neighbours
the *Medes*.

γεια] From γεω, gigno, which laft from γεα, Terra,
it being the opinion of the ancient uncivilized Greeks, that
the original men fprung from the earth, according to the
doctrine of Mofchus, Democritus, and Epicurus, which was
introduced afterwards, and formed upon the fame opinion.
The radical term is the Hebr. *gia*, vallis.

*Gaudeo* is, I believe, deduced from the Hebrew *gaah*,
fuperbire; whence *gavah*, exultatio, which produces the Gr.
γαω and the Lat. *gaudeo*, originally *gaveo*. The Scots
word *gaff*, to laugh immoderately, belongs to the fame family. They feem to be originally *onomatopœas*, formed in allufion to the found of the human voice in an extafy of joy.

Ver. 4. *Ludge*] Celt. *Lug*, *Log*, a place; whence Lat.
*Locus*; and the Scot. *Logie*, the name of feveral villages.
Hence alfo *Kil-logie*.

Ver. 5. *Night*] This word, in various forms, pervades
all the Northern dialects. With a fmall variation, we have
Lat. *nox*, *noct*; Gr. ιυξ; Hebr. Chad. Syr. *nuch*; quievit,
requievit.

*Wat*] Perf. *ab*, *av*, *aw*, a river; the very fame with
the Celtic word *av*, fignifying the fame thing. Of *au* and
*phrat*, the Greeks made Ευφρατης, Euphrates.

Ver. 6. *Ingle*] The origin of this word is very obfcure.
In many places o Scotland they have no other fuel but peats,
furze, broom, heath, and brufhwood. Fires confifting of
fuch materials muft be fed by continual fupplies, which they

call *beeting*. The Welch vocable *inghilſt* ſignifies *feeding*; this I take to be the origin of the word *ingle*, alluding to the conſtant *feeding* of the fire. In like manner, Iſl. *elldur* is fire; *ellde*, to boil with fire; both from *el*, *ool*, *ela*, to feed.

VER. 7. *Dochter's*] This word is purely Perſian, as is generally known.

VER. 8. *Cadgily*] The word *cadge* is probably derived from the Sclavonian *chodge*, to trudge on foot; whence, too, our *ſcodgy*, a little wench, who does the dirty work in a far-mer's kitchen. The word *cadgy*, in the preſent caſe, ſhould, I think, be written *cagy*, or *cagie*, which would agree better with the pronounciation. It imports *merry*, *chearful*, *jovial*, and is, I believe, an abbreviation of the old French word *cagedler*, the ſame with *cajoler*, to cajole, flatter, cox.

## S T A N Z A II.

VER. 5. *Canty*] From Lat. *canto*, *cano*. Hebr. *kanah*, *canna*, calamus, arundo, plainly alludes to playing on inſtru-ments made of reeds, the reed being the firſt ſubſtance uſed for wind muſic. The Hebrew *chanah*, among other ſig-nifications, denotes *to ſing*, *to ſay*, *to ſpeak to*, *to teſtify*, *to atteſt*. The Greek αιſω, in ancient times, implied both to *ſing* and to *ſpeak*. By comparing theſe two ideas, it appears that the ancients uttered their words with a *canting* tone of voice, or in the recitative ſtile. From this circumſtance the orations of the Greeks and Romans may poſſibly have derived ſome part of that influence, which we ſtill admire, but have never ſeen.

VER. 6. *Ken*] This is another word of Perſian extraction. In that language it denotes a learned intelligent man, eſpecially in the Laws of Zerduſht. Hence all the deſcendants of that word in Greek, Latin, Gothic, &c

S T A N Z A

## STANZA III.

Ver. 2. *Daddy*] This word occurs, with little variation, in many different languages; *ab, ap, av-us, at, atta, tat, dad,* &c. and are all mere onomatopæas, fabricated from the early prattle of infants. The sound is formed by an application of the point of the tongue to the roof of the mouth, one of the moſt natural efforts of the organs of ſpeech. It was probably caught by mothers and nurſes, and by them applied to intimate the idea of *father*. This proceſs was natural. The firſt articulate ſound enounced by the child was appropriated to the idea of *father*, he being deemed ſuperior in dignity to the other parent.

*Di*] Mentioned in the notes on the preceding word, ſignifies *bright, luminous, ſplendid, glorious*. It occurs in many of the Eaſtern dialeĉts, and from thence probably found its way into the Weſt. Perſian *div*, a genius, whence Eol. Διβος, Lat. *divus*, Hebr. *zui*, ſplendor; Lat. *diu*, in the daytime; Gr. Δις, Jupiter, originally the *Sun*; Διος, divinus, and ſo forth.

This word makes the firſt part of Διονυσος, the Greek name of Bacchus, a word which has been ſtrangely garbled by etymologiſts. In reality, *dio* ſignifies *bright*, and *naſia*, princeps. The Eolians changed *a* into *v*. Hence Dionyſius will ſignify the *bright Prince*, or the *Prince of Light*, i. e. the Sun, who was indeed the original Bacchus of the Greeks, and Oſiris of the Egyptians.

Ver. 6. *Dyke*] Heb. *deik*, munitio, propugnaculum; Gr. τειχος. Hence all the progeny of that word throughout the Greek and Gothic dialeĉts. Hence, too, the Gr. δεικα, δεικνυμι, *oſtendo*, to point out, as from the top of a bulwark, fort, or tower. This word may be compared with the Lat. *ſpecula, ſpeculor*, to view from a watch-tower. In ancient times

times it was the practice to erect watch-towers, or eminences; round the frontiers of a country, and in these to place a man, whose business it was to *look out*, and, upon the approach of an enemy, to alarm the country by lighting up fires. Hence the *churim*, vigiles, Hebr. Chald. alluding to the kindling up *fires*; the Gr. αγ ε , from the same idea; the Lat. *speculatores*, and the Scandinavian *gokesmen*.

VER. 7. *Clead*] To this family belong the Gr. κλωθω, neo, and Κλωθ , the eldeft of the *Destinies*.

*Braw*] From *brage*, mentioned in the Note on this word, we have the Engl. *brag*, *braggodocio*, importing originally *loud-talking*. The Persian word *brag* signifies *shining*, *sparkling*, and might be metaphorically applied to denote a person of *shining* talents, which exactly suits the Scandinavian *brage*.

*Lady!ike*] *Lady*, compounded of Goth. *lhaif*, bread, and *dien*, to serve, because the mistress of the family used to distribute the *bread* to the guests and domestics.

## STANZA IV.

VER. 1. *Twa*] Scots *twa*, Engl. *two*, Belg. *twee*, Swed. *twa*, Dan. *toe*, Sax. *twa*, *twy*, Pal. *dwa*, Ruf. *twa*, Lat. *duo*, Gr. δυω, Welch *duy*, Ger. *zwan*, Perf. *do*, Beng. *dio*, Malay *duo*.

VER. 2 *Wee*] Little. This word bids fair for being the root of the Greek υιος, a son. Hence, too, we have the Spanish *hijo*, signifying the same thing. This is one of the many Gothic terms still subsisting in the Spanish tongue. Their etymologists tell us, that the word *hidolgo*, which, in their language, signifies a *gentleman*, is compounded of *hijo* and

and *algo*, i. e. *the fon of fomething*. I believe they are miftaken. The word is made up of the two Gothic terms *hijo*
and *idelg*, or *idolg*, which laft, in that language, fignifies a
*gentleman*. A. S. *adel athæling*, nobly born.

*Cock*] The Celtic word *kok* fignifies *red;* whence Greek
κοκκ. , and Latin *coccus*, purple. Perhaps this bird was fo
denominated from the *red colour* of his *creft*, or *comb*. Be
that as it may, the creature is a native of Media, and therefore cannot endure the cold of thefe northern regions, without
fuffering very feverely.

VER. 3. *Shot*] The root is the Scythian *fket*, an *arrow*.
Perhaps it may not be amifs to enquire fomewhat minutely into the origin and connections of this word, for reafons which
will appear by and by. I fhall not pretend to trace it through
the Gothic dialects, all which it pervades, with little alteration
of found or fignification. From the numerous cognates of
this term, I fhall fingle out the word *fkeit*, or *fkout*, which is
nothing elfe but a modification of the original vocable. The
prefent meaning of this word is univerfally known; but, I believe, few are acquainted with its original and primary acceptation.

The Celtic or Gaelic word *fcuta* denotes a *vagabond*, a
*reftlefs wanderer, one perpetually roving about, without fet-
tling in any particular place, or fixed habitation*. From this
definition it plainly appears, that it is of the fame family with
the word *fcout*, mentioned above. This radical term, with
the definition annexed, I owe to the tranflator of Offian's
Poems; and it enables me to afcertain the original import of
two *names*, which have greatly embarraffed a multitude of
critics, of different ages and countries. This word *fcuta* is,
beyond all doubt, the original of the Greek Σκυ α, Scytha,
a *Scythian*. The found and fignification of the Celtic and
Greek

Greek word fix the analogy to a demonstration. It was, no doubt, applied to the Scythians, with a particular view to exhibit the roving, restless disposition of those people, who inhabited all the Northern regions of Asia and Europe. Analagous to this idea, the Persians called the same people Σακαι, Sacæ. Herod. l. 7. cap. 64. Οιδε Περσαι παντας τας Σκυθας καλεςι Σακας; "Now the Persians call all the *Scythians,* "*Sacæ.*" The Persian word *fack* is plainly a cognate of the Hebrew *shakak*, discurrere, discursitare, &c. The monosyllable root of the word is *shak*, or *sheik*, and alludes to the very same restless, wandering disposition, that the word *scuta* does in the Celtic. Both the Σκ.θαι of the Greeks, and the *Sacæ* of the Persians, were terms of reproach, imposed by hostile neighbours ; and, of course, were never adopted by the Scythians themselves, who always assumed a more honourable denomination.

From the same word *scuta,* and for the same reason, was derived the opprobrious name *Scot ;* a name detested by the Aborigines of the country, who always call themselves by the Gentile appellation, *Albanich.* During the lower ages of the Roman Empire, the Aboriginous Britons, whom the Romans, upon their first invasion, had forced to take shelter among the fastnesses of the mountains, gradually recovered their courage, and, sallying from their strong holds, harrassed the Romans, and Provincial Britons, without distinction. As these people were perpetually roving about, and distressing the Province by desultory wars, the Provincial Britons, out of spite, branded them with the infamous epithet of *scuta,* in allusion to their wandering migratory course of life. The Romans soon caught the term from the Britons, and turned the word into *Scotti,* or *Scoti.*

In confirmation of this etymon, it may be observed, that, not many years ago, the Scots borderers used to call them-

felves *fcuytes*, and *fkytes*, as we learn from Cambden. Indeed, lefs than a century ago, the term was current in the
North of Scotland. The Saxon-Scots readily adopted this
name, being ignorant of the original import of it; but the
Scoto-Brigantes, or Highlanders, have always deemed it a
term of reproach, and, confequently, ftill retain their original
denomination, *Albanich*.

From the fame word *Saca*, or *Sak*, explained above,
the Saxons who fettled in the North of Germany feem to
have derived their name. They were probably a colony of
Scythian emigrants, who fettled in that country, and brought
with them the Gentile name *Sak*, which had become the
general denomination of thefe tribes of Scythians who lived
neareft the frontiers of Media, and the other Provinces of
the Perfian Empire. Certainly the etymon affigned by Verfte-
gan, Sir William Temple, and others, who tell us, that it
is derived from *feaxen*, or *feaxes*, is highly improbable.
Thefe *feaxen*, or *feaxes*, were weapons much ufed by the
Saxons. They were crooked after the fafhion of a fcythe,
with the edge on the contrary or outward fide. The plural,
formed by *n*, inftead of *s*, made *Seaxon*, which (fays Verfte-
gan, p. 21.) the Latins turned into *Saxons*.

VER. 4. *Bent*] This fpecies of grafs is feldom produced in
marfhy grounds. It appears in greateft plenty on any fandy
hillocks, efpecially on fandy grounds lying on the fea-fhore,
which we call *links*. In Erfe it is called *ifiiach*, which fignifies *fhort, ill-grown*; Scot. *fitten*. Our anceftors ufed to
twift ropes of it, for feveral purpofes; hence, perhaps, it
might be called *bent*, from Iflandic *band*, Saxon *bandan*,
vinculum.

M STANZA

## S T A N Z A  V.

VER. 1. *Beggar*] To beg, to aſk alms ; from the Goth. *bidgan*, Iſl. *bid*, Sax. *biddan*, to pray ; whence *to bid beads.* Perhaps it may have originated from the practice of beggars, who uſe to pray for alms. The Hebr. *bag* ſignifies *meat*, and is, perhaps, a cognate of this term.

VER. 2. *Strae*] There is an obvious analogy between this word and the Gr. ϛοωα, ϛρονυυμι; Lat. *ſtrao, ſterno*, to ſtraw, to ſpread, to level. In this laſt ſenſe, they ſeem to coincide with the word *ſtrath*, (a level country, lying between two ridges of mountains) ſo common in all the Celtic dialects. *Strath* and *ſtraith* are true Celtic words, a valley lying along a river. Vide Bullet, Dict. Celt. in *Strat* and *Strah.* To the ſame tribe belong Gr. ϛρατος, ϛραπα, ϛ˙ατοπεδον, &c. Theſe words were appropriated by the Greeks to ſigni-fy a *camp*, an *army*, an *encampment*, &c. becauſe the ori-ginal mode was to chuſe large level plains for encampments. For the ſame reaſon, the word *camp*, from the Lat. *campus*, a *plain*, is uſed by the French, Spaniards, Italians, and Eng-liſh, to denote the ſame idea.

The Latin word *ſterno* ſignifies *to make a bed*, which was done by ſhaking, arranging, and levelling the *ſtraw ;* whence appears the relation of the ideas. Both Greeks and Latins call a bed-ſtead *torus*, becauſe it was formed of *thongs of a bull's hide*, employed in the ſame manner as we now do *cords.* Thus Oſſian often mentions the binding of priſoners with *thongs.* We learn, too, that in that Poet's time, thongs of leather were uſed aboard of ſhips for ropes. The Chald. *thor* is a *bull ;* whence the ταυρε of the Greeks, and the *taurus* of the Latins. From theſe two ideas of *ſtraw*, and *thongs of undreſſed leather*, we may infer, that the ancients of every rank ſlept not more ſoftly than our peaſants do at preſent.

VER.

VER. 5. *Koffers*] Ifl. *kofe*, domuncula; *kofa*, *cavea*, conclave. Here again we may recur to the Hebrew *kaph*, *cavum*, *vola*, *manus*, &c. Hence, too, we have the vulgar term *coft*, inftead of *bought*, i. e. *coffed*, put into my *coffer*.

*Kifts*] The root of this word is the Hebrew *kis*, loculus, marfupium, crumena.

## STANZA VI.

VER. 2. *Kirn*] To the Author's numerous collections on the etymology of this word, we may add, that, agreeably to his idea, the Hebr. *geor* fignifies *coire*, *convenire*, in the fame fenfe that the Latins fay, *in circulum venire*. I cannot difmifs this word without venturing a few ftrictures on the very different ideas affixed to it.

*Gur*, a verb, fignifies, among other things, to *fear*, to be *afraid*, to *dread*. *Gur*, a fubftantive-noun, imports a *ftranger*, an *incomer*, a *fojourner*. From the connection of thefe two ideas, we are led to infer the inhofpitable character of the ancients towards people of a foreign tribe, or clan, who refided among them. Their hofpitality to travellers, or paffengers, was indeed almoft unbounded; but with refpect to foreigners who fettled in their country, the cafe feems to have been widely different, as it ftill is in many places of the diftant Highlands: Hence, I fuppofe, the many injunctions we meet with in fcripture, inculcating beneficence and tendernefs towards ftrangers.

From *magor*, or *megor*, a compound of this word, we have *Mægara*, the name of one of the furies of hell, importing terror, difmay, &c.

From another compound of the word *magur*, *habitatio*, *commoratio*, we have the Greek μεγαρο, *domus*, *domicilium*, any large repofitory, or magazine; a word very

common

common in Homer. From *Megurah* we have *Megara*, a
city of Greece, mid-way between Athens and Corinth. *Garuth*,
hofpitium, is the very fame with the Celtic *ghwarth*, a fort or
caftle. The fame word produced the Perfian *gheit*, *guerd*,
a city, from which we have a numerous family of defcendants
in all the Gothic dialects. This word is likewife the parent of
the Lat. *migro*, to remove ; or, as we fay in Scotland, to *flit*.

In the notes upon this word, which indeed fhew a vaft ex-
tent of etymological learning, the Author deduces the Greek
*αγορα*, from the the primitive *gur :* To me it feems rather to
be formed from the prefect. med. of the verb *αγειρω*, congre-
go, which is derived from the Hebrew *ager*, collegit,
congeffit.

VER. 2. *Butt*] This word, with all its numerous progeny,
was imported from Perfia, where it appears nearly in the fame
form, *bad*, *bod*, *bud*, fignifying, in that language, a *houfe*, a
*dwelling*, an *abode*, the very fame with the German and Scandinavian word in queftion. It is indeed the Hebr. *beth*, *beith* ;
Chald. *bith* ; Arab. *bait* ; Egypt. *but*. In Egypt, the place
into which the initiated were put was called by this name.
See Hefych. in voce. Alfo, *βυτις*, *βωτις*, and, without
the Greek termination *but*, *bot*, was a kind of fhip; refembling
a floating-houfe or *booth*. From the fame word we have the
Greek *κιβωτις*, a wooden ark. Comp. of the Hebrew *geb*,
gibbus, and *bot*. This word might be traced through a multitude of languages, and was, no doubt, a primæval term.

VER. 4. *Ben*] To the numerous etymologies of this word
traced by the Author, I fhall prefume to add one more,
which will lead us back to the fame original with *but*, of
which it is the oppofite. In the Chald. we find the word *benin*,
*benina*, Ezr. v. 4. fignifies ædificium, a houfe, a dwelling,
from the Hebr. *bana*, ædificavit. From *benin* we may, with-

out

out any violence, deduce the word *ben*, in the same manner we do *butt* from *beth*.

## S T A N Z A  VII.

V ER. 8. *Bann'd*] This is another word of Persian extraction. In that language the word *bend* signifies a *chain*, and metaphorically an *obstacle*, a *barrier*, a *wall*.

## S T A N Z A  VIII.

V ER. 4. *Frae*] The same nearly with the Gr. παρα. The radix is the Hebr. *pharad*, or *phrad*, separavit, sejunxit. The root is *phar*, *phara* ; or, without the point, *phra*. It is certainly connected with our words *far*, *frae*. Of this word *phar*, and Chald. *bara*, is formed the Greek Βαρβαρος, a Barbarian. In the oriental dialects it signified *agrestis*, *rusticus*, a peasant ; what idea the Greeks annexed to its derivative, is too well known to need to be mentioned.

The Author has somewhere observed, that there is certainly a very strict connection among the particles of almost all languages. This observation is founded on fact ; and I may add, that the not understanding the nature, relations, signification, and original import of these seemingly unimportant terms, has occasioned not only great uncertainty, but numberless blunders, in translating the ancient languages into modern tongues. The Greek language, in particular, loses a considerable part of its beauty, elegance, variety, and energy, when the adverbial particles, with which it is replete, are not thoroughly comprehended. An exact translation of these small words, in appearance insignificant, would throw new light not only on Homer and Hesiod,

Hesiod, but even on poets of a much posterior date. Particles, which are generally treated as mere expletives, would often be found energetically significant. It is, however, altogether impossible to succeed in this attempt, without a competent skill in the Hebrew, Chaldean, Syrian, Arabic, Persian, Phœnician, Gothic, and Celtic languages. Such an extensive acquaintance with languages is, it is true, seldom to be found in one and the same person. I shall here take the liberty to mention a few of the most familiar of these particles, one or other of which occurs in almost every line of Homer, and which, I am persuaded, are generally misunderstood. Such are δη, δα, μεν, ην, μαν, μα, τοι, γε, ος, γαν, αρα, πα. All these particles are truly significant, and, if properly explained, would add considerable energy to the clauses in which they stand; but this disquisition must be left to the learned Philologers of the Universities.

Ver. 7. *Laith*] The Author adduces very plausible arguments to prove, that the Greek word ελγει is derived from *laith*. I shall, however, adduce another etymology, and leave the choice to the judgment of the reader. In the Hebr. and Chald. we have the word *cheleg*, plur. *chelegim*; or, as some pronounce them, *oleg*, plur. *olegim*, *lisping, stammering*. In ancient times, ελεγος signified the same with θρηνος, lamentation. Those who lament use a whining tone of voice; which circumstance, perhaps, gave birth to the word.

## STANZA IX.

Ver. 7. *Town*] To the Author's quotation from Tacitus, may be added another from Cæsar de Bel. Gal. l. 5. cap. 21.

STANZA

## STANZA X.

VER. 7. *Ca'*] Few words pafs through more languages, and with lefs variation than this. Its root is the Hebrew *kol*, vox. Its cognates and derivatives fpread themfelves through the Arabic, Syrian, Chaldean, Perfian, Greek, Latin, and Gothic, and are a ftriking inftance of the univerfality of the primæval language.

It has been obferved, in the courfe of thefe Notes, that the German and Scandinavian tongues abound with vocables of the·fame found and fignification. There are only two ways of accounting for this appearance : Firft, by fuppofing that thefe coincident terms were parts of the univerfal original language fpoken by Noah and his family on the plains of Shinar, and preferved after the confufion of tongues at Babel: Or, fecondly, by granting, that Colonies emigrated from the neighbourhood of Media and Perfia, and at laft fettled in Germany and Scandinavia. Perhaps it might be owing to both caufes. Without entering into a minute difcuffion of this point, which the bounds I have prefcribed myfelf will not permit, I fhall only obferve, that the Median and Armenian tongues were different dialects of the fame language. The Armenians, Syrians, Chaldeans, refembled one another in *features*, *language*, and *manners*. Again, the Phrygian and Armenian tongues bore fo near a refemblance, that many have thought the former were defcended from the latter. The Thracians and Phrygians are·faid to have been the fame people, and therefore fpake the fame language. The Thracians and Getæ likewife fpoke only different dialects of the fame tongue. The latter fpread themfelves far and wide towards the Weft and North; probably they over-ran a confiderable

part

part of Germany, and forced their way into Scandinavia. Some have thought that the Goths and Getæ were the fame people. This, however, is a vulgar miftake, arifing from the ignorance of the hiftorians of the lower ages of the Roman Empire. If the links of this chain fhall happen to be firmly connected, we need not be furprifed at finding a great number of words pervade all the dialeéts fpoken by thefe different and very diftant nations.

**C H R I S T's**

# CHRIST's KIRK

# GREEN.

## TO THE READER.

IN the Preface and Notes to the *Gaberlunzie-man*, I have endeavoured to make my Readers acquainted with the true fyftem of rational Etymology, which confifts in deriving the words of every language from the radical founds of the firft, or original tongue, as it was fpoken by Noah and the builders of Babel. Many of thefe are preferved in the feveral dialects now in ufe over this globe, and every day brings more of thofe roots to our knowledge, as we grow better acquainted with the languages fpoken by the feveral tribes of mankind. But the large collection of thefe radical terms will, one day, be laid before the Public, under the title of a *Scoto-Gothic Gloffary*, if Heaven fhall beftow health and leifure to complete the work.

Mean while, the Reader will be able to form fome idea of my plan from the Notes on the preceding Poem ; and, in the following obfervations, I fhall confine myfelf to a more narrow circle of inveftigation, elucidating our ancient language from the later dialects of the primæval one, the *Gothic, Iflandic, Teutonic,* and *Anglo-Saxon.*

To relieve the Reader from the tedious uniformity of etymological difquifition, I have interfperfed fome obfervations on the manners and cuftoms of our anceftors, during the *middle ages,* which, I hope, will prove not unacceptable to the curious antiquarian.

Mr Ramfay has certainly departed very often from the orthography of Bannantyne's M. S. As I have no opportunity to confult that book, I have given fuch readings as appear to me moft confonant to the phrafeology of the fixteenth century.

The learned Bifhop Gibfon feems to have forgot that he was publifhing a Scottifh Poem—his orthography and idioms are quite Englifh.

CHRIST's

# CHRIST's KIRK ON THE GREEN*.

### I.

WAS ne'er in Scotland heard or feen
  Sik dancing nor deray,
Nowther at Falkland on the green,
 Or Peebles at the pley,

         As

*Chriſt's Kirk on the Green*] It is not eafy to affign the real name of the Author of this truly comic performance.—— Tradition gives it to one of the James's, Kings of Scotland; and we find two of them named, James the Firſt, and James the Fifth. In the *Evergreen*, it has the following note at the end, *Finis, quod K. James I.* Drummond's Hiſtory of the James's, p. 16. fays, "This Prince was well fkilled in Latin "and Englifh poetry, as many of his verfes yet extant do tef- "tify." † While this hiſtorian does not tell us what poetical

     N 2        performances

* Kirk-town of Leſlie, near Falkland in Fife.

† Vide *Joan. Majoris Hiſt. Britan.* in vita *Jacob*, who mentions the firſt two or three words of fome of thefe Poems abruptly, but fur- nifhes his Readers with no more; fo it would appear thefe are all now loſt. But Major is a trivial writer, devoid of all taſte.

performances the King left, we cannot, with certainty, afcribe this little poem to him; efpecially as the language appears rather more modern than the year 1430. James I. was murdered Anno 1436. Maitland * talks as if many of James's writings were yet extant; but, in his ufual way, he only copies Drummond. Vide bottom of the preceding page.

Many different writers have faid that this Ballad was compofed by James V. and many arguments are advanced for this opinion; fuch as, the exact defcription of the manners and character of our Scottifh peafants, with which James V. was intimately acquainted, as he delighted in ftrolling about in difguife, among the lower people and farmers; in which excurfions he fometimes met with odd adventures, one of which he is faid to have made the fubject of his *Gaberlunzie-man*, which we have, therefore, prefixed to *Chrift's Kirk on the Green*; and, indeed, the ftyle and ftrain of humour in both are perfectly fimilar.

The poetical talents of James V. made him known abroad; and it is to him the following verfes of Ariof. do refer † :

    " Zerbino di bellezza, edi valore,
    " Sopratutti Signori era eminenti," &c.

And, in the following Stanza, we find what country Zerbino belonged to:

    " Pero, che data fine à la gran fefta,
    " Il mio Zerbino in Scotia fe ritorno."

Ronfard, who accompanied James's Queen from France, and was his domeftic fervant, defcribes him thus:

                                  " Ce

---

* Hiftory of Scotland, p. 613.
† Orlando Fur. Cant. 13. Stan. 8. 9.

" Ce Roy d'Efcoffe etoit en la fleur de fes ans,

" Ses cheveux non tondus, comme fin or luifans,

" Cordonnez et crefpez flottans deffus fa face,

" Et fur fon cou de lait luy donnoit bon grace.

" Son port etoit royal, fon regard vigoureux ;

" De vertus, et d'honneur, et de guerre amoureux ;

" La douceur et la force illuftroit fon vifage,

" Si que Venus et Mars en avoient fait partage."

Maitland's Suffrage, concerning the tafte of James V. for poetry, were it of any avail, might be added; but he only copies fervikely from others.

There have been a good many different editions of this little Ballad, and the oldeft I have met with is one printed at Oxford in quarto *, and illuftrated with Notes by the learned Bifhop Gibfon, in which he has fhewn much knowledge of the an-cient Northern languages.   As the fpelling, however, of his edition is widely different from that ufed by the beft of the co-temporary authors, I have followed, in this one, the ortho-graphy of the collection called *The Evergreen*, but much cor-rected, as more truly correfponding to the Scottifh idiom and pronunciation.   The Notes of the learned Bifhop are diftin-guifhed from thofe of the Editor by the letter G.

In the edition by Bifhop Gibfon we find two entire ftanzas more than in that of Allan Ramfay, which, he fays, were copied from Bannantyne's M. S. Collection of Scottifh Poems, in Lord Hyndford's library, now in the Advocates library, to whom his Lordfhip prefented it, written in the year 1568. Thefe we have retained, as they are evidently in the fame ftyle and manner as the others, and even appear neceffary for connecting the ftory.   They are alfo warranted by Gibfon's edition, being printed thirty-three years earlier than that of Ramfay.

There

* Anno 1691

There are feveral variations in the reading of thefe two editions, which we have marked in the Notes ; but we have principally followed the fpelling of Ramfay's edition correfted, the
Bifhop having often adopted not only the Englifh orthography,
but even the phrafes of that language.

We have only to add, that if the little fpecimen now given
of our ancient poetry fhall prove acceptable to the real judges
of good letters, and the public in general, it is defigned to
print a full collection of all the Scottifh Poems which appeared
before the feventeenth century, illuftrated with Notes, in the
manner of thofe that follow ; in which undertaking we look for
the kind affiftance of all who love the language and antiquities
of our country, and who wifh to preferve the poems of our
anceftors from oblivion.

" *Nobis pulchrum imprimis videtur, non pati occidere*
" *quibus æternitas debeatur,*" as Pliny the younger fays,
L. 5. Ep. 8.

### STANZA I.

Ver. 2. *Deray*] Jollity and merriment ; *feafting* and
*frolicking*, which are generally accompanied with riot and
diforder.   In this fenfe G. Douglas ufes it * :

    " Of the banket, and of the grete *deray*,
    " And how Cupid inflames the lady gay."

And, fpeaking of the diforder in the enemy's camp, made by
Nifus and Eurialus† :

    " Behaldand al there fterage and *deray*."

Ruddiman

* Virgil, p. 35. l. 12.      † Ibid, p. 288. l. 16.

Ruddiman derives the word from the French *desroyer*, which Pasquier explains, *tirer hors de voye*, ou de roye. Hence *arroy*, and our word *array*; and *disarroy*, *disarray*. From *desroyer* this critic also deduces the Scots word *royd*, or *royet*, romping, frolicksome; taking away the first syllable, as in *skirmish*, from *escarmouche*; *sample*, for *example*; *uncle*, from *avunculus*; *spittal*, for *hospital*.

Thus far Mr Ruddiman, who, had he been better acquainted with the Northern languages, would have known that the origin of this word is of much higher antiquity than the old French he quotes. *Rud*, in the Gothic, signifies *line*, or *order*. Thus, in one of their old books *, *Then kunungr the hawær kuninglikt wald met arsde rad*, That King who succeeds according to the *line* of succession. Islandic *raud* and *rada*, to put in order; Saxon, *na der radt*, according to order. In the Scythian dialects we find this ancient word varied by many different terminations. Alam. *ruava;* Angl. *row;* and the Scots, who, we shall often find, retain the ancient Gothic pronounciation, say, *raw;* Welsh *rigwun;* Fenn. *riwi;* Ital. *riga*. Hence the French *raye*, and, by inserting an *n*, *rang*, whence we form *rank*; Belg. *rege*, *rijge*, whence the Scottish *rig*, a ridge of corn, from its streightness and regularity. In Ulphila we find, *Rathjan* †. *garathanu sind alla izwara tagla haubidis*, Numbered are all the hairs of your heads ‡. In Swed. *rakna*, to reckon or number; Lat. *ratio*.

As the ancients generally used counters in summing up their accompts, disposed in rows, *rad* is the common phrase on such occasions in the dialects of the North. Hence *Attrædur* is he who

---

* Kon. Styr. p. 24. apud Ihre, Lex. in Rud.
† Joh. vi. 10.    ‡ Matth. x. 30.

who hath attained to the *eight line, i. e.* fourfcore years ;
*Nirædur*, a man ninety years old ; *Tha var Haraldur Konung
aatradur at aldoi*, King Harald was then eighty years old *.
And in the Iflandic bible †, *Abram hafdi fex um attræt*,
Abram was eighty-fix years old.

VER. 4. *Peebles at the pley*] In the old writers we find
this word ufed in feveral fenfes. To *pley* is to *plead*, carry on
a law fuit ; Belg. *pleyten.* In Welfh we find the word *pleidioy*
to act as advocate for any. Vide Jun. in *Plead.* Douglas,
Virg. p. 73.

" —— Follow our chance bot *pleys.*"

*i. e.* Without difputing.

And p. 445.

" The auld debate of *pley*, or controverfy."

P. 3. 34. *But pleid*, Without controverfy. Now, as our anceftors always reforted to the courts of law, armed and attended by their vaffals and dependents, it often happened that
their differences were decided by fharper weapons than lawyers tongues. Hence the A. S. *plegan*, to ftrike, to wound
in war ; *plega-gares*, the play of fpears. Cædmon, 45. 11.
*Heard hand-plega*, The hard play of hands. Vide Lye, Lex.
Sax. in *Plega.* Hence Spelman in Archeol. derives *plea* from
*pleah*, damnum, periculum. *Play*, or *pley*, was hence ufed
to denote tilts and tournaments, as at thefe meetings it was
very frequent with the knights to give proof of their addrefs
and valour in mock engagements, which, however, often
terminated in blood. The ladies always were prefent at fuch
meetings, and gave the prizes.

——" of

* Olaf Trygg. Saga. Part. 1. p. 11.      † Gen. xviii.

As was of wooers as I ween
    At Chryſt's Kirk on a day ;
There came owr Kittys waſhen clean,
    In new kyrtills of gray,
            · ·Fow gay that day,

II.

——" of wit and arms, while both contend
" To win her grace, whom all commend."    *Milton.*

The town of Peebles was, in ancient times, a place of ſome
note.   Here was a conſiderable Priory ; and, being the largeſt
town in that diſtrict of Scotland, it is likely that frequent and
numerous meetings were held here.   The open plains, too,
round this city, made it a very proper place for tournaments,
and other warlike exerciſes.   *Pley*, the cuſtomary meeting.
Iſl. *plaga*, Goth. *plæga*, ſolere, alſo exercere.   It is probable
one of theſe exerciſes gave riſe to a Scottiſh Poem ſimilar to
this, entitled *Peebles on the Play*, ſaid to be preſerved by the
Reverend Dr Percy of Carliſle.

Ver. 5..*Ween*] Suppoſe; think.   Sax. *wenan*, opinari ;
Goth. *wenian*, Gibſon.   In the Alemanic it is *wanen*.   The
root is in the Gothic *wenian*.   Thus Ulphila, Luke iii. 15.
*At weniandein than allai managein*, All the people thinking.
Confer Jun. Lex. Ulphil.   *Wende*, in Chaucer, to think or
conſider.   Tr. lib. 3. 1547.

" And in his thought gan up and down to *wende*."

Ver. 7. *Kittys*] Either from *Kate*, *Katis*, the common
diminutive of Catherine ; or from their playfulneſs as *kittens*,
or Scot. *kitlings*, young cats.

Ver. 8. *Kirtle*] Mantle.   Iſl. *kiortell*.   Of old we
find the ſame term applied to the gowns worn by the men.

O                    Thus

## II.

To danſs thir damyſells them dight,
  Thir laſſes light of laits;
Thir gluvis war of the raffal right,
  Thir ſhoon war o' the ſtraits.

                          Thir

Thus Franco-Goth. *Ung aultre lui veſtira un kyrtel du rouge tartarin.* Vide Cange, Gloſſ. Lat. vol. 4. p. 737.

### STANZA II.

VER. 1. *Dight*] Prepared, or made them ready. Sax. *Dightan,* parare, inſtruere ; vox Chaucero uſitatiſſima. Thus, *dighteth* his dinner. To bed thou wold be *dight.* His inſtruments wold be *dight.*—Gibſon.

May it not rather be derived from *deccan?* Sax. Metaphor. *Excolere, ornare.* Alam. *Thecan.* Perhaps, too, we are hence to derive the word *deck* of a ſhip. Mr Ruddiman (Gloſſ. to Biſhop Douglas) obſerves, that in Cheſhire the word *dight* is uſed in the oppoſite ſenſe to foul or dirty ; but this is only provincial, like many other corruptions.

VER. 2. *Laits*] If this word is rightly copied from the M. S. it may ſignify nimble, or light-footed. Goth. *laiſtjan,* ſequi. Vide Jun. Gloſſ. Ulph. in voce. Thus Luke ix. v. 59. *Laiſtei mik,* Follow me. Theotis. Gloſſ. Kalepodia. *leiſt.* Dan. *leſt ;* Angl. *laſt,* on which the ſhoe is formed. Hence Sax. *fotleſt,* veſtigium, footſtep. Vide Pſ. lxxxvi. v. 19.

                          VER.

Thir kirtles were of Lincome light,
    Weel preſt wi' mony plaits;
They were fae ſkych, whan men them nicht,
    They ſqueil'd like ony gaits, .
            Fu' loud that day.

                                III.

VER. 3. *Gluvis*] So our anceſtors ſpelled *gloves*. Sax. *gloſes*. Jun. in Etymol. obſerves, that in Daniſh they are called *baand-kloffuer*, from *baand* and *kloffue*, to ſplit or divide, which gives the true idea of the word *glove*. Hence *gloſar*, *gloar*, *gloſe*, *glove*.

*Raffal*] I don't well underſtand the meaning of this word; but, from analogy, it muſt ſignify gloves of rough leather. Celt. *craſ*, nails of the fingers—a file—every thing that ſcratches. Hence ſkins dreſſed in a rough manner, with coarſe inſtruments, and not ſmoothed. Confer Bullet in V. *Craſ*.

VER. 4. *Straits*] Quære, Is this what we now call Morocco leather, from the Straits of Gibraltar?

VER. 5. *Lincome*] Is this rightly copied from the M. S.?

VER. 6. *Plaits*] Folds. Douglas, p. 298. v. 4.

" And he his hand *plait* on the wound in hye."

*Plait*, nectere, contexere; Gr. πλεκειν; A. S. *plett*, *pletta*, a ſheep-fold, they being of old made of wicker work. The Scots called them *faulds*, for the ſame reaſon, and the Engliſh *folds*.

VER. 7. *Skygh*] Shy. *Skygg baſta*, a ſhy horſe.—Jun.

VER. 8. *Squeil'd*] Shrieked. Sueo-Goth. *ſqwallra*, blaterare; *ſqwæla*, incondite vociferare; Angl. *ſqueak*, *ſqueal*. Douglas, of cattle, p. 254. 40.

" Bayth

" Bayth *fqueil* and low."

And p. 248. 36.

" With loud voce *fqueland.*"

It is ufed metaphorically to accufe ; *Sqwallra uppa en,* aliquem accufare ; Vide Ihre Lex. Sueo-Goth. in *Sqwallra. Sqwalungar,* crying children, fqualing brats. Suio-Goth. *fkall,* found ; Alam. *fcall;* Germ. *fchall.* " Ufurpa- " tur a nobis," fays the learned Ihre, " vel pro fonitu for- " tiori in genere, vel etiam in fpecie, quum multitudo, edito " clamore, feras in caffes propellit." Hence *fkallalæghe,* fociety of hunters ; *fkalra,* to cry out ; *fkalla,* to bark or howl as a dog. Hence *fkælla,* a fmall bell, which was hung to the robes of men in power, that the paffengers might make way for them. Chron. Ryth. Min. in Præfat.

" Kunde han danza, fpringa ok hoppa,
" Han fkulle jw hafwa fkallo, och forgylta klocka."

" If he only could dance and hop gracefully, he had immediate- " ly gilded bells given him." Confer Ihre in *Skælla.* The old French Romance *De la Viollette,* ap. Cange in *Mantum,* defcribing a rich robe :

" Et ot a chafcune flourette,
" Attachie une campanette.
" Dedans fi que rien n'en paroit,
" Et fi tres doulcement fonnoit,
" Quant an mantel frapoit le vent."

The antiquity of this ornament appears from the facerdotal robes of the Jewifh priefts, and thofe ufed by other nations. Apul. Met. Lib. 10. Et piftilibus balthæis, et tintinnabulis perargutis exornatum. Adde Eccard. ad LL. Salic. p. 151. where he obferves, that the Ital. *fquilla* is of the Gothic fami- ly. In the Latin of the middle ages we have *fchilla—*
*efquilla,*

### III.

Of a' thir maidens, myld as meid,

    Was nane·fae jimp as Gillie ;

As ony rofe her rude was red,

    Her lyre was lyke the lillie :

                            But

*efquilla*, and *fquillare*, for *fonare*. It was alfo the cuftom to hang bells to the necks of cattle, that they might be more eafily found in the woods : And hence the penalty in the Salic Law, cap. 29. againft him, Qui fkellam de caballis furaverit. Confer Cange in *Tintinnabulum*.

VER. 8. *Gaits*] Goats. Sax. *geit, gat ;* Ifl. *geit,* capra ; Goth. *gateins,* hædus. —Gib.

This is one of the many examples where the Scots have retained the orthography and pronunciation of the mother language, more exactly than the Englifh.

### S T A N Z A  III.

VER. 1. *Meid*] Mead, hydromel, a favourite drink of our anceftors, and alfo of the Scandinavians, as we learn from Snorro, and all the Northern hiftorians. Mead and ale, called by them *ol,* were the conftant beverages ufed in their feafts ; *Cujus frequentiffimus ufus eft in frigidis terris,* fays Olaus Magnus, lib. 13. cap. 21. where he has given us an account of the different methods they ufed in preparing that liquor, which may be of ufe to our modern brewers. Vide cap. 22, 23. 24. It is called by the Icelanders *mied* ;

                                    Alam.

Fow zellow, zellow, was her heid,

 And ſcho of luve ſae ſilly,

Thocht a' hir kin had ſworn hir deid,

 Scho wald hae nane but Willie,

  Alane that day.

       IV.

Alam. *mede ;* A. S. *medu, meodu ;* Welſh, *meddeglyn,* hydromeli ; Gr. μεδυ, vinum.

 Ver. 2. *Jimp*] Slender, handſome, G. *Gim, gimp,* complus, bellus, concinnus ; Welſh, *gwymp ;* Armor. *coant,* pulcher.

 Ver. 3. *Rude*] Bluſh. Sax. *rudu ;* Cimb. *rode, rubor.* Properly complection, the *verecundus color* of Horace, Epod. 17. Chaucer, Sir Topas, v. 13.

 " His *rudde* is like ſcarlet in graine."

Douglas, Virg.

 " So that the *rude* did in her viſſage glow."

Jun. Etymol. quotes from Joſephus, the ῥοδανον τε ϛωματος, the roſeate colour of the ſkin, which perfectly expreſſes the *rude* of our Poet.

 Ver. 4. *Lyre*] Biſhop Gibſon derives this from the Cimb. *blyre,* or the Sax. *bleare,* gena, maxilla, mentum, facies, vultus, quoting that of Chaucer :

 " Saturn his *lere* was like the lede."

But the learned annotator is certainly miſtaken ; for it comes from A. S. *lire,* which ſignifies (ſays Lye) Pulpan, quicquid carnoſum eſt, et nervoſum in homine, ut *earſlyre* nates,

           ſcanclira,

ſcanclira, ſura. Thus it means in general *fleſh*, as in Wal‑
lace's Hiſtory, b, 7. c. 1.

——" Burnt up bone and *lyre*."

And elſewhere :

" Through bone and *lyre*."

Douglas, Virg. p. 19. 35.

" Syne brocht flikerand ſum gobbetis of *lyre*."

And p. 456. 1.

" Wyth platis full the altaris by and by,

" And gan do charge, and wourſchip with fat *lyre*."

Vɛʀ. 5. *Zellow*] Thus our anceſtors uſed the *z*, though
they always pronounced the words ſo ſpelled as if they had
been written with the letter *y*. The reaſon ſeems to have
been, that the *gh*, to which *y* has ſucceeded in later times, had
been taken by ignorant tranſcribers for an *z*, as it bore ſome
reſemblance to it in the Saxon writing. This ſeems the more
probable, as we find the Anglo-Saxon character ſtill in uſe
after the conqueſt ; and, even under Edward the Third, the
Monks blended Saxon letters with the Roman. See Mande‑
ville's Travels, printed at London 1725, and Robert of
Glocester's Chronicle in 1724, exactly after the original
MSS. Hence, too, we muſt account for the changes we
find in the names of many places. Thus, *Yetland* was the
original name of the iſland which, from the above-mentioned
miſtake, came afterwards to be written *Zetland*, and which is
now corrupted, by vulgar uſe, into its preſent form *Shetland*.

Though the *z* be uſed in the Gothic tongue, (Vide Ul‑
phila's Goſpels *paſſim*) yet it is not found in the Iſlandic
alphabet, nor is it much uſed in the Sueo-Gothic ; ſo that the
learned Ihre calls it *Literam Suecis peregrinam.* The figure

z

## IV.

Scho fkornit Jock and fkrapit at him,
   And murgeon'd him wi' mokks;
He wald hae luvit, fcho wald not lat him,
   For a' his zellow lokks;

He

z much refembles the Saxon *g*, which the later Englifh have changed in moft words into *y*; as *geard, yeard; gea, yea; gear, year; geong, young;* and the Scots ftill more frequently, (as Ruddiman obferves) even where the Englifh retain *g*; as *yate,* for *gate; foryet,* for *forget,* &c. Junius has ranged all the words in Douglas's Virgil, which begin with *z,* under *g.* Vide his Gloff.

### STANZA IV.

Ver. 1. *Skrapit*] So Ramfay's edition. Bifhop Gibfon reads *fkripped,* which he explains, " Made a courtfie to him " in a mocking manner." " Vox deducenda videtur (adds he) per metathefin et fyncopen a Cimbr. *fkapraunade,* opprobrio vexabat. Bibl. Ifland. 1 Sam. 1. 6.

Perhaps this word may be, with more facility, derived from Sueo-Goth. *fkrapa;* A. S. *fcreope,* a fcraper; fcreopan, radære, fcalpere. Hence the faying, *Fa en fcrapa,* to be blamed or mocked. Perhaps our phrafe, *To fall into a fcrape,* may have originated from this. Shall we look here, too, for the root of the Latin *crepo, increpo,* with the *s* prefixed, as the Goths ufually do? Similar metaphor in the French, *Etriller* de paroles.

We

We have further to obferve, that the Goth. *ſkrap* properly ſignifies *uſeleſs fragments* of any thing, which we call *ſcraps.* Hence metaphorically *a lazy uſeleſs fellow.* Anſg. Saga cap. Ihre **Lex.** in *Skrap*, *Thu eſt meſta heims ſkripe*, Tu omnium bipedum ignaviſſimus es. As ſuch people are often vain-glorious, we have the verb *ſkrappa.* Jactare ſe, gloriari, *ſkrappa vet ſkryta.* Hence Lat. *crepare*, in the ſame ſenſe. *Skræp*, jactatio, oſtentatio.

VER. 2. *Murgeon'd*] Made mouths at him, G. The A. S. *murcnung*, murmuratio, querela, querimonia ; Goth. and Iſl. *mogla*, murmurare.

VER. 3. *Luvid*] This may be underſtood in the common acceptation of *loving.* But our anceſtors uſed it for *praiſing.* Thus Douglas, Virg. p. 455.

" How Eneas, glaid of his victory,
" *Lovit* the goddis, and can them ſacrify.'

Bruce's Life, p. 248.

" They *loved* God, and were full fain,
" And blyth that they eſcaped ſo."

Perhaps from the French *louer*, ſays Ruddiman ; but this word is formed from Goth. *lof*, praiſe. The words, in that language, *loſt, luſt, lyſta*, all denote ſomething *high* and *lofty.* *Lofwa*, laudare ; Iſland. *leiva.* In the Havamal, *Atqueld ſkal dag, leiva konu tha kender, make er reindur, is tha yfer um killmer*, i. e. Praiſe the day when evening is come, a wife when you know her, a ſword when you have tried it, and ice when you have paſſed it. *Loflig*, laudable ; *loford*, com-mendation.

He cherifh'd her, fcho bid gae chat him,

   Scho compt him not twa clokkis,

Sae fchamefully his fchort goun fet him,

   His legs war lyke twa rokkis,

       On rungs that day.

               V.

VER. 5. *Chat him*] To go about his bufinefs, G. Properly to take care of himfelf, and not attend to her, from the Gothic *fkota*, curare. Chron. Rython. apud Ihre, Lex. p. 619.

    " Han wille thet intet *fkota*,
    " Parum id penfi habebat."

Ifl. *fkeita*. Job 18. *Thes fem ecke fkeita um gud*, qui deum non curant. The fame learned and moft ingenious etymologift obferves the correfpondence of the Fr. *Il ne me chaut*, I care not; from the old *chaloir*. He adds, Credo noftrum a *fkot finus* fa&tum, ut a *finus* fit *infinuare*, adeoq; propriè ufurpatum fuiffe de infantibus qui in finu portabantur, unde hodieq; *fkoting* dicitur tenellus, quem nondum de finu deponere licet. Hence applied to other things, *Skota fit ambele*, to look after his charge. Adde Douglas, p. 239. v. 30.

VER. 6. *Clokkis*] Beetles, fcarabæi, G. True, the beetle in the Scot. is *clok*; but perhaps it means here, fhe valued him no more than the *cluk* of a hen, which our anceftors pronounced *clok*, from the found the hen makes.

VER. 7. *Schort Goun*] Till the French taught us to wear our clothes fhort in the prefent fafhion, the gown, covering the knees, was univerfally worn both in England and Scotland. Hence Jun. derives it from γυνα pro γυιατα, genua.

                    But

But the etymon is from the Welsh *gwn*, a gown or cloak, from *gunio*, ſuere. In the *True Protraiture of Geoffrey Chaucer, the famous Engliſh poet, as it is deſcryved by Thomas Ocleve, who was his ſcholar*, and is generally put before the title-page in the old editions of Chaucer, we find him cloathed in the true Engliſh gown, cloſe gathered at the collar and wriſts, and flowing looſely down from the ſhoulders to the knees. The form of this garment we had from Germany; and it ſeems to have been imported by the Saxons, as it was worn all over Germany. Vide Spelman in *Guna*. The opulent had their gowns lined with ermine, and other rich furs; the poorer people with hare and ſheep ſkins. Boniface, Archbiſhop of Mentz, epiſt. 89. Gunnam de pellibus lutrarum factum fraternitati væſtrie miſi. Vinca Benedict, cap. 5. Senibus noſtris gunnas pelliceas tribuimus. Sometimes wrote *gonna*. Thus Gul. Major, apud Cange, in *Gonna*; Canonici ejuſdem eccleſiæ in gonnis ſuis. In old French *Gonne*. In the Romance of Guillaume del. Nez:

" Or feraigrè, ſil me tollent ma *gonne*."

And ibid. apud Cange ubi ſup:

" Laiſſa le ſiecle, pour devenir prodhom,
" Et priſt la *gonne*, et le noir chaperon."

As *guna*, or *gown*, denoted the men's garment, the women's was called, in the barbarous Latin of the middle ages, *gunella*, becauſe made pretty near in the faſhion of the men's robe. Ital. *gonella*; Fr. *gotillon, cotillon*. Cluverius Germ. Ant. l. 1. c. 15. derives *gunam* a *gonaco*, quod Varro *majus ſagum* interpretatur, vocem Græcam eſſe ait. Hyſech. καυνακα, ϛρωματα, ἢ επιβολαια ετεϱομελλα, ſtragula, altera parte villoſa. We ſhall, in another work, prove evidently, that numbers of the Greek words are formed from the Gothic, of

which

which this is one, the robe itfelf being of Gothic, and not Greek invention. We find a Count of Angers firnamed *Grife-gonelle*, from his wearing a gown furred with that colour. Vide Cange Gloff. in *Grifeus* color. And we find an Epiftle of Pope John, folemnly addreffed to him, Goffrido *Grifia-gonellas cognominato*, nobilliffimo Andegavorum comiti. The men's gown is fometimes called *cappa*. Baldricus in Geft. Alberonis, ap. Cange, ubi fup. Clericali fe togo induit—et cappa de panno grifco fe fuper induit. Hence the faying of Henry IV. of France : " Je ne fuis q'un pauvre " here. Je n'ai que la *cappe* et l'efpée."

VER. 8. *Rokkis*] *Rock*, in Gothic and Iflandic, properly denotes a heap of any loofe things flung together. Thus *rock boys*, a heap or rick of hay ; and thus it is ftill ufed in Belg. Hence transferred to a heap of lint or wool put upon the ftick for fpinning. The tranfition was eafily made, when *rock* was ufed to denote the piece of wood to which the lint or wool was fixed. Thus the Chron. Ryth. apud Ihre Lex. in *Roak*, p. 496.

" Quinnor tager theras hæft ock harnijfk ifra,
" Ok monde them med *rockin* fla."

" *Women took the horfes and breaftplates from the men,*
" *And beat them with their* rocks."

Ifl. *rock*, and apud Kilian. Lex. Tuet. *rocken*, penfum colo aptare. See the learned Ihre, Lex. Sueo-Goth. in voce. Marefchall Obf. ad Verf. Angl. Sax. 4. Evangel. informs us, that in the times of Paganifm, the belt of Orion was, by the Scandinavians, called *Frygr rock*, colum deæ Fryggæ. Thus the girl here compares Jock's gown to an ill-fhaped heap of lint on the rock. Might not his ill-fhaped legs, if flender, &c. be compared to the rock or diftaff ? Another Scot-

tiſh Poem deſcribes the legs like *barrow-trams*. Perhaps, too, *rock* may here be meant of the gown he
wore, which looked as if it had been hung on a pole;
for *rock* Goth. and A. S. *rocc*, ſign. *toga*, veſtis ex-
terior; Al. *rokk*. In the barbarous Latin, *roccus, rochus*.
Vide Cange Gloſſ. in voce. Gall. *rochet*. Whence we call
the outer-garment of a ſucking-child a *rochet*, or *rachet*, and
the Engliſh, putting *f* before, have formed their word *frock*;
Gall. *froc*. Stadenius derives *rock* from *rauh*, rough, hairy.
Ulphil. *rih*, as our anceſtors firſt were clothed in ſkins, and
after wool came to be uſed, they continued to line their gowns
with furs of different kinds. The Finlanders ſtill call a furred gown *roucka*, and the bed-coverings they uſe, made of
ſheep-ſkins, are named *roucat;* whence our *rug*.

From this origin comes *rocklin*, the linen veſtment worn by
the prieſts; the biſhops *rocket*. Thus Hiſtor. Sigiſmund. ap.
Ihre Lex. vol. 2. p. 450. *Aflagges præſtens hwita rocklin*,
abrogatur ſacerdotis linea toga. This word was uſed in the
ſame ſenſe by the ancient Latins, as we ſee from Feſtus;
*Rica*, veſtimentum quadratum, fimbriatum, purpureum, quo
Flaminæ pro palliolo utebantur—Titinius, *Rica* et lana ſucidei,
alba veſtitus. Our readers will find many learned and critical
miſtakes in the notes on this paſſage, which is quite plain to
thoſe who know that it is a Gothic or Scythian term, as many
more of the ancient Latin words are. Confer Jun. Etym. in
*Rokette;* Spelm. in *Rocketum*.

Vᴇʀ. 9. *Rungs*] Round and long pieces of wood. Vox
in uſu apud Anglos boreales, G.

Properly poles, or long ſtaves like hunting poles, frequent
in Douglas, and our old writers. Skinner ſays the carpenters
call thoſe timbers in a ſhip, which conſtitute her floor, and are
bolted to the keel, *rungs*.

STANZA

## V.

Tam Lutar was thair minſtrel meet ;

   Gude Lord ! how he cou'd lans !

He playt ſae ſchill, and ſang ſae ſweet,

   Quhyle Towſie took a tranſs.

Auld

### STANZA V.

VER. 1. *Minſtrel*] This term was indiſcriminately applied to the harper, the fiddler, or the player on the bagpipe. Fr. *meneſtrier*. It appears to be derived from A. S. *minſter ;* and thoſe called *minſtrells* were employed in the public worſhip of the cathedrals as ſingers, (vide Jun. in voce) in the ſame way the Welſh called muſicians *cler*, as employed in the ſame way. Thoſe minſtrels, during the middle ages, united the arts of poetry, inſtrumental and vocal muſic, their ſongs being always accompanied with the harp. Thus, too, our Poet repreſents his minſtrel, in ver. 3. below, as playing and ſinging. They ſeem to have been the genuine ſucceſſors of the ancient bards, who, under different names, were admired and honoured from the earlieſt ages among the Gauls, Britiſh, Iriſh, and Scandinavians ; and, indeed, by all the firſt inhabitants of Europe, whether of Celtic or Gothic origin. It were eaſy to add many curious particulars concerning this once famed race of muſicians and poets ; but we refer our Reader to the elegant diſſertation on the ancient Engliſh minſtrels, prefixed to the Reliques of Ancient Poetry, where we find it obſerved, that the light of the ſong (to uſe Oſſian's expreſſion) never aroſe without the harp. Douglas, Virg. 250. 18.

" Sync

" Syne the menftrallis, fingaris, and danfaris,
" About the kyndlit altaris."

Du Cange has collected a number of curious anecdotes concerning thefe minftrells, voce *Miniſtelli.* The ufual theme of
their fongs we may learn from an old French romance, quoted
by this lexicographer :

" Quiveut avoir des bons et des vaillans,
" Il doit aler fouvent a la pluie et au champs,
" Et eftre en la bataille, ainfi que fut Rolans,
" Les quatre fils Haimon, et Charlons li plus grans,
" Li dus Lions de Bourges, et Guion de Connans,
" Percival li Galois, Lancelot et Triftans,
" Alixandres, Artus, Godefroy li Sachans,
" Dequoy cil menetriers font les nobles Romans."

VER. 2. *Lans*] To run or fkip ; metaphorically to dance.
Arm. *Lanca*, jaculari, lanceam vibrare. The minftrels, in
general, could acquit themfelves as dancers, as well as fingers
and poets. Douglas, Virg. p. 297. 16.

——" Turnus *lanfand* lightlie over the landis,
" With fpear in hand purfewis."——

Some think the phrafe *to launch a ſhip,* comes from this word.
Vide Effay prefixed to Reliques of Ancient Poetry, p. 41.
This ancient Celtic word has pervaded many dialects. Bafq.
*lancza ;* Gael. *langa ;* Corn. *lancels ;* Alam. *lamze ;* Gr.
λογχη; Hung. *lantfas,* a fpearman. Hence Lat. *lanceare,*
*lancinare.* Confer Voff. Etym. Lat. in *Lancea.*

VER. 4. *Tranfs*] The name of fome foreign dance, perhaps then firft ufed in Scotland, and oppofed to *Lightfute,* a
fpecies of the *hayes,* or, as the Scots call it, *reel,* a *traiu.*
Belg. *trein,* ingens effe clarûm numerus (fays Jun.) qui

ductorem

Auld Light-fute thair he cou'd fore-leet,

   And counterfittet Franfs ;

He held him as a man difcriet,

   And up the Moreis-danfs

         He tuke that day.

                VI.

ductorem fuum comitatur ; une queue trainante, une traine de gens ; of which train Towfie was the leader, or *choragus*, as in this manner the Morefco dances are ftill performed, which are mentioned below.

VER. 5. *Fore-leet*] To outdo, G. This is an error ; for *forlata*, Goth. fignifies to leave off, to defert. Job 4. 3. *Ho kan forlatat ?* Quis illud derelinquere poterit ? Ulphil. *traletan*. So Mark viii. 3. *Jabai fraleta ins laufqui thrans ;* If I fend them away empty. The Iflanders write it *firilata*, and *fyrirlita*. Vide Snorro, vol. 1. p. 103. The prepofition *for*, generally indicates a bad acceptation. Thus *forhæda*, to contemn ; and, where God is fpoken of, to blafpheme. *Forhala*, to delay ; *forhægda*, to deftroy ; *forhalla*, unjuftly to detain what is due to another. An hundred more examples might be given : Thus Towfie here *fore-leets*, leaves off and defpifes the dances of his own country, and betakes him to the French and Morefco tunes.

VER. 7. *Up-tuke*] He took up ; he began. Phrafis eft Cimbrica. Etenim tafia, tafia till, et tafia upp, ap. Iflandos fignificant *incipere*, ut, ogg drottins andetof ad vera med honum, cæpitq ; fpiritus domini effe cum eo. Gib.

Goth. *taga*, in general, to take. *Taga til lans*, to take on credit ; *taga arf*, to take or fucceed to an inheritance ; Ifl. *taka*. The great antiquity of this word may be feen in the

                             Latin

Latin *tagere*, and *tagax*, ap. Ciceron. Qui lubenter capit, rapax. Plaut. Milite:

" *Tetigit* calicem clanculum."

That is, ftole or *took* it. Hence *integer*, from whom nothing is taken. *Taga* alfo fignifies *proficere*. *Han tager fik wackert*. Pulchre proficit. He *takes* to it. Meric. Caufaubon. de Ling. Angl. Sax. p. 366. Ταω vel ταχω, τέ]αχα. Aor. 2. Partic. τέ]αγων. Exponunt quidam τειναϛ, alii τιναζαϛ, alii deniq; λαβων, accipiens, prehendens, quos Steph. fequitur —Certe. Τη imper. ex ταω—omnes exponunt λαβε. Cape. Angl. *take*. It fignifies alfo *to choofe*. *Taka konung*, regem eligere. Snorro, vol. 1. p. 65. *Taga lag*, legem accipere.

VER. 8. *Morris Dance*] Afric or Moorifh dance. A la *Morefca*, It. Fr. *Morefque*: Hence corruptly *Morris dance*. This kind was much ufed by our anceftors, and is included in the catalogue given by G. Douglas, Virg. 476. 1.

————" Gan do double frangillis and gambettis,
" Danfis and roundis trafing mony gatis,
" Athir throw uthir reland on their gyfe,
" Thay futtit it fo, that lang war to devife
" Thare haifty fare, thare revelling and deray,
" Thare Morifis."

Junius explains it—Chironomica faltatio—faciem plerumq; inficiunt fuligine, et peregrinum veftium cultum affumunt qui ludicris talibus indulgent, ut *Mecuri* effe videantur;—becaufe this fpecies of dance was firft brought into Spain by the Moors, and from the Spaniards it was communicated to other European nations, together with the *rebeck*, or *violin*, which is a Moorifh inftrument.

Q                    STANZA

## VI.

Then Steen cam ftappin in wi' ftends,·

    Nae rynk might him arreft,

Splae-fut he bobbit up wi' bends,

    For Maufe he maid requeift ;

                          He

### STANZA VI.

VER. 1. *Stends*] Long paces, or great fteps. G.
In old Scots, *to ftent*, to extend; a Lat. *tendere.* Douglas, p. 39. 34.

  " Cruell Achil here *ftentit* his palzoun.''

Ital. *ftendere.* Hence *ftend.* Douglas, defcribing horfes
running off with the car, p. 338. 31.

  " And brake away with the carte to the fchore,
  " With *ftendis* fell.''——

And p. 420. 53.

  " Quhilk fleis forth fae wyth mony ane *ftend.*"

VER. 2. *Rynk*] Sax. *rinc.* Homo robuftus, fortis, præftans, G. And hence it came to fignify, *a man* in general ;
as *wærcæft rinc*, fidus homo. *Rinc*, alfo ufed for hufband.
Vide Cædmon. 4. 22. Lye, Sax. Lex. in *Rinc.* Here it
means a ftrong man, or foldier, as it is alfo explained by Lye,
Gloff. Sax. in Voce.

VER. 3. *Bobit up*] Jumped, or danced, with many bendings of the body. We find a fet of men, in the middle ages,

                          who

He lap quhyle he lay on his lends,
　　But ryfand was fae preift,
Quhyle he did hoaft at baith the ends,
　　For honour o' the feift,
　　　　　　And dauns'd that day.

VII.

who, from the imperfect accounts given of them, appear to
have been a kind of itinerant dancers, and, like their other
wandering brethren, of no very good character. Urftis. ap.
Spelman. in *bobones*, *bubones*, lixæ, calones—Aliqando ne-
bulones et Furciferi. Ger. *buben*. Chron. Colmar. ap. Cang.
in *Bubii*. Servorum autem pauperum (in exercitu) qui dicuntur *bubii*, tanta fuit multitudo de *bobinare*. Conviciare,
clamiare, ap. Feft. ubi vide Scaliger.

*Bab*, bow often, or fink low, apud Anglos occidentales, to
*bob*, or *bob* down. Gib.

VER. 5. *Lap*] Supped; lapt. A Cimbr. *lepia*. in Imperf.
*lapte*, linqua vel lambendo bibere. G.

Surely our learned prelate has not attended to the obvious
fenfe of the paffage : Our Poet defcribes a clown dancing and
*leaping* with fuch violence as to fall. To *loup* is to *leap*; he
*lap*, he *leaped*. Thus the Bifhop of Dunkeld, p. 418. 47.

　　——" Some in haift, with an *loupe* or ane fwak,
　　" Thamfelf upcaftis on the horfis bak."

Ifland. *ad bleypa*, to run ; Sax. *hleapere*, faltator. Confer
Jun. Gloff. in *Leap*.

*Lends*] Loins. Sax. *lendenu*, *lendena*, *lendene* ; Ifl.
*lendes*, Gib. From Ifl. *leinge*, to extend, this being the
length of the trunk of the body.

## VII.

Then Robene Roy begouth to revell,
    And Towſie to him drugged.
Let be, quo' Jock, and caw'd him Jevel,
    And be the tail him tuggit:

                              **Then**

VER. 7. *Hoſtit*] Anglis Sept. to *hoſt*, eſt tuſſire. Sax.
*hwoſta*, eſt tuſſis; Iſl. *hooſt*; Angl. occident. to huſt, *i. e.* to
cough violently. Gib.

*Hoaſt, hoſt,* cough; A. S. *hwoſta,* from the Iſl. *hooſte,*
tuſſis; Angl. Bor. *hauſte,* id. a dry cough, as Ray explains it.
Belg. *hoeſt n* to cough.

### STANZA VII.

VER. I. *Revell*] To grow noiſy or troubleſome. Belg.
*ravelen, raveelen,* æſtuare, circumcurſare. Skinner's etymology from Fr. *reveiller,* is ridiculous. We may here obſerve,
that of old the word *revel* did not ſignify, as now, riot and
diſorder, but decent mirth and cheerfulneſs. So G. Douglas,
p. 146. 48.

    " With *revele,* blythneſs, and ane manere fere,
    " Troyanis reſavis thaim."

Chaucer alſo uſes it in the ſame good ſenſe; as alſo *riot,* in
which he is followed too by the Biſhop, p. 37.

    " The gild and *riot* Tyrrianis doublit for joy."

And p. 269. 46.

    " The blisfull feiſt they making man and boy,
    " So that thre hundredth rial temples ring,
    " Of *riot,* rippet, and of *revelling*"

                              **So**

So the old French *rioter*, to feaſt and be innocently merry. In this, however, they have departed from the original meaning of the Goth. *reta* ; Iſland. *reitq*, ad iram concitare. *Rede*, *raide*, anger. Inde Scot. *rede* ; Angl. *rate*, et præpoſito, *wrath* ; Alam. *ratan*, irritare. It is more than probable that the ancient Latins uſed *ritare* in the ſame ſenſe ; and hence the etymon of *irritare* and *proritare*, which the modern etymologiſts can make nothing of. From *riot*, the Barb. Lat. has formed *riota*, uſed in its original or bad ſignification. So Statuta Colleg. Corifop. apud Cange, in *Riotta :* Ab omnibus contentionibus, rixis, jurgiis, convitiis, *riotis*. And ibid. Ad invicem tunc inceperunt magnam *riottam*, et fugerunt hinc inde. Ital. *riotta*. Villani Hiſt. l. 9. cap. 304. Venendo tra loro, a *riotta*. Fr. *riote*. So Hiſt. de la Guerre Sacr. ap. Cange. Par cette mariage fut faite concorde du Roi de France, et de celui de Caſtele, de *riote* que eſtoit entre eux. And the Poet, (ibid.)

    " A tant commencent environ,
    " A *rihotter* tout li Baron."

We have in King Rob. Brece's Life, *To riot all the land,* *i. e.* To plunder it.

VER. 2. *Drugged*] Came to him. Eſt phraſis Cimbrica. *At draga till*, eſt venire ad, vel in. Deut. 1. v. 2. *Draga yſer*, tranſire. V. 24. *Draga* ut, egredi. Deut. 3. 1. *Draga fram*, præcedere. V. 18. Gib.

We have little to add to the learned Biſhop's obſervation, but to remark the analogy of the languages derived from the Gothic. Thus A. G. *dragan;* Angl. *draw*. In the ancient laws of Weſter Gothland, ap. Ihre, Lex. in *Draga*, it is written *Draha, Ar eig or huſum dræhit*, ſi ex ædibus portatum non fuit, in the ſame ſenſe as the Latin *traho*, Fr. *trainer*. *Draga wagnen*, to draw a waggon. Aſthmatic people are ſaid *draga andan*, in the ſame ſenſe almoſt as the

                                Latins,

Latins, *fpiritum trahere.* Vide Liv. l. 4. cap. 21. *Draga not,* to draw a net. Whence our fmall net, thrown with the hand, is called a *drag-net.* We may alfo hence derive the name of that fpecies of net, called by the Latins *tragulæ,* a *trahendo,* fays Turneb. Adverf. l. 20. c. 14. Vide Plin. l. 16. c. 8. Ifidorus calls it *tragum.* Metaphorically *Draga fin wæg,* to go away. Lat. *viam ducere.;* Belg. *trecken.* Adde Cange in *Traho,* where he notes the origin of the French *tirer vers un lieu.* It is ufed alfo to fignify *doubting,* the mind being *drawn* hither and thither. *Han nager vid fig,* deliberat de hac re. We find quite a fimilar phrafe, Salluft. Bell. Jugurth. cap. 93. Marius multis diebus et laboribus confumptis, anxius *trahere* cum animo fuo, omitteret ne inceptum, an fortunam opireretur. *Te deceive.* Laur. Petri de miffa, ap. Ihre, ubi fup. *Chriften almoga hafwær latit talje och dragha fig.* Populus Chriftianus fe decipi paffus'eft. Franc. *trahir,* to deceive or betray.

Ver. 3. *Jevel*] Vox blandientis, forfan idem quod jewel. Gib.

We cannot agree with the Bifhop in this interpretation. Thefe people are about to quarrel, and therefore *jevel* muft here be a term of reproach ; perhaps an evil-fpirit or dæmon. Goth. *jette,* giant; Ifland. *gotun.* The Saxons call a giant *Eten ;* and hence, perhaps, the Scots *Redeten,* the name of a Giant or Dæmon ufed by nurfes to frighten their children. *Jettegrytor,* ollæ gigantum, round holes in the rocks, in which (fay the vulgar) the Giants or Dæmons cooked their victuals. Uncertain as we are of the true reading of the MS. we only hazard this as mere conjecture.

Ver. 4. *Tuggit*] Drew. Scots *tugge,* to draw, from the Goth. *tahjan,* lacerare, difcerpere. Ulph. Mark ix. 26. *Filu tahjands ina,* Greatly fearing him. Adde Luke ix. 42. Hence, as the learned Ihre obferves, (in voce) *tugga,* to

eat,

The Kenzie clieked to a kevel,

 God wots if thir twa luggit;

They parted manly wi' a nevel,

 Men fay that hair was ruggit

   Betwixt them twa.

          VIII.

eat, to *tear* with the teeth, as in chewing. Ifl. *toga;* A. S. *teogan,* trahere. Confer Ihre, Lex. 2. p. 973.

 VER. 5. *Kenzie*] The angry man. A. S. *Kene, ken wer,* Vir acer, iracundus.

 *Clieked*] Catched up, or fnatched. Gib. *Click,* in old Englifh, apprehendere, rapere. Ifland. *kla,* frico. *Ad klaa,* fricare. Hence *claw,* and *to claw.* Sax. *clawan,* fcabere. Perhaps *klick* is only a contraction of the Saxon *gelæccan,* apprehendere.

 *Kevel, or Gevel*] So it fhould be wrote, and not erroneoufly, as in Ramfay's edition, *cavell,* It is properly a long pole, ftaff, or fpear. Goth. *gafflack,* jaculi genus, apud Vet. Suio-Gothos, fays the ingenious Ihre, in voce. Snorro, tom. 1. p. 367. *Olafr K. fcaut flundum bogafcoti, enn flundumga flocum,* King Olaf fometimes fought with the bow, and fometimes ufed the dart. A. S. *gafelucas.* Matthew Paris, ad an. 1256. p. 793. Frifones—ipfum Williefmum cum jaculis, quæ vulgariter *gaveloces* appellant—e veftigio hoftiliter infequebantur. Hence the French *javelle, javelot,* and our *javelin. Gaffel,* Ihre explains, *Quicquid bifurcum eft,* as a hay-fork. Hence Scot. *gavelok,* an iron crow, or lever, as it is generally divided into two toes at the lower end. Pelletier, Dict. Celt. derives it from two Celtic words, *galf,* bifidus,

## VIII.

Ane bent a bow, fic fturt could fteir him,
 Grit fkayth wead to haif fkard him :
He cheift a flane as did effeir him ;
 The toder faid, Dirdum, Dardum.
        Through

bifidus, and *flach*, fcipio, ut adeo denotet baculum bifurcum. Welfh *gefa*, il, forceps.

VER. 6. *Luggit*] Pulled each other about. Goth. *lugga*, crines vellere ; A. S. *geluggian*, vellere ; Ifl. *lagd*, villum notat ; *lugg*, villus, fign. any cloth or other thing which has been made rough by carding. Hence, perhaps, the Greek λαγος, hirfutus ; and the name of the hare in that language, λαγωτος, alias δαςυπυς.

It is not eafy to give a reafon for Bifhop Gibfon deriving this Scots word from Cimbr. *liuga*, fingere ; Sax. *leogan* ; Goth. *linga*, mendacium. Nothing can be more foreign to the obvious meaning of the paffage. In old Englifh, *lug* fignifies to draw or pull.

VER. 7. *Nevel*] Alapa, (fays Gibfon, Not. in Polem. Middin.) a blow or box on the ear, qua quis profterni poteft. Verb *nevel*, to box. Cimbr. *hneffe*, pugnus. Scotis *neaf*, (rectius *nief*, or *nieve*) et *fella*, profternere. Angl. *to fell*. Dougl. Virg. 123. 45.

 " And fmytand with *nieffis* her brieft."
Bruce's Life, p. 431.

 " And als their *nives* aft famen drive."

           STANZA

## STANZA VIII.

VER. 1. *Sturt*] Wrath, anger, defpite. *Sturt* is ufed
actively by Chaucer, to ftrive or contend. A. S. Alem.
Cimbr. *ftrid*, and *ftrit*. Gloff. apud Jun. in *Strife*, alterca-
tio. *Strit*, feditio. *Heim ftrit*, dimicant, pugnant, ftrident.
Ifland. *ftryd*; Germ. *ftreiten*, to fight; Ifl. *ftir*, bellum.

In Suio-Goth. *Storto*, præcipitem agere, deturbare. *Storta
en i olycka*; aliquem in infortunium præcipitem dare.
Germ. *ftürtzen, genftortig*, contumax; *paftorta*, irruere. Ifl.
*ftyr*, conflictus. Hence the old French *eftour*, and our
*ftour*, heat of battle, often ufed by the old poets: Douglas,
387. 4.

    " The *ftoure* encreffis, furius and wod."

Life of Bruce, p. 293.

    " The *ftoure* begouth."

He alfo ufes the word *fturt* to fignify *vexation*, 41. 36.

    " Dolorus my lyfe I led in *fturt* and pane."

And p. 238. 21.

    " *Sturtin* ftudy has the ftere."——

Confer Rudd. Gloff. ibid. in *Sturt*.

VER. 2. *Skaith*] Damage, hurt, lofs. In our old laws,
*fkaithlefs to keep*, to preferve from harm. Douglas, 72 23.

    ——" How grete harme and fkaith, for evermair,
    " That child has caught."——

And. p. 41. v. 43.

    " To me this was firft appearance of fkaithe."

A. S. *fkeathian, fcaethan*; Teuton. *fchaden*, to hurt. Vide
Lye, Sax. Dict. Theot. *Skadon*, damnum, noxa; et Goth.
*Skathjan*, nocere. A. S. *fceathe*; Teuton. *fchade*.

*Skar'd*] To have affrighted or hindered him, Douglas,
214. 52.

            Ufed

Through baith the chieks he thoch to chier him,

   Or through the erfs haif chard him ;

Be ane akerbraid it came na' neir him,

   I canna' tell quhat mard him,

        Sae wide that day.

                   IX.

" Ne *fkar* not at his freyndis face, as ane gaift."

Used also actively, to *fcare*, to *terrify* ; *fcare-crow*, a figure used to fright away birds. Hefych. interprets ςκαριζ̑ι]αι, ταρατ]ί]αι, turbatur ; and Euftath. ςκαριζ̑ειν, palpitare.

VER. 3. *Cheift*] Or chefid, *i. e.* choofed. Thus Douglas too ufes it. Alam. *kiefen*, eligere, from the Ifland. *kioofa*, eligere.

*Flane*] Arrow, alfo written *flaine*. Angl. S. *flan*, *flæn*. Perhaps (fays Lye) from *fleogan* or *fleon*, volare. Ifland. *flein*, an arrow. Douglas, 387.

    ——" Fleand with her bow fchute mony ane flane."

*Effeir*] For this is the true reading ; not as in Ramfay, *affeir*. He chofe out fuch an arrow as fuited his hand. This is an ordinary term in old our laws : *As effeirs*, as belongs to, as is proper and expedient. *Efferand*, or *effering*, conform to, proper to. Vide Ruddim. Gloff. ad G. Douglas.

*Efferis* alfo fignifies bufinefs. Douglas, p. 359. 48.

    " The greateft part of our werkis and *efferis*

    " Ben endit now."——

Unlefs this be only another mode of fpelling *affairs*.

VER. 4. *Dirdum dardum*] Term of derifion ; a great ado about nothing. Seems to be formed from the Ifland *dyr*, pretiofus ; or rather from *dyrd*, gloria, *dyrka*, glorifico. The

                  other

## IX.

Wi' that a frien o' his cried, Fy!
  And up an arrow drew;
He forgit it fae forcefully,
  The bow in flinders flew.

Sic

other word feems to be added only, *euphoniæ gratiæ*, unlefs
it be alfo from the Ifland. *daare*, rafh; whence our verb, to
*dare*.

VER. 6. *Chard*] This is another part of the verb *cheir*, in
the verfe before. Perhaps it may come from Goth. *karfwa*,
minutim cædere. Sax. *ceorfan*, *beceorfan*, amputare; *ceorf-æx*,
fecuris. Hence *char* fignifies to *wound*, or *cut*; and our
*carve*, to divide or cut meat into fmall pieces.

VER. 8. *Mard*] Spoilt his fhooting; made him err fo
wide. Sax. *amyrran*, diftrahere, confumere; Aleman.
*merren*, to hinder; Ifl. *meru*, minutim, diffipare; *marde*,
diffipavi.

## STANZA IX.

VER. 3. *Forgit*] Preffed. Ifl. *fergia*. In Præter. *Fergde*,
premere, compingere. G.
  *Farg*, Preffura, apud Verelium. Hence, perhaps, our
word *fardel*, burden. " *Ferg*," (fays Ihre) " vocantur conti,
" qui ad continendum corticem, quo domus ruricolarum te-
" guntur, faftigio utrinq; dimittuntur." From this idea of
preffing,

Sik was the will of God, trow I;

For, had the tree been trew,

Men faid, that ken'd his archery,

He wald haif flain enow,

Belyve that day.

X.

preffing, perhaps the name of a fmith's *forge* is derived; at leaft, this etymology may be as juft as thofe mentioned by Menage and Junius, in *Forge*. Bifhop Douglas calls a fmith *forgeare*, and a forge *forgin*.

VER. 4. *Flinders*] Splinters. Bifhop Douglas writes it *flendris*, and Mr Ruddiman (in Gloff. ad Virg.) deduces it from Lat. *findere*, Fr. *fendre*. But the true origin is the Gothic *flinga*; fruftum, utpote quod percutiendo rumpitur, fays the learned Ihre. *Isflinger*, pieces of broken ice. And thefe from *flenga*, tundere, percutere; Gr. φλαω, ferio. Hence, too, Germ. *flegel*, our *flail*, and the Fr. *fleau*. From this idea, the Icelanders call a wedge *fleigr*, and the Suio-Goths *plugg*, in the fame fenfe as we ufe it, *viz.* a piece of wood driven into a hole. Vide Ihre, Lex. in *Plugg*. This moft accurate etymologift thinks that the ancient Iflanders pronounced *flæc*, fegmentum, fruftum, partem de toto demptam. If this origin be juft, we have here the real meaning of the A. S. *flicce*, and our *flitch*, as exprefling a part of the carcafe of the fow. Ifland. *flycke*. In Trygwaf. Saga, p. ii. p. 23. *Fleickis fneid*, fruftum lardi. Confer Ihre, Lex. in v. *Flaca*, findere, partiri. Jun. in *Flitch*.

VER. 7. *That kend*] Scribe *quha* kend.

Kend

*Kend,* From *kunna,* Goth. *fcire.* Ulphila, *kunnan,* to *know.* Joh. vii. 27. *Kunnum.* Adde John xiv. ver. 4. Hefychius has κοννειν, fcire ; *kunnift,* fcientia, now pronounced *konft; kunnoga,* notum facere ; *kunnog,* fciens, peritus. Knytl. Saga, p. 4. " *Harald K. baud cunnugum* " *mannum;*" " King Harald confulted the Diviners ;" or, as we fay, the *cunning* men. Hence, he who attends to the courfe of the fhip is faid to *cunn* the fhip. Transferred alfo to denote bodily ftrength, if this be not its primary fignification. Al. *chunnan,* poffe, valere, Germ. *chonnen.* Anglice *can.*

VER. 8. *Enow*] Enough, many. Sax. *genog, genoh,* fatis ; Goth. *ganohs,* multus ; Ifl. *gnoght, nogt,* abundance ; *gnogr* vel *nogr,* abundantia. G.

In Ulphila, Joh. xiv. 8. *Gana unfis,* fufficit nobis. Alam. *genuoh,* any, enough.

VER. 9. *Belyve*] Senfus hujus vocis conftat ex Verfione G. Douglas, ubi fic redditur hoc carmen.

" *Extemplo Æneæ folvuntur frigore membra.*"

" *Belive* Æneas' members fchuke for cauld ;" Et iftud,

" *Ut primum lux alma data eft.*"

" *Belive* as that the halefum day wox licht."

Quibus adde :

" How Æneas in Afric did arrive,

" And that with fchote flew feaven hartis *belive.*" G.

Mr Ruddiman would derive this word from Teuton. *blick,* nictus oculi. We in Scotland fay, A thing was done in a *blink,* fuddenly ; from Ifl. *blinka* nictare ; *ogonblick,* nictus oculi. In the ancient Ballad of *William of Cloudeflie,* (Rel. of Anc. Poetry, vol. 1. p. 164.)

" The

## X.

An hasty henfure, callit Hary,
  Quha was an archer heynd,
Tytt up a taikel withoutten tary,
  That torment sae him teynd.

" The fyrst boone that I wold aske,
" Ye wold graunt it me *belyfe*."
Ibid. p. 91.

" He thoght to loose him *belive*."

### STANZA X.

Bishop Gibson places here the Stanza beginning,

" A zape young man that stood him neist," &c.
which is the XII. in Ramsay's edition.

VER. 1. *Henfure*] So Ramsay. Gibson has here *kinfman;*
we know not on what authority. *Hein, heini,* Celt. strong
young man. V. Bullet in *Heini.* It would seem that the
copy followed by the Bishop was very faulty ; or perhaps he
left out this word, because he did not understand it.

VER. 2. *Heynd*] Lord H. in his Gloss. to the Ancient
Scots Poems, explains it *handy, expert.* Douglas, p 363. 53.

——" Eneas *heynd*, curtas, and gude."
And p. 306. v. 3.

——" Clitius the *heynd*."
Skinner writes *hende*, which he explains, *feat, fine, gentle.*

VER.

I wat na' quhidder his hand cou'd vary,
 Or the man was his frien';
For he efcapit, throw the michts of Mary,
 As man that nae ill meind,
    But gude that day.

        XI.

VER. 3. *Tytt up a taikle*] Made ready an arrow. Chaucer:

 " Well could he drefs his *takcle* yomenly."

And :

 " The *tackle* fmote, and depe it went." G.

Douglas ufes the fame often : Thus, p. 300. v. 1.

 " His bow with hors fenonnis bendit has he,
 " Tharin ane *tackill* fet of fouir tree."

And below, (ibid.)

 " Quhirrand fmertly furth flaw the *takyll* tyte."

*Tackle*, Goth. fig. ornamenta navis, rudentes. Ihre, in Lex. *Tackle* ; and hence we fay the *tackles*, the ropes of a fhip.

VER. 4. *That torment fae him teynd*] So Ramfay. The Bifhop reads :

 " I trow the man was tien."

Not having the MSS. we cannot judge which is the true reading. *Torment* is ufed by our old writers to fignify *wrath, anger, indignation.*

VER. 4. *Teynd*] *Tien*, incenfed ; Sax. *teona*, irritatio. G.

         *Teen,*

*Teen*, and, as Chaucer writes it *tene*, injury, vexation. Sax. *teonan*, injuriæ, calumniæ; Belg. *tenenn*, *tanen*, irritare. τειϝεϑαι, vexare. Vide Junius, in *Teen*.

VER. 5. *1 wat na'*] I know not. Goth. *wetan*, scire. Ulph. *vitan*; Island. *vita*; Germ. *wiſſen*. The Latin, with the digamma, hence forms *video*. The A. S. for *vitan*, put often *wiſtan*. Hence our *wiſt*; *I Wiſt not*. Non multum abludit ειδω, ειδεα, quæ de acie tammentis quam oculorum uſurpantur; as the moſt ingenious critic Ihre obſerves, in *Weta*. The Goths diſtinguiſh betwixt *bokwett*, artium ſcientia, and *manwtett*, humanitas; and indeed they are often found ſeparate.

VER. 6. *Or the man was his frien'*] Biſhop Gibſon reads thus:

" Or his foe was his friend."

Which is ſcarcely to be underſtood.

VER. 7. *Michts of Mary*] Through the protection of the Virgin. Every body knows, that the blind votaries of Popery more frequently addreſs themſelves in prayer to the Virgin Mary, than either to God or our Bleſſed Saviour. The Scots ſay *mights*, power, from Ulphil. *mahts*, *magan*, poſſe. Mark xiv. v. 20. *Ni mag qwiman*. Non poſſum venire. Iſl. *At meiga*.

VER. 8. *As man*, &c.] Biſhop Gibſon has it:

" As one that nothing meant."

But I know not on what authority. He has either uſed unwarrantable liberties with the text, or has been miſled by ſome erroneous copy.

STANZA

## XI.

Then Lowry lyke a lyon lap,
An' fone a flane can fedder;
He hecht to perfe him at the pap,
Theron to wad a wedder.

He

## STANZA XI.

VER. 1. *Lap*] Run, a Cimbr. *Hlaupa*, in Imp. *hliop* currere. Vel *leapt*, a Sax. *leapan*, faltare, currere. Imperf.
*Laup*. G.

The laft etymology is the true one; from *laup* we fay,
*to loup*, to jump. Thus Douglas, Virg. p. 418.

———" Sume in haift, with ane *loupe* and ane fwak,
" Thamefelf upcaftis on the horfis bak."

Goth. *lopa*, currere. Hence *lopta*, a flea. Ulphila writes
*hlaupan*, faltare. Mark, chap. x. ver. 5. *Ufhlaupands*, exilians.
Jun. in Gloff. Ulphil. thinks this has fome connection with
λαυρϑαζει, which Hefychius explains ϛπευδει, haftens.

VER. 2. *Flane*] Vide Note to Stanza VIII.

VER. 3. *Hecht*] Hoped. A. Sax. *hiht*, fpes. G.

*Hecht*, he promifed to himfelf, or vowed. So LL. Goth.
cap. 4. 1. (ap. Ihre in *Heta*) Engin ma haita a huathki a
hult epa hauga. Nemo vota nuncupabit, nec luco nec tumulo.
Ulphila *gahaitan*. Vide Mark xiv. 11. Al. *heizan*. Gloff.
Lipfii, *Giheitan*. Ifland. *heita*, unde *heit* votum. *Streinga
heit*, voto fe obligare.

S

VIR.

He hit him on the wame a wap,

   It buft like ony bledder;

But fwa his fortune was and hap,

   His doublet made o' lether

              Saift him that day.

                      XII.

VER. 4. *Wad*] Pawn. Goth. *wad*, pignus; A. S. *wed*, *wedde fyllan*, pignus dare. Fenn. *weden*. We muft obferve here, for the illuftration of this phrafe, that *wad* properly fig-nifies *cloth*; becaufe, in the fcarcity of cafh of old, cloth was given as ready money, and received as fuch for other goods. Hence, when any pledge was given, it was generally *cloth*, wad; and from the frequency of this cuftom, *wad* came to fignify a *pledge*. We ftill fay, the *wadding* of a gun. By the common change of *f* and *w*, the Iflanders pronounce *fat*, and *fot*. Alam. *pfand*; Goth. *pant*, *pans*; Lat. *pignus*. Hence the Goth. verb *wadfætta*, oppig-norare, and the Scots law-term *wadfett*, and *to wadfet*, to lay in pawn. In the middle Latin we find *vadium*, *guadium*, &c. Etrard in Græcifmo, ap. Cange in Vadium.

   " Vado viam, vado quadrupedem, vadio, vadium do,

   " Pro conforte vador; fonat hoc quod fum fidejuffor."

Hence *vadimoniare*. Vide plura ap. Cange in *Vadium*, et in *Plegius*. Alfo called *gagium*, unde Fr. *gage*; and from hence the *gage*, offered by the challenger, and taken up by the perfon challenged, in furety that he was to fight the other.

VER. 5. *Wap*] A blunt or edgelefs ftroke, in oppofition to one that pierces the fkin. The elegant Editor of the Scots Poems, printed Edinburgh, 1770, explains *wapped*, fudden-ly ftruck down, that is, by a *blunt ftroke*, as of a cudgel.

                         VER.

Vrr. 6. *Buft*] Sounded; a dull found, fuch as a bladder filled with wind makes, when ftruck. *Puff* of wind; flatus venti. Fr. *bouffeè* de vent; Belg. *boffen*, to puff up the cheeks with wind. Hence *buffet*, a blow on the cheek. Dan. *puff*, plaga, ictus. *Puffe*, percutere malas inflatas. Hence, too, vain-glorious boafters are called by the Dutch *poffen* and *poechan*. Gr. Ποιφυςςειν, vehementius fpirare. Fr. *piaffe*, pomp, vain glory.

Ver. 8. *Doublet of lether*] Our anceftors wore very commonly clothes made of leather; and anciently the inhabitants of this ifland ufed no other garments. But even long after the ufe of woollens, thofe who lived much in the woods, and the yeomanry, were often clad in fkins. Thus Guy of Gifborn is dreffed, Rel. of Anc. Poet. vol. 1, p. 83.

" And he was clad in his capul hyde,
" Top, and tayle, and mayne."

We in this ifland had this cuftom from our German, and they from their Scythian anceftors, of whom Juftin, l. 2. c. 2. " Lanæ iis ufus, ac veftium ignotus, quanquam continuis fri- " goribus urantur, pellibus tamen ferinis, aut murinis, utun- " tur." Adde Ifidor, lib. 19. cap. 23. and Cæfar of the Suevi, lib. 4. cap. 1. Cluver. Geogr. l. 1. c. 16. We find the Emperor Charlemagn clothed with a fkin above his inner garments. Eginhart, Tit. Car. cap. 23. defcribing his drefs, " Veftitu patrio, hoc eft Francico utebatur,—crura et pedes " calceamentis conftringebat, et ex pellibus Lutrinis, thorace " confecta, humeros ac pectus hieme muniebat." This garment was by the ancient Iflanders called *felldr*, being made of fheep-fkin with the wool on, and ferved them as a cover for their beds at night, as well as a cloke, or robe, through the day. Thus Ara Frode, Libell. de Ifland. cap 7. defcribing Thorgeir going to bed, " Oc bræiddi felld fin a fic, et explicabat

S 2                                   " ftragulym

## XII.

The buff fae boift'roufly abaift him,
   That he to th' erd dufht down ;
The ither man for deid there left him,
   An' fled out o' the town.

The

" ftragulum fuum fuper fe." It is ftill cuftomary in Green-land, Iceland, Finland, and Lapland, to fleep on fkins, and alfo in Norway. Vid. Buff. Lex. ad ara Frode in *Felldr.* Even the women of diftinction wore their *feld* in the day time. So the Norwegian poet of Gudruna :

   " Som det nu lakked till quelden
  . " Indkom Fru Guru med *felden*."

" In the evening came in the Lady Gudruna clothed in her " *feld*."

### S T A N Z A XII.

We give this Stanza from Gibfon's edition. · It is not in Ramfay's, though by the ftile it appears to be genuine.

Ver. 1. *Buff* ] Vide Supra, Stanza 11. *Buff*, fays Gib-fon, a blow or ftroke.

*Abaift* ] Abafed, aftonifhed, fays Gibfon.

Perhaps it fhould be *abafhed ;* confternatus, ftupefactus, Suid. Αβαζος, ησυχος, ηγυυ εςρημενος τυ βαζειν, ὁ εςι λεγειν ; filens, cui ereptus eft ufus loquendi. Chaucer has *abawed* for abafhed. I was *abawed* for merveile,

Jun.

The wives came forth, an' up thay reft him,
   An' fand lyfe in the lown ;
Then wi' three routs on's erfe they reir'd him,
   An' cur'd him out o'. foone,
           Frae hand that day.

                      XIII.

Jun. derives it from Sax. *beap ;* de quo vide Lye, Sax.
Dict. Confer Jun. in *Bafe.*

   VER. 2. *Dufht*] Fell down fuddenly. *Dufch,* contundere,
allidere. Douglas, p. 225. 1.

   " The fharp hedit fchaft *dufchit* with the dint."

And p. 296. 34.

   " The birnand towris down rollis with ane ruche,
   " Quhil all the hevynnefs dynlit with the *dufche.*"

   VER. 5. *Wives*] Women. *Wif,* ap. Sax. et *twif,* ap.
Cimbr. fæminam, vel mulierem fignificat. Gib.

   Thus, Gen. iii. 2. xx. 5. *This wyf*; This woman. Adde
Cædmon, 58. 9. Matth. ix. 20. *An wyf,* quædam mulier.
Jo. iv. 9. *Samaritanifce wyf,* A Samaritan woman. Gen.
v. 2. *Were and wif,* Man and woman, male and female.
Vide plura ap. Lye, in *Wif.* Hence *wiman, wimman,* i. e.
*wif—man,* Mulier, fæmina. Alam. *Uuib, Uuip ;* Germ.
*weif.* The learned Ihre mentions two derivations ; firft, a
*wefwa,* to weave ; or elfe from *wif,* or *hwif,* calantica, a
woman's head-drefs, metaphorically, as the northern writers
fay, *Gyrdle oc linda, Girdel and belt,* for man and woman ;
and alfo *hatt oc hætta,* pileus et vitta, in the fame fenfe.

   VER. 5. *Reft him*] Snatched. Sax. *reafian,* rapere. G.
                                     Henc

Hence Douglas ufes it for robbed, pulled, or forced away, 74. 12.

"The rayne and roik *reft* from us ficht of hevin."

Teut. *rauben*, fpoliare; *raffen*, corripere. Hence *bereave*, *bereft*; and the Scots, *to reave*; and *reaver*, a *robber*, often ufed for a *pirate*. Hift. of Wallace, p. 342.

"Upon the fea yon *reaver* long has been."

And p. 343.

"At ilka fhot he gart a *reaver* die."

*Reif*, rapine, robbery. G. Douglas, p. 354. 30.

"For na conqueft, *reif*, ftayt, nor penfioun."

VER. 6. *Loun*] Rogue, rafcal. Alludit. Eng. *clown*. Douglas, p. 239.

———"Quod I, *Loun*, thou leis."

The old ballad of Gilderoy, Reliq. Anc. Poet. p. 324.

"And bauldly bare away the gear
"Of many a lawland *loun*."

Lye Addit. to Junius deduces it from Cimbr. *luin*; ignavus, piger, iners.

VER. 7. *Routs*] Roarings, bellowings. Cimb. *at ryta*, vel *rauta*; frendere, vel rugire belluarum more. *Angli Bor. dicunt*, The ox *rowts*; et hinc ap. Scotos *route*, eft idem as to make a great noife. Ut habet Douglas:

"The firmament gan rummil, rare, and *rout*."

*Hinc, oborto tumultu dicimus*, What a *rout* is here? Item *orto ftrepitu*, What a *rout* you make? G. Dougl.

"The are begouth to rumbill and *rout*."

Sax. *hrutan*, to fnort, to fnore in fleeping. This is Mr Ruddiman's etymon; but we imagine it comes more immediately
from

## XIII.

A zape zung man that ſtude him neiſt,
  Lous'd aff a ſchot wi' yre ;
He ettlit the bern in at the brieſt,
  The bolt flew owre the byre.

Ane

from the Goth. *bropian*, clamare. Ulphila, Matth. xxvii. 46.
*Uſropida ſtibnai mikilai*, clamavit voce magna. Luke xix. 40.
*Hropjand*, clamabunt. Iſland. *broop*, clamor; Alam. *ruaſan*,
clamare, vociferare. Is *roopy*, hoarſe, derived from this?

VER. 8. *Frae hand*] Quickly, in a little time. Ang. out
of hand. G.

### STANZA XIII.

This is the 12th in Ramſay's edition, owing to the omiſſion
of the foregoing, which we give from the Biſhop's edition;
but this 13th Stanza is omitted by Gibſon.

VER. 1. *Zaip*, or *Zape*] Ready, alert. We have already
ſaid why our old writers always uſe the *z* for the *y* Engliſh,
when it begins the word, as *zeir, yeir—zour, your,* &c.
Douglas, p. 409. v. 19.

  " The biſſy knapis and verlotis of his ſtabil,
  " About thyme ſtude, full *zape* and ſerviabil."

It may alſo mean vaunting, inſulting. Chaucer thus uſes it.
R. R. 1927.

" And

" And fayd to me in great *jape,*

" Yeld the, for thou may not efcape."

Iſland. *geip,* boaſting. Chaucer, Lucre. v. 18.

' ——" Tarqinius the yonge

" Gan far to *jape,* for he was light of tonge." '

Hence it came to fignify jeſting, light talking. Id. Fr. lib. 2. 1167.

" He gan his beſt *japes* forth to caſt,

" And made her fo to laugh."——

*Neiſt*] Next. In Decalog. Angl. Sax. Ne wilna thu, thi- nes *nehſtan* yrfes med unriht ; Ne concupiſcas bona proximi tui injuſte. *Neh,* nigh ; *nehſt,* neareſt. Hence *neh-bur,* neighbour, from Ulphila's *neguha,* nigh. Mark ii. 4. *Neguha gwiman,* To come near. Alem. *nah ;* Bel. *nae, naer.* Whence our Scots *naar,* near.

VER. 3. *Ettlit*] Defigned, aimed, intended. Cimbr. *Atætla,* defignare, deſtinare.

" The goddes *ettilit,* if werdes were not contrare." G.

*Ætla* (fays the learned Ihre) indicat varios mentis humanæ motus, ut dum deſtinatæ ſibi propohit, judicat, ſperat, &c. Iſland. id. Thorſten Wik, S. p. 10. *Dat ætla eg.* Id Spero, vel animo concipio. Lex. Scanica, p. 16. ſect. 21. *Ætla wider frænda ſin ;* Confultare cum cognatis, vel amicis fuis. Con- fonat Gr. εθελω, nec fenfu longius diſtat, quum utrumq; defiderium voluntatis ad quidpiam tendens denotat.

*Barn*] The A. Sax. *bearn ;* Iſl. *barn ;* a *bairan, beran,* parere. Gib.

It is is originally derived from the Goth. *barns.* Vide Ul- phila, Luke i. 41. and ii. 12. We find it even ufed to fignify a girl, Mark v. 39, 40. Hence *barnilo,* a little boy, an in- fant. Luke i. 46. *Jah thu barnilo,* And thou child. Alam.

*barn,*

*barn, bern.* Let us obferve, by the way, that our old authors often ufe *bairn*, to denote young men, full-grown perfons, as the Englifh do *child.* So Pallas, addreffing Æneas, ap. Douglas, p. 244. 33.

" Come furth, quhatever thou be, *berne* bald."

And p. 439. 22.

———" And that awfull *berne*,

" Beryng fchaftis fedderit."———

*Bern time,* the whole number of a woman's children. Id. p. 443.

" Bare at ane birth———

" The nicht thare moder, that *barne time* miferabill."

The ancient Englifh writers apply *child* to knights. Thus the Child of Elle, Reliq. of Anc. Poetry, p. 107.

" And yonder lives the *Child* of Elle,

" A young and comely knight."

Warburton, Not. on Shakefpeare, obferves, that in the times of chivalry, the noble *youth,* who were candidates for knight-hood, during the time of their probation, were called *Infans, Varlets, Damoyfels, Bacheliers.* From this comes the Scots word *chiel,* which is applied to a young man, full-grown.

VER. 4. *Bolt*] Arrow. Sagitta capitata, fays Junius. Cymbr. *Bollt.* Belg. *bolt, bout.* Non abludit βελις, jaculum ; βολιδες, miffilia ; a βαλλω, jacio.

*Byre*] Cowhoufe. Theotif. *Buer* eft cafa, tugurium. Item. *byre* eft villa, fiquidem *bar* eft pagus, villa prædium, Gib.

In the old Gothic *byr,* pagus; a *bo,* habitare. Alfo *by,* pagus. Hefych. βυριο, οικημα, habitatio. Etym. Mag. ευβυριον pro ευοικον, and βυριοθεν, Hefych. pro οικοθεν. " Qumque aliæ olim urbes non fuerint, quam grandi- " ores.

T

Ane cryd, Fy! he had flain a prieft, .

 A myle bezond a myre ;

Then bow and bag frae him he keift,

 And fled as ferfs as fire   -

    Frae flint that day.

       XIV.

" ores villæ, hinc etiam urbes quantumvis ampliores, idem " nominis habuere, et etiamnum inter Danos habent," fays the learned Ihre. Hence *By fogde*, Præfectus civitatis. *By lag*, Jus civitatis, who fornandes de reb. Get. tranflates bellago, *byfwen*, city-officer, or conftable. *Byr*, an inhabitant ; A. S. *bure* ; Germ. *bauer*.

VER. 5. *Slain a prieft*] This was, in thofe days of ignorance, deemed the moft horrid murder that could be committed, and in a manner irremiffible, the perfon of a prieft being held much more facred than that of any layman. Hence, in the laws of the middle ages, we find the fine, or compenfation for the murder of a prieft, much higher than that of a layman, of whatever high rank he might be. They were eftimated according to their feveral degrees ; and hence, in the laws of Kanote, p. 151. we find Tryhyndmon, Syxhyndmon, *i. e.* Homø ducentorum, trecentorum, fexcentorum folidorum ; every man's life, from the king to that of the cottager, having a fixed price fet upon it. This was generally called *wiregild*, *wergild*, and *manwyrd, the price of a man.* By the laws of King Athelftan, the King's life is valued at 30,000 thrymfas ; an Archbifhop's at one half of this fum. A common man's life is bought for 267 thrymfas ; but a bifhop's at 8000 ; and one in fimple prieft's orders at 2000. In the additions to the Salic law, made by the Emperor Louis, anno 819, we find

            the

## XIV.

Wi' forks and flails they lent grit flaps,
  And flang togidder like fryggs ;
Wi' bougars of barns thay beft blew kapps,
  Quhyle thay of berns maid briggs.

The

the compenfation for a prieft always triple to that of a layman ;
and if the offender had not wherewith to pay, he was fold for
a flave.

Ver. 7. *Bag*] The quiver of arrows, which was often
made of the fkin of a beaft.

*Kieft*] Caft.

### STANZA XIV.

Ver. 1. *Flaps*] Douglas writes it *flappis*, ftrokes given
with a blunt weapon, fuch as a flail. Hence Belg. *flabbt*,
colaphus, a fono, fays Ruddiman. *Flap*; fays Jun. extremi-
tas cujufq; rei mollis ac pendula, quæq; ad levem motum fta-
tim concutitur. Ita *throat-flap*, Anglis eft epiglottis. *Flye-
flapy* mufcarium. Teuton. *flabbe*, libens, præfixo D. Hence,
too, Suio-Goth. *flab*, os, labium, de quo vid. Ihre, Lex. in
*Flabb*, who, with his ufual accuracy, obferves the connection
betwixt the Greek and Scythian languages ; rifum nempe, qui
patulo ore, et diductis labiis fit, perinde in illa (Lingua
Græca) πλαῖον γελᾶῖα dici, ac a nobis *flatt laje*. We

T 2                                          fay

say also, a *broad* laugh, a *broad* stare. Perhaps *flatter* may be also derived fro *flat*, de quo vide Jun. in *Flatter*.

Ver. 2. *Fryggs*] Perhaps this is the same as *freik*, ap. Douglas, a foolish impertinent fellow. Teuton. *frech*, protervus, procax. Petulans, says Mr Ruddiman; unde Angl. *freik*, whim or caprice. In the Jus Aulicum of King Magnus, anno 1319. sect. 9. we find some public game or meeting, called *frimark*, prohibited on account of the mischiefs and wrongs they did to each on these occasions. Framledis forbjudher minne herre nokor frimark, &c. ulterius prohibita esse vult dominus meus omnia ludicra, *frimark* dicta, sive equo peragantur, sive alias. Confer Ihre in *Frimark*. These sports were also called *seylemarked*, de quo id. ibid. Vide Jus Aulicum, Dan. anno 1590. sect. 25.

*Friggs*] Forsan eagerly, libenter, a Cimb. *frigd*, libido. Gibs. vide infra, Stanza 21. v. 4. Note.

Ver. 3. *Bougars*] Rafters; probably from A. S. *bugan* flectere, unde *boh*, boga, a bough or branch.

Ver. 4. *Best*] Beat. Thus the word is used by G. Douglas.

*Blew kapps*] Alluding to the blue caps or bonnets our commonalty usually wear on their heads.

Ver. 4. *Briggs*] Bridges. The elegant etymologist Ihre observes, that the original word is *bro*, signifying *stratum aliquod*—Nunc observare lubet (adds he) septentrionem nostrum solum esse, qui hoc primitivum retinuerit, dum cæteri dialecti omnes diminutivum ejus adoptarunt. Such is *brigga*, from *bro*; *bygga*, from *bo*; *sugga*, from *so*, &c. Hence, too, the Suio-Goth. *brosjol*, tabulatum pontis; *brokista*, fulcimentum pontis; *bookar*, idem; *brygga*, a bridge; A. S. *brigg*, *brycge*; Germ. *brucke*. Observe here, that, as in many other words, the Scots have kept more closely to the orthography and pronunciation

The reird raife rudely with the rapps,

   Quhen rungs war laid on riggs;

The wyfis came forth wi' crys and clapps;

   Lo! quhair my lyking liggs!

            Quoth thay, that day.

                  XV.

nunciation of the mother language, than moft of the other northern dialects.

VER. 5. *Reird*] Or *Rerde*, for thus it fhould be wrote; not as in Gibfon's edition *reir*. *Reirde* is properly clamour, noife, and fhouting. Douglas, p. 300. 30.

   " Bot the Trojanis rafit ane fkry in the are,

   " With *rerde* and clamour."——

And p. 37. 12.

   " Syne the *reird* followed of the zounkeris of Troy."

Ruddiman derives it from Sax. *reod*, lingua, fermo, as the primary idea feems to have been that of *fhouting*. Hence, too, *rede*, council, advice. Teut. *raad*, concilium; *raden fuadere*; Angl. *aread*, to pronounce.

   *Rapps*] Stroak; alfo the found made by a ftroak. Dougl. 301. 50.

   " On bois helmes and fcheildis the werely fchot,

   " Maid *rap* for *rap*."——

And 143. 12.

   " Als faft as rane fchoure *rappis* on the thak."

Alludit ῥαπίζω, percutio, fays Rudd. who derives this from

                    *hreppan,*

*hreppan,* tangere. But the truer etymon seems to be from
Goth. *hropjan* clamare, from the *sound* made by the stroke.
In Suio-Goth. *rapp,* ictus ; *gifwa en ett rapp,* to give one a
blow ; *rappa,* the verb, to draw or pull violenty. Ulphila,
Mark ii. 23. *Raupjan ahsa,* spicas vellere.

VER. 6. *Rung*] A rough pole ; Island. *runne,* saltus
sylvæ.

*Rigg*] And *riggin,* the back bone. Goth. *rygg ;* Ant.
*rigg,* dorsum ; Island. *hriggur ;* Goth. *rigben,* spina dorsi.
Notat etiam *dorsum* vel jugum montis ; Gr. ραχις υρειος, the
ridge of a hill. In Scot. the *riggin* of a house ; Goth. *rygg-
knota,* spondilus, vertebræ ; literally the *knots* of the back bone.
Vide Ihre, Lex. in *rygg.*

VER. 8. *Likyng*] My beloved. Theotif. *likon,* placere ;
Sax. *lican, licigian, gelecan,* from Theot. *guodlichan, lik,*
properly *corpus animatum.* Ulphila, Mark x. ver. 8. *Tha-
naseiths ni vind tua,* ak leik *ain,* They are no longer two,
but one flesh, or one *body.* Hence *metaph,* for a lovely girl,
Hawamaal Stroph. 84.

" Annad thotte mier ecke værna
" Enn vid thad *lik* liffa."
" Nil ego pulchrius cogitare potui,
" Quam illo corpore (puella) potiri."

Hence Douglas uses *likandlie,* for pleasantly, contentedly,
p. 253. 14.

" Sae *likandlie* in peace and libertie,
" At eis his commoun pepil governit he."

*Liggis*] Lies on the ground. Ulphila *ligan,* to lie. Luke
ii. 16. *Bigetan thata barn* ligando *in uzetin,* They found the
babe lying in a manger. Isl. *liggia ;* Al. *ligen ;* Bel. *liggen ;*

Suio-

## XV.

Thay girnit and lute gird wi' granes,
  Ilk goffip oder grieved,
Sum ftrak wi' ftings, fum gaddert ftains,
  Sum fled and ill mifchevet.

The

Suio-Goth. calls *immoveable goods*, as lands, houfes, &c. *ligfa*; and *moveable, gangande fa*. In Scot. the immoveable wood of a mill is called the *lying graith*, in oppofition to the *moving* part, which we call *ganging graith*. Douglas, p. 462. 16.

———" They laid this Pallas zing
" Ligging thereon."———

## STANZA XV.

VER. 1. *Girned*] Dentibus frendebant ut folent homines dolore iraque perciti. A. S. *gnirne*, indignatio, mœftitia. Cædmon 52. 19. Mid *gnirne*, cum quærimonia, indignatur. It is written alfo *gnorne*, mœftus, dejeftus, quærulus. Confer Lye, Gloff. Sax. in voce. The Saxon plainly flows from Goth. *knorra*, murmurare; Sax. *gnarren*, quod proprie (fays the elegant Ihre in Lex.) de canibus hirrientibus ufurpatur Ifl. *knurra*, to murmur. Olafs Sag. cap 96. *Buender knurudu illa*; ruftici murmurabant vehementer. *Knurla* and *kulla* denotes the murmur of the turtle dove. Vide Efdr. 38.

58. 14. Secundum hoc (fays Ihre) *knorra* proprie erit, malis fuis ingemifcere.

Gibfon for *girned* reads *glowred,* which he rightly obferves comes from Cimbr. *Att glora,* lippe profpectare ; but we know not his authority here for this alteration. Adde Lye, in *Girnan.*

*Lute gird*] Gave hard ftrokes. Douglas ufes *gird,* the verb, to fignify *ftrike through. Throw gird,* did thruft through. Sax. *gird,* virga. Vid. Exod. iv. ver. 2. Matth. x. ver 10. Leg. Inæ. 67. Virgata terræ, *hoops* being made of rolls, before they were formed of iron. Hence Scots *gird,* fig. a hoop ; and from it comes *girdle. Gird* to deceive or *beguile,* to go *about* one, *to take them in.* In this fenfe, Douglas, p. 219. 22.

" Was it not evin by ane *fenzet gird* ;"

*i. e.* falfe ftory, or trick. Alludit gyrus, gyrare, γυρος γυροα, fays Ruddiman.

*Granes*] Groans. Douglas, *granyt,* groaned. The reader will obferve in this verfe the propenfity of our old Scots poets to alliteration, a fort of ornament they feem fond of adopting as often as poffible, and which was much in requeft with our Scandinavian anceftors, as we learn from Wormius de Litterat. Runica, and the poems of the ancient Skalds ftill remaining.

VER. 2. *Goffip*] Properly *godfather,* pater luftricus ; Sax. *godfibbe,* cognatus ex parte dei. Vide Jun. in *Goffip.* " And " the child was called *Godbearn,*" Gudfon. Chaucer, p. 209. 6. " And certes parentele is in two manners, either " ghoftlie or flefhlie ; ghoftly, as for to dele with his *godfib.*" From the drinking on thofe occafions, the matres luftricæ, or godmothers, were called, in no very good acceptation,

*Goffips ;*

*Goffips;* and *to go a goffiping,* denoted a drinking match. And in this fenfe our poet here ufes it of thofe drunken clowns.

VER. 3. *Stings*] Poles, ftaves. Cimbr. *ftaung;* Plur. *fteingur,* hafta, contus, baculus. Angl. Bor. *Stangs.* Gib. Hence *nid ftang,* the fpear or pole of infamy, erected againft thofe who were called *nidingr, infamous.* In what this infamy confifted, (*nid,* fignifying *infamy* or *reproach*) 'fee in Ihre, Lex. voce *Niding;* and Jus Sueon. Vetuft. p. 346. which paffage Dr Robertfon has tranflated, Hiftory of Charles V. vol. I. chap. 5. p. 291. of the various ceremonies ufed in fetting up the fpear or *ftang* of infamy. Vide Bartolin. Ant. Dan. p. 97. feqq. Steph. in Sax. p. 116. Egill Skallagrim, the famous bard, deeming himfelf highly injured by King Eric Bloddox of Norway, who had profcribed him, refolved, before he left his dominions, to fet up the *nidftang,* or fpear of infamy, againft him. Having furprifed one of his villas by night, and killed one of Eric's fons, and feveral of his friends, with his own hand, juft before he fet fail for Iceland, " Confcenfa rupe quæ continentem fpectabat, " gerens haftile corylinum," (fays Torfæus, Hiftor. Nor. vol. II. p. 177.) " caput ei equinum affixit, formulam hu- " jufmodi præfatus; Hic ego haftam infamiæ (*nidftang*) ad- " verfus regem Eiricum et reginam Gunhildam ftatuo. Tunc " capite equino in continentem converfo, Converto, inquit, " has diras, in Genios qui hanc terram incolunt, ita ut omnes " incertis fedibus vagentur, nec quifquam eorum receptaculi " compos fiat, donec regem Eiricum et Gunhildam tota hac " terra ejecerint, et impreffa fiffuræ rupis hafta, litteris Runi- " cis hanc formulam incidit." The learned reader will at once fee the analogy of this ancient Scandinavian curfe, and that of the Romans, devoting others to the infernal gods.

U         We

We have tranfcribed this curious paffage for two reafons. *Firft*, It ferves to explain a term in one of our English hiftori- 'ans, which our critics can make nothing of, though quite intelligible to thofe who know the meaning of the word *nidingr*. Matthew Paris, in his Hiftory of William Rufus, p. 12. 34. " Rex ira inflammatus, ftipendiarios milites fuos " Anglos congregat, et abfq; mora, ut ad obfidionem veniant, " jubet; nifi velint fub *nithing* nomine, quod latinè, *nequam* " fonat, recenferi. Angli, qui nihil contumeliofius et vilius " æftimant, quam hujufmodi ignominiofo vocabulo notari," *&c.* It is entertaining enough to fee Watts, the learned editor of this Monkifh Hiftory, gravely deducing this word from *nidth*, night. Nor has Spelman fucceeded better (Gloff. in *Niderling*) deriving it from *nid*, a neft, and *ling*, a chicken. " Ac fi ignavi ifti homines (fays he) qui in exercitum pro- " ficifci nolunt, pullorum inftar effent, qui de nido non aude- " ant prodire." Would it not have been better for the learn- ed Knight to own, that he did not underftand the phrafe? We hence, too, explain the phrafe *unnithing*, in the Annals of Waverly, anno 1088. " Rex Will. Junior mifit per to- " tam Angliam, et mandavit ut qui cunq; foret *unnithing*— " veniret ad eum." *Un*, privative, and *niding*, infamous; *i. e.* whoever was brave, and willing to fight.

The *fecond* motive for quoting particularly the paffage of Torfæus above, was to explain a cuftom ftill prevalent among the country people of Scotland, who oblige any man, who is fo unmanly as to beat his wife, to ride aftride on a long pole, borne by two men, through the village, as a mark of the higheft infamy. This they call *riding the ftang;* and the perfon who has been thus treated feldom recovers his honour in the opinion of his neighbours. When they cannot lay hold of the culprit himfelf, they put fome young fellow on the

*ftang,*

*ſtang*, or pole, who proclaims that it is not on his own account that he is thus treated, but on that of another perſon, whom he names.

We may obſerve here how common and familiar the Gothic was to the Engliſh, even in the eleventh century. Eric Bloddox being driven out of Norway, came with his Queen and Court to ſeek for protection from Athelſtan, who gave him Northumberland, anno 935. He lived much at York; and he and his people converſed familiarly with the Engliſh of that age, without needing an interpreter, as did his cotemporary Eigil Skallagrim, the bard, when in the ſervice of King Athelſtan. A century and an half before this period, we find the great Alfred entering familiarly into the Daniſh camp, and diverting them in the feigned character of a bard, without their ſuſpecting him to be a foreigner, which could not have happened, had his language differed from their own.

VER. 3. *Stanes*] Stones, Goth. *ſtains*; Sax. *ſtan*, lapis; Angl. Bor. *ſtean*, G.

The Iſlandic Spelling is *ſtain*. Thus, in all the Runic inſcriptions, *N. riſta ſtain*, N. erected this ſtone, *viz.* to the memory of ſome deceaſed perſon. Sometimes they write it *ſtein*. Worm. Monum. p. 245. Saſi ſati Runir *Stein*. Saſi Runicum lapidem poſuit.

VER. 4. *Miſchevet*] The verb from *miſchief*. The Gothic particle *miſs*, always implies defect, error, or ſomething bad; as miſtruſt, miſlead, miſcall, miſapply, &c. So the French *meſiant*, *mecontent*, *mecompter*, and the like. The Latins uſed *male* in the ſame manner; *malèfidus*, *malèvalidus*, *effeminatus*. The Barb. Lat. Misfacere, malè agere, peccare. Confer Jun. in Gloſſ. Ulphil. p. 256. Iſl. *miſſater*, people who differ, among whom concord is wanting. *Misfoſdſel*,

an

The menſtral wan within twa wains,

    That day fu' weil he prievit;

For he came hame wi' unbirs'd bains,

    Quhair fechtars war miſchieved,

            For evir that day.

                            XVI.

an abortion. Vide Ihre, Lex. in *Miſs*. *Miſſtyrma*, malè et ignominioſè traƈtare. Bibl· Iſl. Judg. xix. ver. 26. *Og ſeir kiendu hennar, og miſtyrmau henne alla pa nott*. They knew her, and abuſed her all the night.

VER. 5. *Wan*] Got within, or betwixt two waggons. So Douglas uſes the phraſe, *Wan before*, He got before. Sax. *wendan*, to go; *wendan hidar ac thider*, to wander hither and thither. Vide Lye, in *Wendon*.

*Wains*] Contraƈted from *waggon*, as from the Sax· *wægen* is formed *wæn* and *weign*. Alam. *wagan*; Iſland. *vagn*; alludit ὀχειν, ὑχμηϭ, vehiculum.

VER. 6. *Prievit*] Proved, found. Iſland. *profa*, to examine or try. Hence Sax. *profian*; id. *prof*, an experiment. Hence Germ. *prufen*; Fr. *preuve*, *eprouver*; Ang. *proof*. Kon. Styr. p. 14. *Prowa med ſullom ſkælom*, Prove by evident reaſons. *Profſhen*, a touchſtone.

The pronunciation here belongs to the Scots; nor is it in uſe in any of the ſiſter dialeƈts. Thus Douglas, Prol· to Book 10. p. 309.

" Thocht God be his awin creature to *prieve*."

*To prieve* ſuch a diſh, *i. e.* to taſte it.

                                  VER.

## XVI.

Heich Hutcheon wi' a hiffil ryfs,
    To redd can throw them rummil;
He muddilt them down lyk ony myce,
    He was nae baity bummyl.

                                        Thocht

VER. 7. *Unbirs'd*] Unbruifed bones. *Birr*, force, violence; alfo the noife an arrow makes in its flight. Douglas ufes thus the word *birrand*. Ifland. *bir*, ventus fecundus; *mier biriar*, oportet me. Hence Sax. *me byriad*, vel *gebyriad*; all which include the idea of force and ftrength: And this is furely a more natural etymology than that from *vir*, or *vires*, which the reader will find in Ruddiman's Gloffary. Confer Voff. Etymol. in *Brifa*. Cimbr. *brifim*, a bruife. Hefych. βριζει, πιεζει, ftringendo premit.

VER. 8. *Fechtars*] Here is another inftance of the old pronunciation retained by the Scots. Alam. *fehtan*, *vehtan*, to fight; and the Sax. *feohtan*.


## STANZA XVI.

VER. 1. *Ryfs*] Bough, twig, or ftake. A. Cimbr. *Hriis*, quod virgam ramum, vel virgultum, fonat. *Vil eg tyfta hann med marnanna* hraife; Caftigabo eum cum virga virorum. Bibl. Ifl. 2 Sam. vii. 14. Hinc *hreifar* apud Ifland. loco virgultis obfita; et *breys*, virgultis confita domus, cafula. Danis
                                        quoq;

quoq; *Hriis foftr*, eft ftrues e ramis arborum congefta, et a *rice dyke*. Apud Anglos Sept. eft fepes ex cæfis ramis et virgis texta. Gib.

A. S. *bris*, vimen, frondes; Al. *ris*; Germ. *reis*; Hib. *ras*; Fen. *rifu*. Alludit 'pı↓ vimen, fays the learned Ihre, in *Ris*. Ulphila ufes *raus*, to fignify a reed, which he and Wachter derive from *rifa*, furgére, in the fame manner as the Latin *furculus*. Suio-Goth. *rifa*, virgis cædere; *rif-bad*, verbera.

VER. 2. *Redd*] We cannot guefs the Bifhop's meaning in his note on this word *red*; Sax. *to rath*, confeftim, prefently. *To red*, in Scots, fig. to loofe, to unravel, or unfold. So Douglas, 127. 43.

" This being faid, commandis he every fere,
" Do *red* thair takillis, and ftand hard by there gare."

Confer p. 339. 44. where *rede* fig. to make way. So we fay, *To red the way*; to clear the way. To *rede* marches, fettle boundaries betwixt contending parties; figuratively (as Rudd. obferves) to make peace. To *redd* a fray; to interpofe betwixt two combatants; and often thofe who do get *the redding ftraik*, get a blow from one or other. Sax. *hreddan*, liberare; *briddan*, repellere. Hence Engl. To *rid* one's hand of a thing. *Riddance*, *raed*, expeditus; *reyden*, parare. Hence E. *ready*. Suio-Goth. *reda*, numerare, fyno-nimous with *rækna*: Whence *reckon*, *reckoning*. Hence our *ready money*; and the Goth. *reda penningar*, id. But the Scots *redd*, as here ufed, comes immediately from *reda*, explicare, expedire, ordinare. *Reda ut fit heir*, to comb out, or, as we fay, to *redd* out the hair. Ifl. *greida*. Snor-ro, vol. I. p. 99. *Tha let Haraldur greida har fit*; Tum Haraldus comam fuam explicandum curavit; which, in confequence of a vow, he had worn uncombed, till he fhould become mafter of all Norway; Snorro, ubi fup. Vide omnino Ihre

Ihre, in *Reda*. We fay alfo, to *rid* one out of the world, *i. e.* to kill him. So Knytling. Saga, p. 212. *Han red fwarba Plog*, He killed Plog the black. Snorro, voll. II. p. 245. *Ratha af liß*, to red one out of life. And hence *rad*, flaughter.

VER. 2. *Rummyl*] Gibfon explains it of *thundering*; but this is a miftake, though he quotes that of Virgil, *Intonuere poli*, tranflated by Douglas :

" The firmament gan *rummyl*."

Properly it fig. to *rumble, grumble, roar*, or *bellow*. Douglas, p. 151. v. 7.

" Hillis and valis trimblit of thundir *rumuyl*."

p. 200. v. 26.

" And landbirft *rumbland* rudely with fic bere,
" Sae loud nevir rummyft wyld lioun nor bere."

Suio-Goth. *ramla*, from the Ifland. *rymber*, murmur. *Rym*, verb, raucam voce edo.

VER. 3. *Muddilt*] Or *muddeled*, *i. e.* threw them down, fays Gibfon. Ifland. *mill*, in minutas particulas divide. Præterit. *mulde*, unde a *mill*, and to *mull*. Vide Hickes. Dictionar. Ifland. in *Mill*.

VER. 4. *Baity bummil*] Effeminate fellow. Gib.

It fhould be wrote *Batie*, that being a name our country people, in fome parts of Scotland, give to their dogs. The word *bummil* we remember not to have met with in any old writer. *Bulgia*, Goth. fig. intumefcere ; *bula*, tumor; *bulna*, intumefcere. If thefe have any affinity with this word, the meaning may be, that he was no vain boafter—that he was not a *baty*, or dog, that would fnarl, but durft not bite.

Thocht he was wight, he was na' wyfs,

    With fic jangleurs to jummil;

For frae his thoume they dang a fklyfs,

    Quhyle he cried, Barlafummil!

             I'm flain this day.

                      XVII.

VER. 5. *Wight*] We imagine the learned Bifhop has miftaken the fenfe of this word, explaining *weighty*, ftrong,
ponderous, from Ifl. *wift*, libra, pondus. We rather deduce
*wight* from Goth. *wig*, pugna, certamen. Unde Sax. *vig*,
*vige :* hinc *vigian*, pugnare ; *vigend*, bellator ; Al. *wigand*,
id. We find *vigan*, pugnare, employed by Ulphila, Luke iv.
31. Ifland. *wig*, pugna ; Celt. *gwych*, vir ftrenuus, bellator.
The elegant and accurate etymologift Ihre, juftly thinks he
has here found the root of the old Latin *vicis*, as ufed for
*pugna*; and that it was ufed in this fenfe, we have the tefti-
mony of Servius, in his Notes to thefe words of Virgil,
Æneid, 2. 433. Nec ullas vitaviffe *vices* Danaum. Hence,
too, *pervicax*, quod *contentiofum* proprie notat. Ifidorus tells
us, that the old Latins faid *vicam*, for victoriam. The God-
defs of Victory was called *Vica Pota*. Suio-Goth. *wega*,
certare, cædere ; *enwig*, certamen fingulare.

VER. 6. *Jangleurs*] Gibfon reads *jutors*, (we know not
on what authority) which he explains from Cimbr. *Jodur*,
Titan, gigas, Cyclops. To *jangle*, is to quarrel, gannire, blaterare, altercari, a Teut. *jancken*.

*Jummil*] Juftle. G.

*Jummil*] Collidere, infundere, in fe mutuo irruere; forte
a *jump*, infilire, fays Skinner. Chaucer writes *jombre*; Germ.
                                        *jumpen,*

*jumpen*, micare, exilire. Sicambris, *gumpig*, lascivus, sport-
ful or playful.

*Sklyce*] Oftimes written *slyce*, from Island. *slita*, dif-
rumpere, lacerare. Hence Sax. *slitan*, and Alaman. *slizzen;*
idem. Otfrid, lib. 4. cap. 19. 29. of Caiaphas, *Sleizer sin gin-
nati*, He rent his clothes. Tatian, cap. 56. 7. *gisliz*, rup-
tura. Sax. *slyten* under, to slit and slice. Ulphila uses
*gasleithjan*, perdere, Mark viii. 36. Gasleitheith *sik saivalai
seinai*, perdit animam suam. Plura vide ap. illustriss. Ihre in
*Slita*. Island. *slyss*, damnum, infortunium.

Ver. 8. *Barlafummil*] Vox concertantium, nam in singu-
lari certamine apud Scotos, agonista, ictu gravi læsus, porti-
nus exclamat, *barlafummel*. Vox videtur deduci ex *bardla*,
ictus, verber, et *fimbul*, grande, vehemens quid. G.

The original signification of this word is to be found in the
Suio-Goth. *famla*, which the learned Ihre interprets, Manibus
ultro, citroq; pertentare, ut solent qui in tenebris obambulant.
The Islanders say *falma*, which is certainly the original word,
as Alaman. *folmo*, fig. the palm of the hand; and thus, in
the passage of Esaias (quoted by Ihre in *Famla*) *Huner wak
himila sinero solmo*, Quis ponderavit cœlos palmo suo. Hence,
too, the Lat. *palmus ;* Ang. *palm* of the hand. Goth. *fumla*, manibus contrectare, attrectare; Fr. *patiner*, im-
probe contrectare ; Belg. *fommelen*. To *fumble* (says
Jun. in Gloss. Angl.) proprie dicitur de iis, qui rem aliquam
inscitè, infabrè tractant, quod Succis est *fumla*. Douglas
seems to use *fumbler* to signify a parasite, p. 482. 34.

" I am na caik *fumler*, full weil ye knaw."

Ruddiman here ingeniously imagines *caik fumler* means a
*cake-turner*, a fellow that will do any mean thing to get a
bellyful ; or an avaricious person, who *whumbles*, i. e. turns
and hides his cake, lest others should share with him. But

X                                     the

## XVII.

Quhen that he faw his blude fae reid,
 To fle micht nae man let him;
He weind it had been for auld feid,
He thocht ane cry'd, Haif at him.

         He

the firft is certainly the beft interpretation. The other word *barla* is plainly derived from *parley*, a ftop or ceffation in order to fpeak. It was held ungenerous to refufe this of old, when demanded by one combatant of another. Hence we ufe the word *parley*, and to *beat a parley*, *i. e.* to make a fhort truce, in order to propofe terms of accommodation; and this phrafe is often ufed even by boys in their games. Or may we not fuppofe *barla* to be derived from, and a corruption of Suio-Goth. *barma*, mifereri? Chron. Ryth. p. 165.

 " Gud *barme* then omilde hempd
  " Deus mifereatur immitis vindictæ."

Ulphila has *arman*. Mark x. 48. *Armai mik*, Miferere mei, And this from *barm*, finus, ibid. Luke xvi. 22. quod quæ nobis indeliciis funt, in finu fæpe foveantur, fays the elegant Ihre (in *Barm*.) Hence Lat. *infinuare*, and our *infinuate*. Hence we may explain that unintelligible paffage in Auguftin, Epift. 178. Si licet, dicere non folum Barbaris lingua fua, fed etiam Romanis, *fi hora armen*, quod interpretatur, Domine miferere, &c. Lege, *Si Frauja* (or *Froja*) *armai*, Domine miferere; *Frauja* fignifying *Lord* in the Gothic. Vide Ulphila, Matth. xxvii. 63.

       STANZA

## STANZA XVII.

VER. 2. *Let him*] Hinder or prevent. Sax. *lettan*, *ge-lettan*; orig. from Goth. *latjan*, tardare, morari. Hinc Island. *latur*; Al. *laz*; Dan. *lat*; and Angl. *late*. Alludit (fays Jun.) λησθομαι, Dor. λαθομαι, oblitus fum. This proves Junius's fondnefs for Greek derivations, where the originals are to be fought and found at home.

VER. 3. *Weind*] Thought or imagined. Gibfon here reads *trow'd*, which he rightly derives from the Sax. *truwian*, credere. *Ween* comes alfo from the fame fountain; *wenan*, exiftimare; Al. *wanen*. The root of all thefe is found in Ulphila's *wennyan*, or *wenjan*, or *gawenjan*, putare. Luke iii. 15. *Atwenjandein than alai managein*, exiftimante omni populo. Adde Luke vii. 43. Confer. Jun. in Gloff. Ulphil. *wenjan*. It is alfo ufed for *expectation*, becaufe this depends on *opinion*; *Thu is fa quimanda, thau antharanu wenjaima?* Art thou he that fhould come, or look we for another? Luke vii. 19. Douglas, 222. 19.

" It ftands not fo as thou *wenys*."

——*i. e.* thinkeft. He ufes *wenys* elfewhere for *tokens* and *figns*; as marks to point out the way, and determine our courfe. P. 100. 6.

" I knaw and felis the *wenys* and the way."

VER. 3. *Feid*] Enmity. Cimbr. *faide*; Sax. *fahth*; Lat. Barb. *faida, feida*, inimicitiæ; Angl. *fewd*. G.

*Fec*, Sax. inimicus; Island. *faad*. Hence *foe*, and *feud*, enmity. Leg. Athelftan, 20. *Sij he fa wid done Cyng*, Sit inimicus regis. In the Saxon laws, *fah* properly fignifies that capital enmity that fubfifted on account of murder com-

mitted

He gart his feit defend his heid,

   The far fairer it fet him ;

Quhyle he was paft out of all pleid,

   They fould bene fwift that gat him,

           Throw fpeid that day.

                 XVIII.

mitted. Vide Jun. in Gloff, et Leg. Ecclef. Canuti, 5.
Spelman obferves the fame in vuce *Faida.* This favage cuftom of obliging the male relation to revenge the flaughter of
his friend, is as ancient as any thing we know of the ufages
of our Germanic anceftors. " Sufcipere tam inimicitias (fays
" Tacit. de Mor. Germ.) feu patris, feu propinqui, quam ami-
" citias, neceffe eft." Obferve, it was not left to their choice,
but under the moft fevere penalties they were *obliged*, to pro-
fecute this vengeance, by every mean in their power. The
excefs of this barbarity at laft brought on a cure, though the
lapfe of many ages was neceffary to foften the fierce manners of
our anceftors. We find many laws among the Salic, Langobard,
and Francic ftatutes, calculated to check this cuftom ; and
King Edmund in England, about an. 944, complaining in one of
his laws much of this evil, and fuggefting feveral remedies for
it, and ordering compenfations to be made by the aggreffor.
However, we find it ftill prevailing even in the Norman times ;
but how this inhumanity gradually loft ground, and by degrees
was annihilated, would lead us into a hiftorical deduction, too
extenfive for thefe notes, but we may perhaps give it in another work. Confer. Cange in *Faida.*

                                  Out

## XVIII.

The town foutar in grief was bowdin,
   His wyfe hang at his waift;
His body was in blude a' browdin,
   He grain'd lyk ony ghaift.

Hir

Our poet here mentions *auld fied*; for thofe feuds of old ftanding, being fharpened by their progrefs from generation to generation, were, of all others, the moft deadly.

VER. 7. *Pleid*] Gibfon has totally miftaken the meaning of this word, explaining it by *reach*; getting beyond their reach. *Pleid* fignifies here the *quarrel, broil,* or *contention.* Thus Douglas, p. 111. v. 54.

———" Bot gif the fatis but *pleid,*
  " At my pleafure fuffered me life to leid."

Adde p. 454. 42. where it fignifies oppofition, controverfy. In Suio-Goth. *pleet,* ictus lævis; Sax. *plæt, handplætas,* ictus in vola. *Plætan,* ferire, unde Fr. *playe*; and the Bremen *pliete,* vulnus. Ifland. *plaaga,* cruciatus. Alludit πλητͺͺ.

## STANZA XVIII.

VER. 1. *Soutar*] Shoemaker. G.
The word *fhoe,* now in ufe, is foftened from the ancient Gothic *fko,* which is properly *tegmen,* (fays the learned Ihre)

id

id quod rem quamlibet tuetur—fpeciatim ufurpatur pro eo quod extremitates munit, et fpecialiffimè de indumento pedum. Leg. Dal. p. 15. *Skærper fko a foti,* fi calceus pedem urit, *i. e.* If the neceffity be very preffing. Ulphil. *fkote,* fhoes; Mark i. 7. Sax. *fco, fchoh;* Ifland. *fko;* Aleman. *fcu.* May it not come come from *fkya,* tegere? unde *fky.*

—————"quod *tegit* omnia, cælum."

As the Latin *nubes,* a *nubendo,* i. e. *tegendo.* Ifl. *fkyla,* to cover; *fkyfwe,* tegmen. Whence the Scots *fcoug,* a fhade or cover; *under the fcough of a tree.* Be this as it may, we find the Gothic *fkand,* a fhoe, and *fkauda raip,* fhoes ropes; or, as we better pronounce, *raips,* i. e. fhoe latchet. *Skohe is fkaudaraip and bindan,* calceamentorum ejus corrigia folvere, Mark i. ver. 7. Alludit ςκυ]ος, *corium,* fays Junius; as if our Scythian anceftors had no name for a thong of leather, till they got it from Greece. If there is really any connection, the latter certainly comes from the former. *Skotwange,* the thongs or *whangs* of the fhoes. *Gloves* are called in German *handfchuk;* and, in fome parts of Denmark, *boots* are called *knæfko.* Ihre obferves, that Harpocration has the word ςκυϑιρος, which he explains ειδος τι ὑποδηματος, genus calceamenti.

We find here the origin of the title, *Skofwen,* an officer in the courts of the ancient Scandinavian monarchs. He was a kind of Lord or Gentleman of the Bedchamber, whofe duty it was to give the King his fhoes; but being always near his perfon, he was generally a rich and powerful courtier.

Thus, in Trygw. Saga, p. 2. p. 316. the rich Kali is called *Skofvein Einars,* though he was a man of great power, and a near relation of Einars.

*Bowdin*] So we think it fhould be read, and not as Gibfon has it, *bowen,* which he explains as if it had been *boun,*

or

or *bown, prepared to go,* from the Iſlandic *bwen,* contr. *bun,* paratus.

*Bowdin* ſignifies *filled, ſwelled,* from Goth. *bulgia,* intumeſcere. Kon. Styr. p. 212. *Ta wardir han giarnt trutin ooh bulgin,* Tum fere inflatur et intumeſcit. *Bulgot,* flaccidum. Alludit Gr. βολοι, which the Gloſſographers explain by φυμαʃα, tumores. *Bulna,* intumeſcere ; *bula,* a tumor or ſwelling raiſed by a ſtroke. A number of words are hence derived, which include the idea of *ſwelling* ; as *bolde,* ulcus, our word *bolſter; bolja,* a wave. *Bulla,* a ſort of round bread uſed in Sweden ; whence the French *boulanger,* and our *bowl, bullet.* The Latin *bulla,* hung about children's necks, is alſo from it. Vide Juvenal Sat. 5. 164. Goth. *bulle,* poculum, Hiſtor. Alex. M. ap. Litteratiſſ. Ihre in *Bulle.*

" Nappa och ſwa alla *bulla.*"
Cyathos et omnia pocula.

*Bullra,* tumultuari, ſtrepitum edere. Hence, too, *bolt,* a nail or pin, with a *large round head.* Ihre informs us, that the large wooden or iron cylinder, or roller, uſed for breaking the clods, is, in many places of Sweden, called *bult.*

VER. 3. *Browdin*] Browden, ſwelled, or embroidered. Gib.

We find *browdin* in Douglas, which Rudd. explains *forward, bent* ; and alſo *brudy,* abounding with ; from *brood,* broody. Perhaps it may come from the Scots *bruche,* ſignifying a gold chain, or bracelet, as if his body, ſtreaked with his own blood, had appeared as if adorned with gold chains. Douglas, 146. 2.

" The *bruche* of gold or chene loupit in ringis,
" About thare hals doun to the breiſt hingis."

Vide ibid. 215. 25. Chaucer writes it *broche* or *brooch* ; or

perhaps

Hir glitterand hair, that was sae gowden,
  Sae hard in lufe him laist,
That for her sake he was nae zowden,
  Seven myle that he was chaist,
    And mair that day.

XIX.

perhaps from Sax. *bradan*, affare, De quo Lye, in Lex. Saxon.

VER. 4. *Grain'd*] Groaned. Douglas writes it *granyt* ; Sax. *granan* ; Cimbr. *grwn*, gemitus columbarum ; Hibern. *gearan*, gemitus, querela. Alludit (fays Jun.) γρωνος, explained by Hefych. τ8ς ακσον]ας, και τ8ς μη λαλ8ν]ας, audientes, fed non loquentes.

*Ghaift*] Sprite. Sax. *gaft*, spirit. G.

Douglas writes it *gaift*, *gaifts*, which is nearer the Saxon orthography. Alam. *geift*. Hence Engl. *gaftly*, αγασος, ειδος αγασον, ap. Homer, which Euftathius explains εκ-πληκ]ικον, species terribilis. Hence probably Scots *goufty*, ufed by Douglas, wafte, defolate, and lonely places, becaufe *ghofts* were thought to haunt fuch. Armor. *goafta*, vaftare, *to wafte*. I find in Lye *gaftoine*, ager incultus. Lat. Barb. *gaftina*, de qua vid. Cange, Gloff.

VER. 5. *Gowden*] Liquefcente. *l* in *w*, ex *golden*. Hinc *rufum* Scoti vocant *gowdy* locks, fcil. pro more gentium feptent. apud quas rutili et flavi capilli in maximo pretio habebantur. Hinc Cædmon vocat Saram, *Bryd blonden feax*, ponfam flavi comam. Lothum etiam appellat, *Blonden feax ;* et in Edda Snorronis legimus Saturnum in taurum rutilum fe con-
                                            vertiffe,

vertiffe, cujus pilus quilibet aureo nitebat colore, *Var fagur gulz litur a huortu har.* Memnon etiam omnes anteiffe pulchritudine dicitur, utpote cujus cæfaries fupra aurum nitebat, *Har hanr var fegra en gull.* Et uxor ejus fatidica, omnium formofiffima, dicitur habuiffe capillos *auro* fimiles, *Hun var alftra Kuenna fogurft har hennar var fem gull.* Cap. 3. Præfat. Eddæ. Neq; mirandum quod feprentr. fcriptores rutilum cæfariem tot elogiis celebrant, cum multiplicem Gothorum nationem, Vandalos, Wifigothos, Gepidas, ipfofq; Gothos proprie fic dictos comas rutilos effe fcribit Procop. Hift. Vandal. lib. 1. Gib.

All the northern nations were remarkable for blue eyes, and yellow or fair hair. Of the Germans, *Tacit. Mor.* c. 4. " Truces et cæruli oculei, rutilæ comæ." *Juven. Sat.* 13.

 " Cærulea quis ftupuit Germani lumina? flavam
 " Cæfariem."

Confer Cluver. Ger. Ant. p. 118. Ariftot. Problem. fect. 14. 8. Conringius de Hab. Corp. Germ. p. 11. 12. From this mark, Tacitus (Vita Agricolæ, cap. 2.) infers the German origin of the Caledonians; " Rutilas Caledoniam " habitantium comas, et magnus artus Germanicam originem adfervaffe." Lucan, Pharfal. l. 10. fpeaking of Cleopatra's flaves:

 " Pars tam flavas gerit akera crines,
 " Ut nullus Cæfar Rheni fe dicat in arvis
 " Tam rutilas vidiffe comas."———

So fond were the Germans of this colour of hair, that they ufed different ointments, both to give and to preferve this ornament; as Plin. informs us, lib. 28. cap. 12.

VER. 7. *Zowden*] So it ftands in Ramfay's edition, but whether according to the M.S. we cannot fay; nor is the meaning of this word very eafy to difcover. In the Gloffary

                   to

## XIX.

The millar was of manly mak,
  To meit him was nae mows ;
There durſt not ten cum him to tak,
  Sae noytit he thair pows.

                                        The

to Ramſay's edition, we find *zolden*, explained *holden*. In Douglas we have *zoldin*, which ſeems to come neareſt the ſenſe
here, ſignifying *yeilding*, or *yeilded*. But we think it better
to own our ignorance, than to fill the page with idle conjectures.

### STANZA XIX.

VER. 2. *To meit him*, &c.] Gibſon reads this verſe,

  " With him it was nae mows."

*Mows*] Mockery, or jeſt. Thus Lindſay of Pitſcottie,
of Sinclair, when the Lords ſeized him, " Is it *mows*, or ear-
neſt, my Lords ?" Battle of Harlaw, ſtan. 19.

  " Their was nae *mowis* there them amang,
  " Naithing was hard bot heavy knocks."

  The French ſay, *Faire la moue*, to laugh at one ; and hence
Chaucer, Tr. lib. 4. 1. of Lady Fortune ;

  " And whan a wight is from her whele ithrow,
  " Than laugheth ſhe, and *maketh him the mowe*."

Hib. *magam* illudere, deſidere ; *magadh* irriſio, deriſus.

                                           *Mow*

*Mow* alfo fignifies properly the *mouth*. Gothmund. Thus *faire la mowe*, is to diftort the mouth, as is done in looking contemptuoufly at any perfon. In Sui-Goth. *mopa*, illudere, vexare, Chron. Rythm. (apud Ihre in *Mopa*.)

" Jak feer Erik will ofs *mopa*.
" Video Ericum nobis illudere velle."

Our elegant etymologift remarks the affinity betwixt this and the Englifh *mope*.

Among the Ætolians, *mova* fignified *cantilena*, a fong ; and in Celtic, *moues* denotes the fame thing. Hence *Mofai*, the *Mufes*, who made and fung verfes. Vide Pezron, Antiq; p. ad voc. Μῦσαι. Μωχος, a *derider*, comes from the Celtic *moch*, a fow, from the action of that animal in turning his fnout up into the air, and men doing fo, as a gefture of contempt; μωχια, fannia, derifio; and the Celts fay, *moccio*, for *deriding*. Hence the French *moquer*, and our *mock*. Again, the ancient Gauls faid *gore*, for a *fow*. Hence γοριαω, irrideo, fubfanno; and from the fame origin, Χοιρος, fus. The ancient Scholiafts truly remark, that this word was *feminine*, among the ancient Greeks ; but they did not know the reafon, which is, that *gore* in the Celtic properly denotes *fus fæmina*, a *fow*.

VER. 3. *There durft not ten*] Gibfon reads the verfe thus :

" There durft nae tenfome thair him tak."

VER. 4. *Noytit*] Gibfon reads *cowed*. Goth. *nod*. neceffitas. Inde *noda*, cogere; *nodde*, coegit. Vide Gen. 33. v. 11. Ulphila, *Nauthjan*, uibi vid. Jun. Douglas ufes *noy* for hurt, annoy, and *noyfum*, hurtful, noxious. Thus pag. 191, 11.

" Sa fer as that thir *noyfum* bodyis cauld."

Ray

The bufchment hale about him brak,
  And bikkert him wi' bows,
Syne traytorly behint his back
  They hew'd him on the hows
    Behind, that day.

XX.

Ray (Collect. of words) obferves, that in Lancafhire they
fay *note*, to pufh, ftrike, or gore with the horn, as a bull or
ram. This he derives from the Sax. *Hnitan*, to pufh or
gore, Exod. xxi. 28. Gif oxa *hnite*. And this from the
Ifland. *Hniota* ferire, which is the true origin of our *noyt*.
Vide Hick. Diction. Ifland. in *Hnyt*.

*Pows*.] So the Scots pronounce *Poll*, cacumen, vertex
capitis. Hence to *poll at election*, to have each head reckoned ; *poll-money*, capitation tax ; a *pole* of ling, caput afelli
pifcis faliti. Skin.

VER. 5. *Bufchment*] Contracte from Fr. *embufchement*,
ambufcade. We find *bufchement* ufed by Douglas. *Am-
bufh* may perhaps be derived from *bufh* ; and in woody places
*ambufhes* were generally placed. And this, too, is the opinion of Jun. Gloff. in *Ambufhes*. Hence the Italian *imbof-
cate*, and the Lat. term *fubfeffores*, vid. Serv. ad Æneid v.
ver. 498.

VER. 6. *Bikkert*] Laid a load of *rattling* blows on him.
It would feem, that in this fenfe the word is ufed in the old
poem of *Chevy Chace*. Reliq. of Ancient Poet. vol. 1. p. 5.

  " Bomen *bickart* uppone the bent
  " With ther brow'd arras cleare."

*i. e.* their

## XX.

Twa that war herdmen of the herd,
  On udder ran lyk rams,
Then followit feymen, richt unaffeird
  Bet on with barrow trams;

But

*i. e.* their arrows *rattled* in the quiver as they moved. In an old tranflation of Ovid, quoted in the Gloffary on this poem, we find thefe verfes :

  " And on that flee Ulyffes head
  " Sad curfes down does *bicker*."

Hence it came to fignify *fighting* or *fkirmifhing*; and here, fay our boys to each other, *Let us bicker*, i. e. *fkirmifh*.

VER. 8. *Hows*] The hams. *How*, from Angl. Sax. *hog* and *boh ;* and from this laft the Scots fay ftill *hoch*, as in Douglafs. Belg. *Haeffen*, verb to *hoch*, to cut the back finews of the leg, *fuffragines fuccidere*. Hence Jun. derives the phrafe, *hoxing* of dogs, *genu fciffio canum*. Adde Spelm. in *expeditare* canem. Ifland. *huka ;* incurvare fe modo cacantis. Perhaps, too, the *huckle-bone* had its name from hence. Belg. *hucken*, defidere, in terram fe fubmittere. Vide, Lye Addit. to Jun. Gloff.

### STANZA XX.

VER. 1. *Herdmen*] Headfmen, G.

VER. 3. *Feymen*] Lege *faemen*, i. e. *enemies*. Douglas fometimes writes it *fa*, which is nearer to the Saxon *fah*,

inimicus ;

inimicus; as from *feond*, fiend. Leg. Athelſtani R. 20.
" Sy he *fa* with done lyng; *Sit inimicus regis.*" Vide LL.
Edmundi R. 1. et Jun. Gloſſ. in *Foe.* From *fab* comes
*feebld*, feud betwixt two families on account of the ſlaughter
of a kinſman; Angl. *feud;* Iſland. *fead;* Dan. *feyd.* The Latins of the middle ages formed hence their *faida*, de qua
Spelman in Archæol. B. Rhenanus Rev. Germ. l. 2. p. 95.
" *Faidam* vocabant Franci ſimultatem apertam, qua unus ali-
" quis uni vel pluribus bellum denuntiat. Ab hac Gallicani
" ſcribæ *faidoſum* appellat, qui *faidam* exercet. Germanis
" notum nimis vocabulum eſt." Every difference, however,
was not called *faida*, but only that capital hatred which could
not be appeaſed, but by the blood of the malefactor. Hence
Gloſſ. *faida*, vindicta mortis. *Faidam* portare alicui, to de-
clare private war againſt any perſon. The dreadful conſe-
quences of this right of private war, and the numerous ſta-
tutes againſt it, are to be found in all the writers of the middle ages. See many curious particulars concerning it, ap.
du Cange in *Faida.* Hence the poor Albigenſes, while
cruelly perſecuted and murdered by the Papiſts, were called
*Faididi*, quod profugi et exulantes erant.

*Unaffeired*] Unaffrighted, without fear, or as we ſpell it,
*feir.*

VER. 4. *Barrow*] From Sax. *berewe*, which comes from
Goth. *bairan;* Sax. *bæran*, *beoran.* Hence *bier*, on which
the dead are carried; and thoſe who carry them are called
*bearers*, and the ſpokes on which the coffin reſts, *bear-trees.*

*Trams*] Tram, or trum, is Gothic, and thus explained by
the elegant and learned Ihre: " Pars arboris longioris in
" plures partes diſſectæ, ut commodius plauſtro injici queat."
Germ. *trumm*, fragorem; Iſland, *trumba.* With the German lawyers, *tramrecht*, or *traumrecht*, denotes that right
which

which one neighbour has of letting the beams or joists of his house into the nearest wall. Bohem. *tram*, trabs. Stadenius (Explicat. Vocum Bibl. p. 663.) obferves, that the Germ. *thramen* fignifies *beams*, and the crofs joists on which wooden stairs are fupported, which leads us to the *thramfteins* of Ulphila, Mark i. v. 6. by which he tranflates the ακριδες of the Greek, which our verfion renders *locufts*, the food of John Baptift in the defert. Many of the ancients, as well as the Gothic Bifhop, underftand this paffage of the facred writer, not of locufts, but the tender tops of fome fhrub, or fpecies of plant, unknown to us; as Bengelius obferves in his note on this verfe; and therefore he deduces the laft part of the word from *teins*, virga, ramus tenerior. Adde Wachter in *Tram*.

May we not attempt, from what is faid of this word *tram*, to explain the word *ftraba*, ufed by Jornandes, when defcribing the funeral of Attila Getica, cap. 39. " Poftquam " talibus lamentis eft defletus, *ftrabam* fuper tumulum ejus, " ingenti commeffatione celebrant." Wormius (Mon. Dan. p. 36.) quotes a paffage from Plac. Lactant. ad Stat. Theb. lib. 12. in the following words : " Exuviis hoftium extruebatur " regibus mortuis pyra, quem ritum fepulturæ hodie quoque " Barbari fervare dicuntur, quem *ftrabas* dicunt lingua fua." Now we know that nothing is more common among all the people of Gothic origin, than to put *f.* before their words. The word *trafwe*, the learned Ihre fays, " ufurpatur de " rebus quibufvis exaggeratis, wed *trafwe*, eft ftrues ligno- " rum," a *heap*, fuch as the funeral pile. *Trafwe* alfo denotes a heap of corn cut down ; and hence our *thrave*, confifting of twenty-four fheaves, as we fhall more fully explain in our Gloffary of the ancient Scottifh Dialect ; vide Ray's Collect. of Words, p. 75. Of this the barbarous Latin has made *trava, trava bladi*, de quo Cange. The cuftom of the Goths

drinking

But quhair thair gobs thay were ungeir'd,
　　They gat upon the gams ;
Quhyl bludy barkit was thair bairds,
　　As they had worriet lamms
　　　　　　Maiſt-lyk that day.

　　　　　　　　　　XXI.

drinking largely at the funeral of their chiefs, is too well
known to need enlarging on in this place.

　Ver. 5. *Gobs*] Roſtrum, beak, uſed of birds of prey.
Celtic, *gob*, roſtrum. Hence our *gab*, uſed to fig. the mouth ;
and *gobble*, to devour greedily. Fr. *gober*. Junius obſerves,
that the Gr. Καβλεϰ has ſome affinity to our words ;
and is explained by Heſychius, Καϊαπινεϰ, devorat, ob-
ſorbet.

　*Ungeird*] Unprepared. Sax. *gearwian*, præparare ; and
this comes from the Iſlandic *giora*, parare, facere. *Eg
ſkal giora*, or *eg мun giora* ; faciam, vel faϭurus ſum.
Hickes (in Diϭ. Iſl.) thinks, that hence is derived the Scots
to *gar*, to *oblige*, or *force* one to do a thing. *Gear*, Scot.
*furniture*, *apparatus*. Iſland. *gearo*, *gearwe*, paratus.

　Ver. 6. *Gams*] The *gumms* ; Teut. *gaum*, *gum*, palatum ; A. S. *goma*, gingiva. Douglas 345. 31.

　" His gredy *gammes* bedyis with the rede blude !"

Iſland. *gomur*, palatum. Theſe ſtrokes they got on the mouth
explains what the poet adds, that their beards were all be-
ſmeared with blood.

　Ver. 7. *Bludy barkit*] Gibſon, on what authority we
　　　　　　　　　　　　　　　　　　　know

## XXI.

The wyves keift up a hideous zell,
  Quhan all thir zounkers zokkit;
Als ferfs as ony fire-flauchts fell,
  Freiks to the fields they flokkit.

The

know not, reads *bludy-burn;* the meaning of which we are ignorant of.

*Barkned*] Covered with congealed blood, as hard, and in the fame manner, as the bark covers the tree. Skinner derives *bark* from Teuton. *bergen*, tegere.

Ver. 8. *Worried*] *Worry*, vexare, dilacerare, vide Lye, Gloff. Sax. in *Worian*. We find the original meaning of this word in the following paffage of Alfred's Verfion of Bede's Hift. Ecclef. l. 4. c. b. " Seo hreownes thæs oft ewedenan " woles feor & wide eal wees *worigende* & fornimende ; *Sæpe* " *tempeftas dictæ cladis latè cunita depopulabatur.*" Such was the general fignification in the mother tongue ; but in Scotch it is always reftricted to tearing with the teeth, as a dog does. Ray informs us, it is ufed in the fame fenfe in the north of England.

## S T A N Z A  XXI.

Ver. 1. *Keift*] Caft. Gibfon reads *gave.*
*Zell*] A doleful cry, indicating deep diftrefs. Sax. *gealpan*; jactare, gloriari, exclamiare. The root is the Ifland. *giell*, vociferor ; *gall*, vociforatus fum. We find in the
Z                                    fame

same language *yle*, ejulo ; *ylde*, ejulavi. From *gielle* the Danes say, *at gielle*, resonare. Junius, in his idle fondness for Greek derivations, would bring it from ηλεμος, or ιαλεμος, cantio funebris. In the old English we also find *yawl*, lugubriter vociferari ; Island. *Gala*, vociferari ; Armor. *jala*, lamentari. If we must have a Greek derivation, may we not suppose it to come from αλαχαζω? but it is needless to go from home on this occasion.

VER. 2. *Zounkers*] Young men, a Cimbr. *junkiære* (says Gibson) vel *jonkiere*, generosus vir juvenis. Goth. *jugga* ; and Island. *ung.* Hence Sax. *giung, jung* ; Welsh, *jevange*, or *jesange* ; Angl. *young*, inde *younker.*

*Zokkit*] Joined together in combat, as when oxen are joined together by the yoke. *Toke*, from Sax. *geoc. joc.* ; and this from Goth. *gajuk*, Alam. *joch.* We cannot guess what the learned Gibson was thinking of, while he explains *yokkit*, ready to vomit. *Yoake*, in the north of England, sig. *to vomit* ; the *yoakes*, the hiccup. But sure this cannot be understood in this passage, as the true meaning. *Yex*, Angl. sig. singultire ; *yexing*, convulsio ventriculi ; Belg. *huckup* ; Suio-Goth. *hicka.* Confer. Jun. Gloss. *Hick.*

VER. 3. *Fire-flauchts*] Fire flying. Angl. Bor. fulgura *fire-flaughts*, vocant, G. And so do the Scots. The origin is from the Goth. *fleckra* and *fleckta*, motitare, from the quick and versatile motion of the lightning. Tobit. cap. 11. ver. 9. *Ta lopp hunden framfor at, och* fleckrade *med sin rumpo* ; Then the dog went before them, wagging his tail, Ezekiel xi. 22. *Ta* flecktade *cherubim med sinom wingom* ; Tum cherubim alas suas motitabant. Hence the English *flicker, flickering*, de quo vid. Jun. etymol. From this action of a dog fawning on his master, we find *fleckra*, adulari. Kon. Styr. p. 57. *Han sum ar falskr ok flikrar* ; Qui sub dolus est,

et

et adulatur. *Flikert* adulatio, ibid. p. 53. Alaman. *flechen*, adulari ; *flechara*, adulatores. Hence Scot. *fleech*, to flatter. Douglas has *fleicband*, flattering, which Ruddiman, for want of a better etymon, derives from Lat. *flectere*.

VER. 4. *Freiks*] Bold, petulent fellows, who love to quarrel ; also *foolish* and *impertinent*. Thus Douglas, Prol. to Æneid 8. p. 239.

" Ha, wald thou fecht quod the *freik*."

Teuton. *frech*, protervus, infolens, procax. Hence our *freak*, *frakish*, capricious. Suio-Goth. *fræk*, tumidus, infolens. *Eu* freek *uppsyn*, Vultus infolentiam præ fe ferens. Island. *fræckr*, infolence. Hence in Scots *fractious*, troublefome, quarrelfome. Gud. Andreæ Lex. Island. They fay alfo, *frakur*, fævus. Herraud's Saga, cap. 1. *Frækur i heimtum*, fævus in exactionibus. Knitlyng. 5. p. 8. *Oc var that ed fræknafla*, Erant hi milites fortiffimi. The learned and ingenious Ihre derives the Latin *ferox*, from the Goth. *fræks* or *fracks*, with great probability, in Lex. tom. 1. p. 585. This elegant writer alfo afferts (in voce *Frankrike*) that the Franks were called in the ancient language *Frakr*, from their ferocity. All the German writers agree in this. Gothofred. Viterb. Chron. part 17. in Proem. talking of the origin of the empire of the Franks, " Germani adverfus Alanos movent exercitum, eos vincunt, et " omnio extinguunt—et propter eandem victoriam a Valenti- " niano Imp. *Franci*, id eft *feroces* funt perpetuo appellati." Id. Catalog. Reg. Franc. " Poft modum ab Imperatore Va- " lentiniano vocati funt Franci, *i. e.* Feroces." And Ricardus Epifcop. tit. de Leone 3tio Imp. " Sed quia tempore Valen- " tiniani Imp. ejus mandato vicerunt Alanos, vocavit eos Fran- " cos, id eft *Feroces*." Rigordus in geftis Philippi Augufti, p. 74. " Quos cum multis poftmodum idem Valentinianus " præliis attentaffet, nec vincere potuiffet, proprio eos nomine

Z 2

" Francos,

The carlis with clubs did uder quell,

 Quhyl blude at breifts out bokkit;

Sae rudely rang the common bell,

 That a' the fteipill rokkit

    For reid that day.

        XXII.

" *Francos,* quafi *Ferancos, i. e.* Feroces appellavit." The reader will find more to the fame purpofe in Cange, voce *Francus.* *Frekner,* Ifland. fignifies *alacer,* ftrenuous. Olafr. Tryg. S. p. 2. pag. 298. *Tho at badi væri fterker oc frekner,* Quamvis robufti fimul et ftrenui effent. *Freki,* ferocia. Confer Ihre Lex. vol. 1. p. 586.

Ver. 5. *Carlis*] Clowns; Sax. *Eorl* and *Georl,* Gib. The true origin is found in the Iflandic, not in the Saxon; for *eorl* properly denotes a nobleman, whence *Earl;* but in the mother dialect, the Iflan. *Karl,* fig. a ruftic, or man of mean condition, as here. So too Alaman. *karl.* Voffius in Etymol. voce *Androfaces,* brings another etymology, but not a probable one. The Germans fay, *Ein hapfer karl,* a ftrong man. Hence too our *churle,* de qua vid. Jun. in voce, who obferves, that in the Sax. *ceorelboren* and *thegeaborn* are oppofed to each other; the firft fignifying a *plebcian,* the fecond a *gentleman.* It is from this idea of ftrength that the Englifh fay a *karlecat, carlehemp, &c. Carlifb* is clownifh, ruftic. Thus in the ancient ballad, the Childe of Elle, Reliq. of Anc. Poet. p. 112. vol. 1.

 " And foremoft came the *carlifh* knight,
 " Sir John of the north countràye."

             *Quell*

*Quell*] Alam. *quellen*, Belg. *quellen*, domare, fubigere. Sax. *cwellan*. It is ufed alfo to fignify *killing*. Thus Douglas, 153. 50.

" Thre vilis tho', as was the auld manere
" In wourfchip of Erix he bad doun quel.".

and p. 263. 1.

" —— with this famyn rycht hand quellit and flanc."

Hence *kweller*, carnifex.

Ver. 6. *Bokkit*] Burft forth. *Bock* properly to *vomit*, and fo ufed by Douglas. " Vox agro Lincolnienfi familiaris" (fays Skinner) " alludit Hifpan. *boffar*, vomere ;" melius a Belg. *booken*, *boken*, pulfare.

Ver. 8. *Rokkit*] Shaked. Rock a *cradle*; agitare, motitare cunas. Douglas 157. 30.

" How that the fchyp did rok and tailzeve."

He elfewhere ufes *rokkand* for rolling or toffing. Junius brings it from the Tuton. *rucken*, trahere, loco movere. But the true origin is from the Iflandic *krocka*, (as alfo Ruddiman has obferved in Gloff. to Douglas) cum impetu quodam moveri. It is ridiculous enough to find Mer. Caufaubon going to the Greek οργαζειν ανοργαζειν, where there is not the fmalleft affinity of found. Vide Hick. Dick. Ifland. in *Hrok*.

Ver. 9. *Reid*] I fufpect it fhould be *reird* or *rerde*, noife or clamour. Douglas, p. 300. v. 30.

" With *rerde* and clamour of blythnefs."

and p. 37. 12.

" Syne the *reird* followit of the zounkeris of Troy."

Confer ibid. 324. 25. Ruddiman brings it, with probability

enough,

## XXII.

Be this Tam Tailor was in's gear,
  When he heard the common bell ;
Said, he wald mak them all a' fteir,
  When he cam there himfell :

He

enough, from Sax. *reord,* lingua, fermo, as originally it denoted the *clamour of tongues.*

## STANZA XXII.

VER. 1. *Gear*] Bifhop Gibfon obferves, that *gior,* in the
Iflandic, fignifies to *prepare.* True ; but that has nothing
to do with the word here ufed. *Gear,* in our ancient language, denotes all kind of goods and poffeffions, among which
arms were reckoned by our warlike anceftors the moft valuable. Primarily it denoted a fheep fkin in the Iflandic; and
as that was the ufual garment ufed by onr forefathers, it was
afterwards ufed to fignify *cloathing* in general; and hence *armour,* as we ftill fay a coat of armour. Vide our remarks on
this word, Preface, p. 13.

VER. 3. *Steir*] The Englifh *ftir,* from the A. S. *ftyran,*
movere. It is ufed here for violent commotion, as by Douglas, p. 34. ver. 53.

  " But ardentlie behaldis all on *ftere.*"

Junius

He went to fecht with fik a fear,

   While to the erd he fell ;

A wife that hit him to the grund

   Wi' a grit knocking-mell

       Feld him that day.

                       XXIII.

Junius has obferved the affinity betwixt this and the ςΙυρακι-
ζειν, of Hefychius, to ftimulate or prick forward. Ulphila
has a fimilar verb, (only compounded) Mark xiv. ver. 5.
*And—ftauridedun tho*, they murmured againft her ; where
fee the Gloffary of Juuius.

   VER. 8. *Knocking-mell*] *Mell*, from the primitive *mal*, denoting force, power; and hence metaphorically what occafions
*fuffering*, or evil. This is the meaning it carries in the oriental
dialects. Thus the Perfian *mall*, denotes anxiety, fuffering ;
*moul*, patience; *malul*, difquiet ; Arab. *mell*, patience ; Celtic
*mall*, bad, corrupted. But this is not the place for thefe in-
veftigations, which we referve for our Scoto-Gothic Gloffary.
Of the fame family with our *mell*, is the Fr. *mail, maillet* ;
whence the Englifh *mallet*. The Latin *malleus* comes from
the fame origin.

   Our poet here alludes to the large wooden beetle, made
ufe of by our anceftors, to bruife and take the outer hufk from
the barley, to fit it for the pot, before barley mills were in-
vented. This cuftom of *beeteling* the barley, has not ceafed
yet in fome places of the Highlands; and many of the hollow
ftones, ufed as the mortar, are ftill to be feen about our farmers yards, though they are no longer applied by them to the
former purpofe.

                                *Mellie*

## XXIII.

When they had beirt like baited bulls,
   And branewod brynt in bales,
They war as meik as ony mulis
   That mangit ar wi' mails,

                For

---

*Mellie* is, by our poets, ufed for *combat*, fighting. Life of Robert Bruce, p. 121.

  " That men may by this *mellie* fee."

Douglas has it frequently. Fr. *melée;* whence the L. B. *melleia,* and *melletum;* and, from the Fr. Chaude, *mellée,* the barbarous writers of the middle ages formed their monftrous *calida melleia,* as Ruddiman has obferved. Vide Cange in *Melleia.* We have, too, in our old law books, *chaudmella.* Skene de Verb. Sig. though he knew nothing of the origin of the word, has rightly explained *melletum,* by ftrife, débate; as we fay that ane has *melled* or *tulzied* with ane uther.

*Mell* is ftill ufed in the north for a *mallet* or *beetle,* as Ray informs us.

Ver. 9. *Felld*] From the Ifl. *fella,* to beat down. So the Englifh now apply it to trees, *to fell timber.* Alam. Fellen *befillan.* Junius's derivation of this word from *velt,* a field, is almoft as ridiculous as that of Cafaubon, who brings it from βέβλημενος; and yet thefe men were etymologifts.

## STANZA XXIII.

Ver. 1. *Beirt*] Roared and fought with noife, like to that of bulls when baited with dogs. Douglas ufes the word *bera*

               for

for crying or roaring. *Bere* and *birr*, according to Ray, fig. *force* or *might;* and in Chefhire they fay, *with aw my beer*, with all my force. In Scotland too we ufe this word *birr*, for might or ftrength, Hib. *Baireadh*, quod effertur *baireah*, denotat fremitum, et *bairim*, fremere.

In the old Englifh we find *béray*, berayed with blood or dirt, befouled. Teuton. *bern*, *merda*. vid. Jun.

*Baited*] This word is ftill in ufe, though its origin is not fo generally known. With Chaucer *baye* is the ftake to which the bear or bull is tied, in order to be baited. Plowm. T. ver. 87.

" As boiftous as is bere at baye."

They then pronounced *baight*, which is now corrupted into *bait*. Chaucer, ibid. v. 588.

" He fhall be *baighted* as a bere."

The root is the Iflandic *beita*, agitare, incitare. Suio-Goth. *bekeya*, irretire, impedire. " Proprie dicitur" (fays Ihre) " de " illis, quæ cancellis aut caveis inclufa funt."

VER. 2. *Branewod*] Roaring like madmen. *Braie*, fremere, vociferari, barrire, rudere. Hence Fr. *braine*. βραυωςα Hefych. exponit κεκραγυια, vociferans. Lye deduces it from Cambr. *brevy*, to cry out. Douglas ufed *braithlie* for noify, founding.

Perhaps it fhould be wrote *braynewode*, and then it will fignify *mad*. Douglas ufes *brayne* by itfelf in this fenfe, p. 438. ult.

" Quharfore this Turnus half, myndlefs and *brayne*, " Socht divers wentis to flie out throw the plane."

*Brynt*] From *bræn*, ardere; Goth. *brinnan;* Ifl. *ad brenna;* Aleman. *brennan;* Sax. *byrnan*. Hence amber is by the Dutch called *bernfteen*. Douglas ufes *brent* for *burned*.

*Bales*] *Bale*, forrow. Ifl. *bal, bol,* malum ; *bolua,* maledicere ; *boluan,* maledictions. Douglas, 408. 2.

" Have reuthe and pitie of my wofull bale."
Chaucer, P. T. v. 68.

" Thou fhalt be brent in *baleful* fire."
Gothic *baldwyan* torquere, Mark v. 7. *Ni balweys mis.* Do not torment us. Matth. viii. 29. *Quhampt hek faur mel balwyan unfis ?* Art thou come to torment us before the time ? Now Junius (ad voc.) properly obferves, that the torment fpoken of in the New Teftament is always reprefented as by fire ; hence the origin of the Af. *beel,* rogus ; Ifland. *baal,* incendium. Had we room here, we could prove hence the origin of *Beltyne,* the folemn fire kindled by our anceftors in May, at which time the Celts began their year. Vide Macpherfon, Ant. p. 164. Smith Gaelic Ant. p. 31. Pennant's Tour, p. 94. From *tine* comes *tinder,* fomes ; Alaman. *zundere,* item *tundre.*

VER. 4. *Mangit*] Ramfay interprets it *maimed* with carrying ; Gibfon reads *wearied* for *mangit* ; Douglas fometimes writes it *menzeit,* confounded, marred, maimed. Thus of Andromache fainting, p. 78. 15.

" —— to the ground all *mangit* fell echo doun."
and 440. 27.

" Bot then Turnus half *mangit* in affray."
Ruddiman brings it from S. *mangzie,* or *manzie* ; Fr. *mehaign.* Hence, too, our *maim,* per contract. In our old lawbooks it is written *mainzie.* Reg. Majeft. l. 4. c. 3. " He " quha is accufit in fic pleyes, may declyne battle, be reafon of " an *manzie,* or of his age." From *mainzie,* the writers of the middle ages formed the barbarous Latin term *mahamium ;*
though

For faintnefs thae forfochtin fulis
Fell down lyk flauchtir fails ;
Frefh men cam in and hail'd the dulis,
And dang them down in dails
Bedeen that day.

XXIV.

though Ruddiman erroneoufly derives our word from it. Charta Henrici 2do. " Hæc omnia conceffi cum murdro, et morte
" hominis, et plaga, et *mabaim*, et fanguine." Charta Philip 3.
Req. Fr. ann. 1273. " Quod percuffus membrum amitteret
" feu vitam, vel etiam *mabainium* incurreret." Plura vide ap.
Cange, in *Mahamium*.

*Mails*] Burdens.

VER. 5. *Forfochtin*] Wearied with fighting. G.   We
obferve here, that in the Gothic dialects, and all its daughters, the particle *fore*, or *for*, increafes the fignification. Thus
*hindre, forhindra*, impedire ; *minfka, forminfka*, minuere ; and
often imports a worfe meaning than the original word. Thus
*rakna* numerare ; *forakna*, fig. to err in the fum. *Gora*, facere ;
*forgora* perimere.   *Arbeta*, laborare ; *for arbeta* fig. to over-
labour one's felf.   Hence too Engl. *done*, *foredone* ; fworn,
forfworn.   In the Latin, *per* and *præ* have a fimilar meaning.
So *oro, peroro ; facio, perficio ; potens, præpotens, &c.*

VER. 6. *Flaughtir fails*] Thefe are the thin fod pared off
the green furface of a field, with the inftrument now called a
*breaft plough*, but anciently a *flaughter fpade*, which, as it
were, *flays* the foil ; from the Ifland. *ad flàa*, excoriare, cutem
detrahere ; Dan. *flàe ;* A. S. *beflæ*, excoriatus.   Hence too

A a 2                                                *Bakes flakes of snow*, from their broad thin shape. Sax. *flacea*, flocci nivis. Alludit, Gr. φλοιος cortex, and φλοιεω, corticem aut pellem detraho ; Sax. *flean*, to flea. Confer. Jun. Etymol. in *fell*. Ray says, that the surface of the earth, which they pare off to burn in Norfolk, is called *flags*. This sort of firing is still common in all the moorish countries of Scotland. The word *fale* or *feal*, turf, cespes, is found in Douglas's Virgil ; and Ruddiman thinks that *feal* is only a contraction of *fewel*, as being a common kind of firing in Scotland.

Ver. 7. *Hail'd*] To *hail*, Scot. is a phrase used at football, when the victors are said to *hail the ball*, i. e. to drive it beyond, or to the goal ; and as they may thus be said to *cover* the goal, it may, perhaps, come from the Isl. *hill*, tego ; *hulde*, texi ; as this from the Gothic *huljan*, tegere, operiri. Matth. viii. 24. *Gahulith wairthan fram wegim*, Covered with the waves. Hence *hell* is called by Ulphila *halje* ; as *theol*, *hell*, from *helen*, tegere, occultare. Thus *heal* in old English signifies *to conceal*, from Sax. *helan* celare. We call the husks of corn the *hull*, from the same origin. In Northumberland a *swine hull*, a sow house, or swine stye.

*Duiles*] The goal or boundary of the course. We imagine it comes from the Island. *duel*, moror, the stopping-place to which the ball was to be driven by the victorious party. *Dualde*, moratus sum ; *dyel*, mora. Hence *to dwell*, or make abode.

Ver. 8. *Dang*] Perf. from *ding*, cedere, detrudere, to beat down, " Haud dubie," says Lye, " ab Hibern. *dingim*, " pellere, urgere." Douglas 229. 52.

" —— and with bir awin handis
" *Dang* up the zettis ——."

Teuton. *dringen*, from *ding*, *dint*, a stroak or blow ; Sax. *dynt*, ictus. Infra St. seq.

" For

## XXIV.

The bridegrom brought a pint of aile,
And bade the pyper drink it.
Drink it (quoth he), and it fo ftaile ;
A fhrew me, if I think it.

The

" For he durft *ding* nane addir."

*Dails*] In parties, eight or nine together ; from Sax. *dæl*,
a part or portion. Gib.

Vide Luke xv. 12. *Be dale*, ex parte. Greg. Dialog. ex
Verf. R. Alfredi, 2. 23. *Sume dæl.* partim. Thus too Chaucer ufes it, Prol. to W. of B. Tale :

" But fhe was *fome dele* deaf, and that was fkaith."

Hence *dælan*, dividere, Luke xxii. 17. to give alms ; *dæled*,
divifus.

Ver. 9. *Bedeen*] or *bedene* ; for thus it is wrote by Douglas,

" Werpe all thir bodyis in the deep *bedene*." And
" How Æneas with the rout *bedene*."

This word is common alfo to the old Englifh writers ; Ruddiman brings it from Germ. *bedienen*, præftare officium, *q. d.*
affoon as defired.

## STANZA XXIV.

Ver. 4. *A fhrew me*] So it ftands in Gibfon's edition. It
fhould undoubtedly be read *befhrew me*, a very common
phrafe

The bride her maidens ftood near by,
 And faid it was na blinked ;
And Bartagafie, the bride fae gay,
 Upon him faft fhe winked,
    Full foon that day.

## XXV.

When a' was dune, Dik with an aix
 Came furth to fell a fudder.
Quod he, quhair ar yon hangit fmaiks,
 Richt now wald flain my brudder ?
         His

phrafe all over South and North Britain in the fixteenth century.

 Though I have not Lord Hyndford's M. S. at hand; yet I do take this whole ftanza to be an interpolation. It is not found in Ramfay's edition ; and the language has fomething more modern in it than the reft of the poem. *Bartagafie*, a name (as far as I can learn) unknown in Scotland, ftrengthens the conjecture I have formed, that it is fpurious. Whence the Bifhop got it, I cannot fay; but the whole of his orthography is fo faulty and modern, that it appears he was but moderately acquainted with our Scottifh idiom ; and this has probably led him to think this ftanza genuine, and to commit many errors in his notes on the poem itfelf.

### STANZA XXV.

Ver. 2. *Furth*] Gibfon reads *cut* ; but we judge this the true reading, as it adds another letter to the alliteration of the
            verfe ;

verfe ; an ornament, or rather jingle, our old poets were very fond of.

*Fudder*] A load, a great heap. Gibfon writes it *fother*. Ray fays it is commonly ufed fpeaking of lead, and expreffes 8 pigs or 1600 weight. But *fudder* certainly means a cart load. Germ. *fuder*, et hoc fortè (fays Skinner) a Teuton. *fuehren*, vehere, ducere. And this feems the true meaning of the word in this paffage, though Ruddiman will have us to feek it in Hib. *fuidhre*, a fervant or valet. We find *futhir* ufed by Douglas to fignify a *trifle*, or thing of no value, p. 311. 29.

"I compt not of thir pagan goddis ane *futhir*."

But this has no connection with the other, nor are we to confound with it *foder*, fignifying beafts meat, from *foda* nutrire; nor the Gothic *fodr*, fignifying the fheath of a fword, ufed by Ulphila, John xviii. ver. 11. Hence A. S. *fodder*, *boge foddr*, a quiver, perhaps, becaufe the firft quivers and fheaths for fwords were made of fkins, as *foder* fig. vellus, pellis ; Fr. *feutre* ; Lat. barb. *fodrum*, de quo vid. Cange; Germ. *futher* ; Angl. *fur*; confer. doctift. Ihre Lex. vol. 1. p. 511, 512.

VER. 3. *Smaiks*] *Smaik*, filly, pitiful fellow. Douglas, 239. 38.

"Quod I, *Smaik*, lat me flepe ——."

From Teuton. *fchmach*, contumelia. Belg. *fmade*. id Teut. *fchmachlich*, contumeliofus. The root is the Ifl. *fmaa*, to contemn ; *Eg fmaae*, I defpife ; *fmaa*, *fmaar*, little, *fmall*, better pronounced, and nearer to the original, by the Scots *fma* ; Goth. *fmal*, gracilis, tenuis; *fmalna*, gracilefcere. Hence *fmale* denotes the fmaller cattle, as fheep and goats. Alam. call fheep, *fmallfecho*. The ingenious etymologift Ihre thinks

His wyfe bad him gae hame, Gib Glaiks,
  And fae did Meg his mudder ;
He turn'd and gaif them baith their paiks,
  For he durſt ding nane udder,
     For feir that day.

thinks the Greek μηλα, *ſheep,* is nothing but the Gothic term
wanting the *s*. *Smæda,* contumelia afficere ; *ſmædeord,* con-
vicia; Belg. *ſmaeden, ſmadden,* deturpare. And hence the
words *ſmutſa, ſmeta, ſmitta ;* unde Angl. *ſmitch,* and our
*ſmit,* to infect or defile. In the parent dialect we find *ſma-*
*rede,* reculæ, minoris momenti res; *ſmaher,* vile, abject.
Alfred. lib. 1. cap. 25. 10. *Smaher ſcale thin,* Vilis ſervus
tuus. Iſl. *ſma hluter,* res viles ; *ſmæcka,* minuere. Findur
Norr. ap. Ihre in voce. *Toku ſwa riki ad ſmæckaſt,* Incipie-
bant regna tum minui. Hence the true idea of the name given to Magnus, ſon of Eric king of Sweden, called in deri-
ſion *Smæk,* not (as it is generally rendered) blanditiis delini-
tus, *flattered ;* but denoting a weak, contemptible fellow, who
allowed the whole province of Scania to be taken from him
by the Danes, and thereby *ſmeckad,* diminiſhed his heredita-
ry kingdom, contrary to the oath taken by the kings of Sweden when crowned. Vide Locceni, Hiſt. Suet. p. 106.

From this word *ſmæcka,* the barbarous Latin writers formed *ſmaccare,* to mutilate or maim, de qua vide Cange Gloſſ.

VER. 4. *Wald ſlain*] For would have ſlain. Gibſon reads,
*that* hurt my brother.

VER. 5. *Glaicks*] An idle ſauntering prattler. *Glaſſe,* or
*glave,* is *ſmooth,* according to Ray. Hence *glavering* is uſed
for *flattering.* In the Cheſhire dialect *glaver,* to flatter; A. S.
*gliwer,* ſcurra, paraſitus ; a *gliwan,* ſcurram agere, ſmooth.
                                   Iſland.

Ifland. *glær* mare, from its clearnefs; and *gler*, vitrum  Hence
Fr. *glaire d' un œuf*, white of an egg; and Angl. *giare*. Confer Jun. Etymol. in *glayre*.

VER. 7. *Paiks*] Blows, repeated ftrokes.  Angl. *paice*,
verbarare. I fhall well *paie* him, I'll beat him.  This is not
to be confounded with *pay*, folvere debitum.  Jun. derives
*paie* from Greek παιειν, verberare; but the true etymon. is
from Cambr. *pwyo*, ferire, pulfare, percutere.  In looking
into the learned Ihre's Lex. we find *pak*, fuftis; and hence
perhaps we have *paik*, to beat with a cudgel.  Pezron Celt.
Ant. takes notice of *bach* in the Celtic, fig. *fuftis*.  The
Ang. Saxons, changing *c* into *t*, fay *bat*. Fr. *baton*.  Our
moft ingenious etymologift obferves, that it is more than probable that the ancient Latins ufed *bacus* for a *ftick* or *pole*,
from the diminative *baculus*, ftill in common ufe.

We have thrown thefe notes haftily together, they being
only meant, (as well as thofe on the Gaberlunzie-Man) as
a kind of fpecimen to a Gloffary of the ancient Scotifh language
we intend, at fome future period, to publifh, provided thofe
who are the proper judges of fuch an undertaking, fhall deem
fuch a work ufeful for promoting the knowledge of the anti-
tiquities and language of our country.

*F I N I S.*